"Diane Vallere has stitched up an engaging new series with an intelligent, resourceful heroine in Polyester Monroe, plus a great supporting cast and a clever plot. Vallere's knowledge of the fashion business adds an extra layer of authenticity. *Suede to Rest* is a strong addition to the cozy mystery genre."

—Sofie Kelly, *New York Times* bestselling author of the Magical Cats Mysteries

"Toile, taffeta, and trouble! There's a new material girl in town! Poly may have an eye for fashion, but she's also a resourceful and gutsy sleuth. Diane Vallere skillfully blends two mysteries in this smart and engaging tale that will keep you guessing to the very end."

—Krista Davis, *New York Times* bestselling author of the Domestic Diva Mysteries

"In the Material Witness Mystery series, Diane Vallere weaves a tapestry of finely knit characters, luxurious fabrics, and . . . murder."

—Janet Bolin, national bestselling author of the Threadville Mysteries

"In *Suede to Rest*, Diane Vallere has fashioned a terrific mystery, rich with detail and texture. Polyester Monroe is a sassy protagonist who will win your hearts with her seamless style and breezy wit. The first in the series promises readers hours of deftly woven whodunit enjoyment."

—Daryl Wood Gerber, Agatha Award–winning author of the national bestselling Cookbook Nook Mysteries

continued . . .

Berkley Prime Crime titles by Diane Vallere

SUEDE TO REST
CRUSHED VELVET

Crushed
Velvet

DIANE VALLERE

BERKLEY PRIME CRIME, NEW YORK

BERKLEY
PRIME
CRIME

An imprint of Penguin Random House LLC
375 Hudson Street, New York, New York 10014

CRUSHED VELVET

A Berkley Prime Crime Book / published by arrangement with the author

ISBN: 978-0-425-27058-5

PUBLISHING HISTORY
Berkley Prime Crime mass-market edition / August 2015

PRINTED IN THE UNITED STATES OF AMERICA

10 9 8 7 6 5 4 3 2 1

Cover illustration by Brandon Dorman.
Cover design by Sarah Oberrender.
Interior text design by Tiffany Estreicher.

Penguin
Random
House

To Josh Hickman,
who constitutes the fabric of my life.

ACKNOWLEDGMENTS

Thank you to the thousands of readers who forgave Polyester Monroe for having a weird name and took the time to read her story in *Suede to Rest*.

Special thanks to Melanie McMichael, who was in the satellite office with me when Vaughn was born; Richard Goodman, who I trust implicitly with my manuscripts; and Kendel Lynn, my creative co-pilot and soul sister.

Thanks to Katherine Pelz for giving Poly a home at Berkley Prime Crime, Janet Robbins for your eagle eye, and Jessica Faust, for making it all happen.

And, of course, the biggest thank-you goes out to my mother, Mary Vallere, for introducing me to fabric stores at an impressionable age.

One

The crash was louder than I expected.

Two men stood on the top rung of their respective stepladders on either side of the Land of a Thousand Fabrics sign, or rather, where the sign had been ten minutes ago. The man on the right had lost his grip on the *L* in *Land*, and it fell to the sidewalk in front of the store, cracking the concrete. The effects of weather and time, a decade since the store had closed for business but almost half a century since the store had first opened, had rusted the cursive iron letters in the logo. Bird poop and leaves were almost indistinguishable from the decorative font, and one of the metal posts that anchored the massive sign to the storefront had broken sometime in the past week. Since then, *Thousand* had hung in a diagonal slope downward. The men on the ladders were hired to remove the rest of the anchors so the sign could be replaced with my new sign, *Material Girl*, before I opened for business in six days. They'd rescheduled the job twice, and now I had less than a week before the registers were scheduled to ring.

It was eleven thirty on a Monday morning. The first time I'd scheduled this job had been on a Monday, too, because I knew most people would be at work, and the handful of hair salons on the street would be closed. I'd alerted the businesses on either side of me: Tiki Tom, who sold Polynesian ephemera to my left, and the Garden sisters, Lilly and Violet, who ran an antiques shop called Flowers in the Attic to my right. They'd both agreed to close for the day. The construction crew canceled at the last minute, leaving my neighboring stores out of a day's business. I made it up to each of them with ten yards of a fabric of their choice. You work with what you have.

Two weeks later, an unexpected February downpour kept the crew from showing up for the job, which meant it was today or nothing. I didn't love that a sidewalk of tourists and nosy neighbors had a front-row seat to my sign troubles, but the small town of San Ladrón had codes and zoning regulations, and a job like this had to happen Monday through Friday between the hours of ten and four. If it wasn't today, I wouldn't have a proper sign when I opened on Sunday.

"Polyester Monroe?" said a voice to my left. I turned to see a man in a red plaid shirt, faded jeans, and a yellow construction hat. He held a clipboard under one arm. His phone was Velcroed onto his belt below a generous belly. "Zat you?"

"Yes, I'm Polyester Monroe," I said. "But call me Poly."

"Is your legal name Polyester?"

I nodded.

"Then that's what I need you to sign. Here, here, and here." He pushed the clipboard in front of me and tapped the paper three times with the end of the pen.

I scanned page one of the documents. "I already signed the contract for the sign removal and a few notices from the city. What is this for?"

"Release form for the contractors. If anyone is hurt in the course of the job, you're responsible. If any property is damaged in the course of the job, you're responsible. If any—"

I pushed the clipboard back at him. "I applied for a petition through the city council. I have all the forms I need. They recommended you for the job because you have experience with this sort of thing."

"Still gotta sign the release," he said.

"And you still have to finish the job. The store opens on Sunday. I need a sign."

"Lady, this is San Ladrón, not Times Square. You turn on your lights, you open the front door, and you hang out a shingle. If people want what you're selling, they'll come in and buy it."

I took the clipboard, signed my full legal name by the *X*s, and wrote the date after my signatures. "You should have had me sign it before you let it crash to the ground," I said, and pushed the clipboard back at him.

The rest of the construction workers were scattered around, moving large chunks of concrete that had broken loose when the large iron *Land* had hit the sidewalk. My attempt to make the fabric store look new again, to make it more of a shining star than a sore thumb on Bonita Avenue, wasn't exactly going according to plan. Tiki Tom and the Garden sisters were already conspiring against me. I had decided to placate them both with gourmet tea baskets from my friend Genevieve's tea shop, who was heading this way now.

"You look like you could use a pick-me-up," Genevieve said after handing over two of the three baskets she held.

Genevieve Girard was the owner of the small, French-themed tea shop called Tea Totalers. It was about two blocks east of my fabric store. I'd befriended her a few months ago when I first inherited the store. She and her husband, Phil, had met at the World Tea Expo, and after a typical courtship that involved flowers, candy, and twenty pounds added to her curvy frame, they married and set up shop in San Ladrón, Phil's hometown. They plunked their savings into the tea store, but a poor economy kept them from making it the joint project they'd hoped. He went back to driving a taxi and occasionally picking up delivery jobs and she ran the store. A nice patchwork résumé, the new reality for the small business owner.

"Genevieve, you have no idea how happy I am to see you."

She set the picnic basket on a public bench and flipped the wooden handles open. When she lifted the lid, the scent of buttermilk biscuits and mulled cider filled the air. Mugs, saucers, flatware, and napkins were attached to the inside lid of the picnic basket by elastic loops that had been sewn to the red-and-white checkered interior. She removed a mug and saucer, filled the mug with cider, and handed it to me. I took a sip, savoring the rich apple-and-clove flavor.

"This is heavenly," I said.

"Try the biscuit. It's a new recipe: I added pureed loquats to the batter."

I took a bite. The flavors of loquats and cranberries complemented each other perfectly. "You're a genius," I said.

"Can you take out an ad in the *San Ladrón Times* and tell people that? I could use the endorsement."

"Business is still slow?" I was mildly surprised. "I thought it picked up after you started promoting your proprietary blends of tea."

"The only person who's responded to those ads is a food distributor who wants me to sell out to the big grocery stores, and that's not what I want for Tea Totalers. I need to get people to the store. Right now I have about five regulars—not that I'm complaining, so don't you even think about not showing up tomorrow!—and a handful of walk-ins a week. It's barely enough to pay the bills, let alone buy the supplies I need."

Out of the corner of my eye I saw two men standing on

scaffolding that had been suspended from the roof of the fabric store. They looped thick ropes around the iron letters of the parts of the sign that hadn't crashed to the sidewalk and slowly lowered the word *Thousand* to the ground. When I turned to watch what happened next, I saw another group of men move the iron word to the back of their truck, where they'd put *Land*. It was after twelve now, and there was one word left. I'd specifically asked that they take *Fabric* down last in case there were any snafus. Better branding than *of* or *a*. Now they could remove the iron bolts that jutted out from the façade and mount the sign I'd designed during the nights when I was too excited about the prospects of opening the store to sleep.

I did a quick calculation. At the rate the construction crew was working, they'd be at it for hours. Removal of the sign was one thing, but removal of the scaffolding was another.

"Wait here," I said to Genevieve. I walked over to the foreman.

He held up his hand palm side out. "Hard hat," he said, and pointed to a yellow helmet resting on the back of the truck.

I tucked the front of my auburn hair, cut in a style made famous by Victoria Beckham a few years ago, behind my ear and set the half-lemon-shaped hat on top of my head. The hat was bigger than my head and almost covered my eyes. I tipped it back so I could see. The foreman waved me forward.

"How long do you think you're going to be?" I asked.

"This is an all-day job."

"How can that be? The words are down, and that had to be the hardest part."

"We gotta finish removing the iron. Then we gotta get your new sign in place and run the electrical. Then we gotta test everything. Then—"

"So, what does that mean? Three? Four?"

"At least. We go into overtime at five."

"Zoning laws say you have to be done by four."

"Then we're going to need to pick back up tomorrow."

I put my hands on my hips. "Not. Acceptable. This is a one-day job. You said so when you gave me the quote. You canceled on me twice."

"Once. Couldn't do much about the rain, lady."

"You started at ten. You will finish at four. And by finish, I mean finish. Gone. Cleaned up. Out of here."

"Those wall mounts are pretty rusted through," he said. He pulled his hat off and rubbed the back of his arm across his forehead.

"Good. That means instead of trying to save them, you can save time by just cutting them off."

He looked at the picnic basket behind me. "We could work a lot faster if we had food."

"Don't worry about food. I'll take care of that. But this job? Done by four."

He scratched his head and pulled his hard hat back on. "Deal." He turned around and yelled to the workers. "Hey! Pick up the pace! We're on a timetable."

Genevieve was halfway through her third biscuit when I returned to the bench. "Can you do lunch for"—I twisted around and counted the various colors of flannel—"nine men on short notice? I'll pay menu prices."

"Poly, I can't let you be my savior. You're putting all of your money into the store."

"Let me worry about my money. You worry about lunch for nine."

"Fine. Lunch for nine. Can you drive to the store in half an hour? Phil took the truck to LA to pick up your fabrics."

"See, you guys are my savior, too."

When the lease had come due on their Saab, Genevieve had convinced her husband to turn it in and invest in a van they could use for deliveries. She'd had the logo for her tea shop painted on the side and hoped it would help raise her shop's profile. As it turned out, most delivery orders could be handled by bike and the van spent more time sitting behind the shop than cruising the streets of San Ladrón. Ever pragmatic, Phil still took the occasional moving and delivery jobs in the greater Los Angeles area to justify the price of the vehicle.

When I'd first decided to reopen the fabric store, my parents had helped me sort through the bolts of fabric that had been in the store for decades. My uncle Marius had closed the store ten years ago, but left the interior intact. A surprising amount of fabrics were still in sellable condition. I hoped to one day be able to take the kind of trips that Uncle Marius and Aunt Millie had taken—Thailand for silk, France for lace, Scotland for cashmere—but until I established a cash flow, I had to do what I could on a shoestring budget. I sorted through the old inventory and then contacted many of the dealers in New York and New Jersey, spending hours selecting whimsical cotton prints, Pendleton wools, and a glorious spectrum of silk de chine. I offered to buy any bolts they had with less than five yards if they'd make a deal on the price and a few of them did. A few of them remembered my aunt and uncle and deepened my discount when I told them I was reopening the store. It was a start.

Still, I needed a hook, something to make people come to me. After two weeks of stopping by Tea Totalers every morning for a cup of Genevieve's proprietary blend of tea, I got my idea. A proprietary blend of fabric.

It was no coincidence that I owned a fabric store and my name was Polyester. The store had been in my family for generations and I'd been born inside on a bed of polyester. Growing up, I'd been teased on a regular basis and often wished I'd been born on a less controversial fabric. Was there a person alive who didn't think of the seventies when they heard the word *polyester*? Still, it was what it was. Instead of fighting my name, I decided to use it for a PR opportunity. I reached out to all of my contacts and finally found a mill willing to weave a custom blend of velvet using ninety percent silk and ten percent polyester.

I had experience working with blended fabrics in my former job at To The Nines, a somewhat sleazy dress shop in downtown Los Angeles, and I knew that ten percent of a synthetic woven into a fabric could change the drape and wearability of the cloth without dramatically altering the appearance. Fabrics that were woven with a synthetic blend resisted wrinkles and held color better than their pure counterparts. My former boss liked to use mostly synthetic fabrics that came cheap (and sometimes defective). Having grown up around the best fabrics in the world when Land of a Thousand Fabrics was in its prime, I'd always wanted to work with top-quality weaves. This was my opportunity.

My custom velvet had arrived at a distributor in Los Angeles late on Friday afternoon. The warehouse was closed for the weekend. Genevieve had mentioned that her husband was going to Los Angeles for supplies for Tea Totalers today and I'd arranged for him to pick up the fabric. It was a win-win.

Even though the store was locked up tighter than a drum, I had a few misgivings over leaving the crew to pick up lunch. The foreman saw me watching them and gave me a thumbs-up. I smiled a thin smile and walked around the back of the store to my yellow VW Bug. Five minutes later I was parked in front of Tea Totalers.

The tea shop was actually a small house that sat away from the street. A narrow sidewalk led to the front door. Small white iron tables and chairs with mismatched, faded cushions were scattered around the front interior. Inside, Genevieve had hung checkered curtains on the windows and tacked a few French posters featuring roosters and chickens on the walls.

Genevieve was a self-professed Francophile, and her shop

was a testament to her love of the country. I'd secretly been working on a makeover for her store, including curtains, cushions, aprons, placemats, napkins, and tablecloths from linen toile, gingham check, and other French fabrics. I even found a bolt of place-printed cotton canvas, too heavy to use for apparel, with images of roosters on it. I planned to stretch the images over wooden frames and suggest she hang them like art. I couldn't wait to surprise her with the concept, but I wanted to get it all together before it was done, and I wanted to find a way to use the new velvet in the design.

Genevieve was stacking sandwiches wrapped in parchment paper, sealed with stickers that featured the Eiffel tower on them, into a wooden crate.

"I hope you don't mind that I didn't go fancy. I'm low on a couple of supplies. *Jambon* sandwiches with brie and Dijon mustard on croissants, with a side of *pommes frites*. Is that okay?"

"That's not fancy?" I asked with a smile to my voice. "I think it'll do. What time is Phil expected back?"

"Hopefully soon. He left yesterday so he could avoid traffic and be at the suppliers first thing this morning."

We loaded jugs of iced tea into a separate crate and packed them into the backseat of my Bug. I returned to the store and parked out front so we could unload. Two men lowered the scaffolding, and sign removal ceased while a line formed by Genevieve. I stood behind, assessing the work that was left. In the background, a white van turned the corner. It pulled up to the curb behind the flatbed. The logo on the side of the truck, a white rectangle that covered the area to the left of the passenger side door, said *Special Delivery*. Underneath it said *Have We Got A Package For You! Call Us 24 Hours A Day*.

The driver of the van cut the engine and got out. "Is there a Polyester Monroe around here?" he asked.

"I'm Polyester," I said.

"Rick Penwald. Have I got a package for you. A bunch of fabrics?"

Genevieve approached the van. "My husband was supposed to pick up her fabrics. Where's Phil?" She looked at the logo on the side of the vehicle. "Where's his van?"

"This is his van. He called this morning, made arrangements for me to come get it and make the delivery for him. He said he had some business in Los Angeles and wasn't coming back right away."

"But that doesn't make any sense," Genevieve said. "Phil's a deliveryman. Why would he hire you to make his delivery?"

"Not sure." Rick pulled his black mesh hat off his head and wiped his forehead with his palm. "He probably wanted to surprise you with something."

He held out a clipboard with sheets of paper attached and handed me a pen. "Sign by the Xs."

I glanced at the form and then back at Rick. "I already paid for the fabric and I paid Phil for the delivery up front."

"If I make a delivery, I have to have proof I made the delivery. This is proof of delivery. The form's in triplicate. You sign the top one and take the pink copy in the middle. Press hard."

The top copy was white, the middle pink, and the bottom yellow. Along the upper left side, a white sticker with the logo, website, and phone number for Special Delivery had been affixed to each copy. Across the center of the page, written in ball-point pen in surprisingly neat printing that tipped slightly backward, it said "12 rolls velvet. Prepaid. Signature for delivery confirmation only." I zeroed out the totals field and signed my name at the bottom. I tore the pink page from between the white and yellow and set the clipboard inside the open window on the passenger-side seat.

I folded the paper up small enough to fit into my pocket and followed Rick around to the back of the van. He flipped through a ring of keys and tried three in the padlock before he found one that worked. He took the lock off and hooked it on one of the belt loops of his jeans, and then flung the back doors open.

Sunlight hit twelve large rolls of multicolored velvet, propped along the left hand side of the van. On the right were crates of vegetables, spices, and dry goods.

"Where you want it?" he asked.

"Inside the store," I said. I unlocked the hinged metal gate in the front of the fabric store and propped the entrance open with a small black vintage sewing machine I used as a doorstop. Behind us, the colorful flannel army of construction workers sat alongside the building watching. Nobody volunteered to help. Rick grabbed a roll of velvet by the end and yanked on it, then positioned it over his shoulder and carried it inside the store. Behind him, Genevieve screamed. I ran to the back of the van and looked inside.

Jutting out from under the bolts of fabric was an arm.

I scrambled inside the van and rolled the fabric out of their stacked lumber formation to the side of the van with the dry goods. The arm belonged to a body that had been crushed under my new inventory.

And the body belonged to Genevieve's husband, Phil.

TWO

Phil's eyes were closed and his face was an odd shade of green. By his head, an empty jug with the Tea Totalers logo rolled into the crate of dry goods. Crumbs and flakes from some sort of pastry were scattered around his outstretched hand next to unused white plastic zip ties. I checked his carotid artery for a pulse but found none. "Somebody call nine-one-one," I called to the construction crew behind me. The foreman grabbed his phone from his belt and made the call.

Genevieve cried out again. Rick ran out of the store and put his arms around her from the back and held her still. She fought against his embrace until she went limp from exhaustion. He let her go but kept his hands on her upper arms, as if to keep her grounded. He guided her to the bench, where she collapsed.

I remained in the van with the body. Even though I silently urged the paramedics to hurry up and get there, I was sure Phil was already dead. Minutes later I heard the sound of sirens growing louder until they were deafening. Strong hands landed on my shoulders and pulled me out of the van. Men and women in navy blue jackets and pants took my place. I stood on the sidewalk by the crack where my sign had landed earlier that morning and waited with Genevieve. Neither of us spoke.

Phil's body was taken from the van by gurney. It was covered with a dull blue-gray blanket made of thick felted wool that would have itched if Phil could feel it. His body was moved to the back of the waiting ambulance. Doors were shut and the ambulance drove away. The lack of lights told me one thing. There was no reviving Phil Girard.

I looked back at the bench where Genevieve sat with Rick. Her hands were over her face and her body was slumped down. My heart went out to her. She'd moved to San Ladrón because Phil had family here, and her life was rooted in the life he had already made for himself. Without him, she was an outsider like me. Did whoever killed Phil know they'd created a widow in the process?

A black-and-white police cruiser pulled into the space that the ambulance had vacated. Deputy Sheriff Clark, San Ladrón's resident police officer, who manned the mobile sheriff's unit, spoke to a few of the construction workers who remained behind, eating their sandwiches. The foreman looked at me and said something to the deputy sheriff, who looked at me, too. He said something to the foreman and shook his hand. He turned to Rick. They turned their backs to me and shared a few words. They parted ways, with Rick moving to the side of the scene by the construction crew, and Sheriff Clark walking toward me.

I'd met Deputy Sheriff Clark a few months ago when a murder behind the fabric store raised questions we both wanted to answer. When the truth came out, I accepted that he had been searching for the same information I'd sought. Deputy Sheriff Clark was here to do a job, and I respected that.

"Ms. Monroe," he said.

"Deputy Sheriff Clark," I said back.

"What can you tell me about the man in the truck?"

"He's dead, isn't he?" He nodded once. "He's Phil Girard, Genevieve's husband. He went to Los Angeles last night to pick up some fabric for me."

"What kind of fabric?"

"I ordered twelve rolls of a special weave of velvet, and they arrived on Friday. The warehouse was closed over the weekend. I knew Phil and Genevieve could use the money, so I hired Phil to pick it up for me."

"What makes you think they could use the money?"

"Genevieve is my friend and she told me," I said. "It's not common knowledge," I added.

"Did you pay his expenses?"

"What expenses? I hired him to pick up my fabric and drive back. His van is electric, so there's no gas expense. Besides, I don't think deliverymen expect you to pay for their gas."

"I'm talking about his overnight stay."

"No, he must have arranged that himself. Genevieve said he left yesterday so he could pick up dry goods for her first thing this morning, get my fabric, and get back before rush hour."

"So he was already going to Los Angeles to pick up supplies for her store?"

"I guess so."

"But you hired him anyway because they needed the money."

"Sheriff, don't make this into something it isn't. If I were to hire a delivery service to drive to Los Angeles and drive back, it's entirely possible they'd be couriering something for someone else, too. That doesn't change the fact that they're picking up something for me. It's not like sharing a cab."

"Ms. Monroe, I appreciate your loyalty to your friend.

I'm trying to establish a time frame for where this man has been. Is Mrs. Girard here?"

"Yes, she's by the food," I said. I turned around, but Genevieve wasn't there. "She was here a second ago. Maybe she went inside to sit down?"

Clark followed me inside the fabric store, past the velvet that Rick had left there before we discovered Phil's body. I was in the process of figuring out how I wanted to lay out the interior for the best possible shopping experience. The walls were lined with white wooden shelving, stacked full of silk, taffeta, satin, moiré, and other luxury fabrics. The center of the store was filled with large bins, about five feet square, piled high with their own colorful assortments: brightly printed jersey, polyester, cotton, gingham, calico. I'd been lugging the fabrics in poor condition to the back door of the store so I could toss them in the Dumpster out back, but so far hadn't been able to bring myself to do it. Who knows, I reasoned, maybe once I peel off the first couple of yards, I'll find that I can do something with what's left.

When I didn't see Genevieve immediately, I called out for her. She didn't answer.

"I don't know where she went." I said.

"She left?" asked Clark.

I turned around and found him standing by the velvet.

"I said I don't know where she went. Maybe the bathroom. With all due respect, Sheriff, she just saw her husband's dead body. She probably didn't take it very well."

"Is this the fabric from Los Angeles?" he asked. He used the end of a pen to tap it.

"Yes."

"You said twelve bolts. Where are the rest?"

"The others are probably still in the van out front. As soon as I saw the arm jutting out from under the bolts, we stopped unloading."

Clark poked his head out the front door and beckoned someone over. "Tag this fabric and take it to the unit."

"Sheriff—"

"Ms. Monroe, you know how this works. Until you hear otherwise, this fabric is evidence. Did anything else come out from inside the truck?"

"No."

"If you hear from Mrs. Girard before I do, tell her to call me." He headed outside to the truck and I followed him. He walked to the back doors and used his iPhone to snap pictures of the interior. I turned off the sound on my phone and did the same. He turned around, and, too late, I shoved my phone into the pocket of my sweatshirt.

"Ms. Monroe, what are you doing?"

I went with the truth. "I'm taking pictures of my fabric. I already paid for it. I know you have to take it, but I want proof of what I'm owed."

He studied me for a moment, then, as if satisfied with my answer, nodded. "In light of circumstances, I'm going to have to ask you to reschedule the balance of your work on the exterior of the store."

"But it's been rescheduled twice already!"

"That isn't a request."

"Fine."

I found the foreman and explained the situation. He communicated to his crew, who finished their sandwiches and then packed up their tools. Sheriff Clark spoke to Rick by the driver's side of the van. I tried to listen in to their conversation, but the sound of the construction crew loading up their truck with cones and hard hats drowned them out. Rick climbed into the van and pulled it away from the curb.

"Where's he taking the van?" I asked Clark.

"The police station. Like I said about your fabric, until we figure out what happened here, it's evidence."

The men in flannel piled into the back of the flatbed and the foreman drove it away, leaving me alone with the store, the scaffolding, and a mess of parchment paper and empty tea containers. Clark's men carried the remaining roll of velvet out of the store. After I cleaned up the street, I went inside. I locked the front door behind me and climbed the stairs to the small Victorian apartment over the store.

Home.

I was met at the door by Pins, a small gray striped kitten I'd adopted after he and his brother were found in the Dumpster behind my store. He was about six months old and had grown out of his kitten appearance and into that of a frisky kitty. He maintained his playfulness, much like Needles, his orange tabby brother. I scooped Pins up, kissed him on his head, and carried him to the kitchen. He wriggled out of my arms and jumped onto the counter, onto a chair, and down onto the floor, where he buried his nose in his bowl. Needles scampered into the kitchen and joined him.

I fished my phone out of my pocket and called Genevieve. "It's Poly." I paused for a second and thought about what kind of a message to leave. "Call me back as soon as you can."

I poured a cold glass of lemonade and sank into a chair by the table. Phil's body in the back of the van sickened me to the point that I couldn't think about anything else. This wasn't the first time I'd experienced a murder since coming to San Ladrón. I'd learned how the small town treated its residents and its outsiders. It was one of the reasons Genevieve had become friendly to me in the first place.

I'd met Phil Girard on a few occasions, but I'd never gotten to know him other than through Genevieve. I had gotten the feeling that Genevieve would have been happier to have him with her in San Ladrón than constantly on the road. The rare times I'd seen him at her tea shop, he'd been less friendly than tolerant. I'd tried to overcompensate with my own level of friendliness, but we'd never warmed to each other. Truth was, I didn't think he deserved Genevieve.

Phil had been Genevieve's ticket to acceptance in local circles. So what did that mean for her now? Was she enough of a part of San Ladrón's community to be accepted on her own, or was she an outsider like me?

I also knew her financial troubles were worse than she'd let on, and now—well, I didn't know what would happen now. I wanted to tell her that I would help her however I could. Friends need friends in hard times, I knew that. It was harder to go through something like this alone than with people to lean on. I had been lucky. Not only had I found a friend in Genevieve, but I had my parents to lean on, too.

I thought about what my dad had said when I first told him I wanted to reopen the store. *Land of a Thousand Fabrics is a thing of the past. The world has changed since the store's heyday. It won't ever be the same.* I knew he was right, but that didn't mean I couldn't make it something new.

In the weeks after inheriting the store, I wrote up a business plan, applied for a loan, and moved into the apartment upstairs. My parents gave up their nights and weekends and helped me get the interior into shape. I wasn't sure, but I suspected they were proud of my determination. Our hard work paid off, and the store was ready to open earlier than I'd planned. I thanked them with tickets for a cruise up the California coast. I assured them I could handle any last-minute emergencies that popped up. If only I'd known.

I spent the next couple of hours cleaning up the apartment. I didn't think of myself as a sloppy person, but living alone in my aunt Millie and uncle Marius's apartment, as opposed to living with my ex-boyfriend Carson in Los Angeles, gave me the freedom to toss my blazer on the sofa, leave my shoes in the living room, and only do the dishes once every couple of days. Tidying up turned into full-on cleaning. By the time the kitchen floor was scrubbed and all of the dark cherrywood trim had been Murphy-oiled, I knew I wasn't just keeping up with neglected cleaning. I was burning off nervous energy.

I went downstairs. I'd been spending a lot of time getting the store ready to open, sorting through the inventory that I had, tagging some things with discount prices and acquiring others from my contacts in Los Angeles.

Inside the door was a wall of empty shelving. I'd taped a sign there a month ago. *Polyester Velvet*, it said. I wanted it to be the first thing people saw when they came into the store. But thinking about the velvet brought me back to thinking about Genevieve's husband.

I'd seen his body in the back of the truck. He'd been buried under a dozen bolts of fabric. What did that mean? You couldn't get a body under twelve bolts of velvet unless you started with the body first. That told me whoever had put the fabric in the truck had purposely stacked it on top of Phil. And that meant that person had something to do with Phil's murder.

Was he killed over the business opportunity that Rick Penwald had mentioned? Or did his murder have something to do with the food he picked up for Genevieve? Was my fabric a convenient way to hide the body, or had someone known what he'd be couriering? And why had Phil hired another deliveryman to make the delivery to San Ladrón? He could have called Genevieve and told her if he was running late or if something had come up. Why had it been such a secret?

I picked up the phone and called Sheriff Clark. When he answered, I identified myself.

"Sheriff, does the medical examiner know if Phil was dead before the fabric was put on top of him?"

"I'm sorry, Ms. Monroe; that information is part of my investigation."

"It's just that, I was thinking, isn't there a thing called a death mask? Can't you test the fabric to see if someone was suffocated with it?"

"What are you getting at?"

"If you test my velvet, you should be able to determine if it was used to suffocate Phil Girard or if he was dead before the fabric was stacked on top of him."

"And what do you think that will tell us?"

"I'm not sure, but it should tell you something."

"Ms. Monroe, I appreciate the phone call, but I'd like to ask you to leave the investigation to me."

"Have you heard from Genevieve?" I asked.

"Not yet."

That concerned me more than I wanted to admit. I wished the sheriff good luck with the investigation, then hung up, walked downstairs, and headed to Tea Totalers on foot.

When I reached the shop, it was locked up tighter than a canister of *herbes de Provence* that needed to maintain freshness. Lights were off and chairs were upside down on top of tables. I checked my watch. It was approaching two.

It appeared as though Genevieve had come back to the store, but I had a hard time picturing her thinking rationally enough to do much more than turn off the lights and lock the door. But if not her, then who had closed up? And at whose direction?

Too many questions cropped up in my head. I walked around the back of the store, looking for signs that Genevieve had returned. I found a young woman outside of the building, stacking wooden crates like the ones Genevieve had used to pack the lunches.

"Excuse me," I called out.

The woman looked up. She was a pretty blonde, her highlighted hair pulled into a ponytail on top of her head. Bright blue eyes and skin that seemed untouched by the California sun greeted me. She wore a shrunken aqua T-shirt with a picture of a Troll doll on it over a long-sleeved thermal. Faded jeans hung off her hips.

"I'm Poly Monroe. Who are you?"

"I'm Kim Matheson. I work here." She looked at the back

door. "I got a flat tire this morning and ended up running late. I called the store and left a message. Genevieve called me back and said she'd meet me here this afternoon to show me around."

"When was that?"

She checked her phone. "Around nine." She looked up at me. "She called me half an hour ago and apologized, said she had a family emergency. I told her I was here and she asked me to close up."

"Did she tell you what the family emergency was?"

"No."

I looked at the empty crates Kim was stacking. "What are those?"

She looked embarrassed. "There was a set of keys in the Dracaena plant by the back door. When I got here, there were about a dozen crates of produce sitting outside. I didn't think Genevieve would want them to go bad, so I unlocked the store and put everything away in the kitchen. I thought it might make up for me showing up late on my first day."

"Today's your first day?" I asked. "Genevieve never mentioned anyone else working here."

"I saw the ad on Craigslist when I was on vacation. I'm taking a year off from school and I needed a job. We had a phone interview. We talked for forty-five minutes. Before we hung up, she told me the job was mine and I started today. I got the feeling she would have hired the first person who answered the ad, so I'm glad I didn't wait until I got home. This place is perfect for what I have in mind."

I studied Kim. She seemed sincere, but I wondered what exactly she thought she was going to get from working at Tea Totalers? I didn't think Genevieve could afford to pay her much more than minimum wage, and it was possible she couldn't even afford that.

"That probably sounded funny, didn't it?" Kim said. "I want to open my own restaurant someday. I can get hands-on experience here, and Genevieve said if I did a good job she'd be willing to write me a letter of recommendation for—well, for what I need it for," she finished.

"Genevieve's great," I said. "You'll love working here."

"Do you work here, too?"

"No, I own a fabric store down the street." It still gave me a thrill to say those words. "If you get a chance, you should come to the grand opening. I inherited the store a couple of months ago and it's been closed for a long time." I pulled a coupon out of my pocket and handed it to her. She folded it without looking at it and pushed it into her jeans pocket.

I helped her move what was left of the crates to the kitchen. She locked up and looked around, confused. "Should I leave the keys in the plant?"

While I knew that San Ladrón had the appearance of a small, cozy town, I'd lived through my own nightmare and wasn't as trusting as others might be. "Why don't you give them to me? I'm going to see Genevieve later today." *I hope*, I silently added.

"Okay, thanks. You'll tell her I was here, right? And that I put the produce in the kitchen? And cleaned up a little, too, because it looked like she left in a hurry."

"Sure, I'll let her know."

"Okay, thanks. Bye!"

I said good-bye and slipped the keys into my pocket. Kim walked around to the front of the store. She pulled a bicycle from alongside the restaurant and shook a few leaves loose from the handlebars. She pulled on a pink-and-white helmet and straddled the bicycle. A piece of paper fell from her back pocket and fluttered to the ground.

"Kim, you dropped something!" I called. She flipped up the kickstand and walked the bike forward until she reached the path in front of the store. "Kim!" I called again. She didn't appear to hear me.

I jogged forward and stumbled over an exposed tree root.

Kim turned around and looked at me, and then glided down the path out front of Tea Totalers and into a break in traffic.

The paper rested in the dirt. I picked it up by the corner and it unfolded. Along the top was the seal from the city of San Ladrón. Before I could stop myself, I scanned the page. It was a notice of a date and time to meet with a parole officer. The letter was addressed to Kim Matheson.

Three

I folded the paper back up and tucked it into my pocket next to the keys, then thought better of it. It wasn't mine to take. I let myself into the back of Tea Totalers and went to Genevieve's desk. I pulled a blank sheet of paper out of her printer and wrote her a note: *G—I came by to check on you. Your new employee dropped this after she left. Call me—Poly.* I considered adding a note about the produce in the fridge, but didn't. There was more than just a report of activities for me to talk to Genevieve about, and I'd tell her when I saw her.

I left the note on the keyboard and set Kim's letter, folded, on the side. I drew an arrow as if there was any mistaking what I was referring to. When I set down the pen, my hand bumped the mouse. The computer made a chugging noise, and the monitor lit up.

Files had been left open. One was a database of the costs of running the tea shop. Expenses were listed in red; income was listed in black. I had no business snooping around

Genevieve's financial situation, so I closed the file and turned the monitor off.

I moved to the first of three large refrigerators that lined the wall inside the kitchen and looked inside. Plastic tubs were stacked on the shelves. Small labels identified the contents of plants and herbs I knew Genevieve used in her various blends of tea. A large bin labeled "catnip" surprised me. Did she grow it herself or buy it at the local pet store?

I closed the door and looked inside the second fridge. Two dozen plastic dollar-store pitchers of iced tea stood like an army ready to attack. The third fridge had been hastily packed with fruits and vegetables. Lemons, limes, oranges, and tomatoes filled uncovered plastic tubs like the ones used in the first fridge. Apples, pears, carrots, and celery jutted out from shelves. Bunches of radishes were pushed along the interior wall, and avocados filled the door. This must be the produce Kim had brought inside, because Genevieve would have known better than to refrigerate half of these items.

Having grown up in California, I knew how abundant different fruits and vegetables could be. I also knew how to store them until they were ready to eat. Half of the produce in the refrigerator needed to be removed and stored differently. If it had remained in the refrigerator overnight, most of it would have been worthless by morning. How did someone who wanted to work in a restaurant not know that?

I tucked the avocados into a brown paper bag, folded it up, and set it on a shelf next to a set of silver mixing bowls and then transferred the lemons and limes to a blue and white ceramic bowl that had been empty on the counter. The tomatoes went on a flat tray with an inch between them. I spaced out the remaining produce on the now-empty refrigerator shelves and checked my phone between storing each different fruit and vegetable, rebooting it between the limes and the tomatoes. Still no calls from Genevieve.

When I was done, I surveyed the kitchen. A plastic bag

filled with individually wrapped croissants was tucked in the corner under the cabinet. I didn't know that there was a proper way to store croissants, but since Genevieve had been the one to pack the lunches for the crew at the store, I assumed she'd been the one to put them away. Everything else seemed to be in order.

The paper Kim had dropped was still there. Feeling slightly guilty, I unfolded it and snapped a picture with my phone, folded it back up, and locked the store up behind me.

A steady stream of cars lined up behind the traffic light at San Ladrón and Bonita Avenue. Between cleaning my apartment and rearranging food at Genevieve's, I'd burned up a fair portion of the day. Rush hour was officially on. I latched the gate in front of Tea Totalers and turned right. It was four blocks to the fabric store. I crossed the street and stopped off at The Earl of Sandwich, ordered a cucumber and avocado with sprouts on whole wheat toast for me and a side of sliced turkey for the cats. I added a bottle of water and waited while the woman behind the counter wrapped the turkey in tinfoil and put it and my sandwich in a brown paper bag. She handed it all to me and I left.

As I waited at the crosswalk for the light to change, I overheard a raised female voice come from Charlie's Automotive, next door to the sandwich shop. A fiery redhead in a skintight leopard-print dress and red stiletto heels stood on the sidewalk in front.

"He wasn't afraid for people to know. Why would he be? Half of San Ladrón would have killed to be in his shoes," she said.

The traffic light changed. I had been planning to cross the street, but curiosity kept me where I was. I approached a wooden bench in front of one of San Ladrón's many hair salons and ignored the *Walk* sign. The woman out front hadn't seen me, which I thought was for the best.

Charlie, local mechanic and all-around tough cookie, stood

facing the redhead. Charlie was dressed in standard blue coveralls. She wiped her hands on a rag that had long ago lost any semblance of color and smiled at the angry woman. Her lips moved, but her voice was lower than the redhead's, so I couldn't make out what she said. I uncapped my bottle of water and took a swig while watching the scene.

The redhead pointed a finger at Charlie. "Don't mess with me, Charlie," she said loud enough for her voice to carry to me. She pivoted on her high red heels and got into a shiny green Mustang. Seconds later the engine sprung to life and the car pulled out, cutting off traffic and causing an explosion of angry honks. I took another swig of my water, recapped the bottle, tucked it back into the bag, and stood up. Charlie noticed me and headed my way.

"One of these days I'm going to learn to leave well enough alone," she said.

"Who was that?

"Babs Green, San Ladrón's local showgirl."

"I didn't know San Ladrón had showgirls."

"She has a burlesque show at the Villamere Theater. Pretty racy stuff for this town. She's not happy because she found out I have some dirt on her." She wiped her hands with the soiled rag.

"I thought you'd be the type to mind your own business?" I said as a question.

"Nah, I'm as opportunistic as the next person." She jutted her chin toward the front of the fabric store. "You couldn't leave well enough alone, either, could you?"

Since meeting her, I'd come to learn that Charlie wasn't big on hello, good-bye, or small talk in general. With her it was either straight to the point or the tail end of a conversation we'd started days ago. If she wanted to talk about something, we'd talk about it. If not, I'd have to wait until she was ready.

I liked Charlie. She wore her hair in thick braids, mostly

black but currently some colored in shades formerly only known to Crayola, her eyeliner heavy like Cleopatra, and her lipstick burgundy. She had at least nine piercings: seven in her ears, one in her right eyebrow, and one in her navel. I hadn't seen any others and didn't really want to know about them if they were there. You'd never know she was the daughter of one of the wealthiest men in San Ladrón. She'd tried her best to keep it a secret from the town, and had been mostly successful.

"I wish I could say I knew what you were referring to, but today's been the kind of day where you could be talking about a number of things," I said.

"The sign." She pointed to it like her hand was a gun.

We both turned and looked at the front of the fabric store. The words had been removed, but the rusted bolts that had held them in place still jutted out like the ones that protruded from the neck of Frankenstein's monster's. The exposed façade looked dirty and bare without signage, and the sidewalk was buckled from where *Land* had, well, landed. Traces of the construction crew in the form of scaffolding and a few yellow hard hats left behind were still there, despite my attempts to clean up after the men on the job.

"I had the permits. I had the construction crew. Everything was in place to get that sign down today."

"What happened?"

"Phil Girard happened."

"What did that idiot go and do now?"

"He got himself killed."

Charlie looked at me, her normal quick comebacks temporarily silenced. When she found her voice, the tone had changed from tough girl to concern. "You, me, details. Give me a sec to lock up and I'll come to the store."

"I'll wait here."

Being new to San Ladrón, I knew that most people knew more about everybody in the town than I did. Charlie's reaction reiterated that feeling. She knew something about Phil Girard that I didn't. If she was willing to tell me what it was, I wasn't going to give her the chance to change her mind.

About a minute later Charlie slammed down the gate to the auto shop and locked it from the outside. She'd changed out of her coveralls and now wore a cropped Billy Idol T-shirt that showed off her belly button piercing, and a pair of baggy blue jeans. She yanked on the other exterior door, checking that it was locked, too. The light changed and we crossed the street. Charlie stepped over the crack in the sidewalk and waited as I unlocked the gate and the door. I headed upstairs. It wasn't until I reached the kitchen that I realized I'd lost her somewhere along the way.

"Charlie?" I called.

"Give me a minute," her muffled voice called back. A few seconds later I heard the flush of a toilet and the sound of running tap water.

I unpacked my cucumber sandwich and sat down at the table to eat. Charlie poured herself a glass of water and sank into a chair opposite me. "The Earl of Sandwich?"

"How'd you guess?" I said with a mouth full of the cucumber and avocado sandwich.

She rolled her eyes at me. "I don't know how you eat that healthy crap."

"Healthy? This is my third form of bread today. What do you get from Earl's?"

"Basket of onion rings and a roast beef sandwich. So, what's the deal with Phil?"

I swallowed. "I hired Phil to pick up some fabric for me when he was in Los Angeles today. When the truck rolled up in front of the store, some other driver was behind the wheel and Phil's body was in the back buried under my fabric. Those bolts weigh like twenty pounds each. I don't know if he was dead before he was put in there or not, but you're talking about over two hundred pounds of fabric on top of him. If he was alive, he might not have lasted the trip from Los Angeles."

"So Clark was here?"

"Yes, Sheriff Clark was here. I tried to get him to tell me something, but he wouldn't."

"What do you want to know?" she asked. "Maybe I can help you out."

I leaned back against the bench. "How? Five minutes ago you didn't even know about this. How did you not know about this? Your shop is across the street."

"I was out of town this morning. Personal business."

I knew better than to ask. When it came to her personal life, Charlie would tell me what she wanted me to know when she wanted me to know it. It was her version of control. She hated that I'd figured out part of her secret within a week of being in San Ladrón, and now did what she could to maintain what was left of it.

"Okay, so what can you tell me about Phil Girard?"

"For starters, he was cheating on his wife with the woman who just left my garage."

I wasn't sure what I expected Charlie to tell me, but it wasn't that. "He was—on Genevieve—with the stripper?"

"She prefers *showgirl*, if you ever end up in a face-to-face conversation, but yes."

"Are you sure?"

"Phil brought his van in last month. I found a pink garter belt under the floor mat on the passenger side. I told him Genevieve didn't look like the type to wear a garter belt and he turned as red as the beet soup she serves on Thursdays. At first I thought it was funny, you know, this normal couple who lives in this normal town gets their kicks by spicing things up in the back of the delivery van."

"Maybe they do," I said.

"Not on your life. The next day I made sure to detail the whole car and I found a flyer for Babs Green's show. There was a kiss mark on the back of the flyer—same shade of pink as the lingerie. I made a crack to Phil about Babs matching her lipstick to her underwear and he got mad. He said if I ever told anybody about the two of them he'd come after me. I told him to make it worth my while to keep my mouth shut."

"You blackmailed him?" I asked, shocked at her admission.

She waved her hand. "I negotiated. Needed a couple of parts so I could rebuild the transmission on a '72 Hornet. I made enough on that job to pay my rent and then some. Guess that was short-lived. Babs found out that I knew and that he'd paid me to keep quiet."

"Is that what she was so mad about?"

She nodded. "What's weird is that she wanted the world to know about her and Phil. She was more mad that he'd paid me to keep quiet than that I'd blackmailed him. All things considered, you'd think it would be the other way around."

"Does Genevieve know about them?"

"If she does, it's not because I told her. I was planning on milking that cow for a good long time. But if you want my opinion, she's better off without him. She knows that, right?"

"I don't know. I haven't seen her since we found the body."

"She skipped?" Charlie asked.

"I don't know where she went. I left her a couple of messages and I went to her tea shop. Her new employee was there, but she wasn't. The shop was locked up."

"How'd you get in?" Charlie asked.

"Genevieve left a set of keys in the plant behind the café. I went inside and left her a note. The computer had a couple of files open, like someone had been in the middle of something and was interrupted."

"Did you tell Clark?"

"Tell him what? That Genevieve left some files open on her computer? I hardly think that's his business."

"He wants to talk to her, I bet."

"Yes. I don't know why she left. I mean, I'm sure she was upset. He was her husband. But where did she go? And even if she wants to be alone, why is she avoiding the police? It's not like she could have had anything to do with it. He was killed in Los Angeles."

"You don't know that."

"Charlie," I started. "The van pulled up in front of my store and Phil was dead in the back."

"That doesn't mean he was killed in Los Angeles." Charlie picked up a strip of turkey from the tinfoil and held it down for Needles. "I don't think Frenchy killed her husband any more than you do, but she's not doing herself any favors by avoiding Sheriff Clark."

Pins swarmed around our ankles, meowing for his own piece. I held my sandwich down toward the floor. He sniffed it and walked away.

"I don't know what Genevieve's going through right now, but I feel like I need to talk to her. Phil was her connection to the San Ladrón community. Without him, she's all alone," I said.

We both grew quiet. I finished my sandwich and put my plate in the sink. I looked out the back window and noticed a woman in the parking lot. She was wrapped in a blanket that covered her head, making her look like a monk. Her eyes darted left and then right. The blanket shifted back on her head and I recognized Genevieve's soft blond curly hair.

I unlocked the window frame and pushed it up. "Gen?" I called.

She looked up. Even from the distance of two stories above the parking lot I could tell she'd been crying. She put a hand up in front of her and waved it side to side, and pointed to the back door.

"Wait there," I said. I turned to Charlie. "Genevieve's in the parking lot. I'll be right back."

I ran down the stairs and across the exposed concrete floor of the fabric shop. I skidded around the corner of a display of silk and tulle I'd been working on and reached the back door. When I opened it, Genevieve stood in front of me, bundled up like a dethroned princess from one of Grimm's fairy tales.

"Come in, hurry," I said. She bustled past me and I locked the door behind her. "Where have you been?" I asked. "I've been calling you all day."

"Poly, you have to help me," she said. "I'm afraid—"

"Don't be afraid, Genevieve. I know it's scary to think you're on your own now, but it'll be okay."

"No, that's not it. I'm afraid I killed my husband."

Four

"Come again?" said Charlie from the bottom of the stairs. Genevieve looked past me at her, then back to me. Despite the blanket, she was shaking.

"Charlie, go upstairs and get the brandy," I said. "It's in the cabinet in the living room."

Charlie turned around and climbed the stairs. I looked for something for Genevieve to sit on. The only chairs in the fabric store were in the front by the work station, but there was a small plastic stepstool by the shelves I'd been clearing off early last week. I moved the stool to her, guided her down, and handed her a package of tissue paper from the register. I rolled an already-dirty bolt of burlap in front of her and straddled it like it was a log.

"Genevieve, why do you think you killed Phil?"

"I'm almost sure of it. And now the sheriff's office wants to talk to me, and I can't go to jail, Poly! I'll lose the shop and the house and everything I have." She sniffled.

"Slow down. Tell me what happened."

Charlie returned with a heavy cut-crystal glass that held an inch of amber liquid. She offered it to Genevieve, who took it with both hands and drank. She lowered the glass, looked up at Charlie, then raised it again and finished it off. She set it on the floor. Charlie stooped down and picked it up.

"Poly, can I see you for a second?" Charlie asked. She set the glass on the white laminate wrap stand and walked to the back of the store.

"Wait here," I said to Genevieve, even though she showed no signs of moving. "I'll be right back." I followed Charlie to the back door.

"I'm going to take off," she said in a low voice. "Frenchy's not going to talk around me. That's fine. I'm going to the sheriff's office. Clark can't show up here if I've got him detained there. If she needs a place to stay, she can stay with me. Nobody will look for her there. I'll call you when I'm back at my place and we'll work something out."

She unlocked the door and slipped out. I locked it behind her and went back to Genevieve.

"Tell me what happened, Gen."

"I was mad at Phil when he left yesterday. We had a fight at the tea shop. That's why he went to Los Angeles a day early instead of leaving Monday morning. Remember I mentioned the food distributor? His name is Topo di Sali. Phil wanted me to sell to him. I accused him of setting up a meeting without me. He didn't deny it. He said I was being selfish by not considering what it would do for us. I was so mad, I wanted to punish him."

"What did you do?"

"Before the fight, before everything, I was planning to make him a basket of food to take on the trip—you know, sandwiches like the ones I brought you this morning. That's how I knew I had the supplies to make them when you asked. I thought if Phil realized what a considerate wife I was, he'd start to appreciate me more. But after the fight, he stormed out of the store. I got mad. I packed his basket with sandwiches and a batch of catnip tea."

"Catnip?"

"I read about it on a tea blog. It's very relaxing, and I thought Phil needed to calm down. When I first experimented with it, Phil complained that it made him sick. This was a different blend from that first one, but, Poly, if he got sick from the catnip, I might have killed him!" She doubled over, her face in her hands, her shoulders shaking with sobs. I held out a piece of tissue paper to her. She took it and blew her nose like a foghorn.

"When I looked in the back of the van, I saw the empty container. He drank it. All of it. And he's dead. People are going to think I did it because I was mad at him. They're going to think I killed him on purpose!"

"What about Rick, the man who drove the truck? Do you know him?"

She sniffled. "His name is Rick Penwald. He lives in the town next to San Ladrón. He has his own delivery company, and he helped get Phil started. Sometimes he borrows Phil's van when he wants to make smaller deliveries."

"Isn't that like taking business from Phil?"

"No, he only borrows it when he knows Phil is on his taxi route, so it's no bother. And he throws business to Phil all the time. I always thought when the tea shop took off, Phil would turn his delivery route over to Rick."

I thought about the van that I'd seen. "But the truck said *Special Delivery* on the side."

"That's Rick's company. He has a magnetic sign that he can put on whatever vehicle he needs."

"So that was your van? And he put his sign on it and drove it here with Phil in the back?"

"That's what he usually does when he borrows it," she

said. She wiped her face with the edge of the blanket. A fresh wave of tears poured forth.

"What else did you see when you looked in the back of the van?"

"I saw Phil's arm and I saw the tea container rolling around. I knew what happened. Poly, I have pitchers of that stuff at the shop. The police are going to put it all together and come after me. I can't let that happen, Poly. What am I going to do? I lost my husband. I can't lose my business and my home. I can't lose my whole life. I'm all alone now. I'm going to lose everything!" She buried her face in her blanket-covered hands and her shoulders shook with sobs.

I closed my eyes and thought back to what I'd seen inside the back of the van. Genevieve was right, there had been an empty tea container next to Phil's hand. I wasn't certain, but thought there had been a logo from Tea Totalers on the outside of it. There had also been crumbs scattered on the floor around it. Had he eaten the contents of the picnic basket when he drank the tea? And if so, would the police be able to determine anything from the contents of his stomach?

But after he ate or drank whatever she had packed for him, his body had been buried under the fabric. No matter what was in the picnic basket that Genevieve sent him to Los Angeles with, there was no way he would have buried himself under the fabric after being poisoned. Maybe Genevieve had accidentally slipped Phil a Mickey, but that wasn't what killed him. And as long as Sheriff Clark was holding my fabric hostage as part of his investigation, I was going to do my darnedest to figure out what did.

I moved from the burlap to the stool and put my arm around Genevieve's shaking shoulders. "It's going to be okay," I said. "You don't know if Phil was poisoned. You don't know how he died. I know you feel scared and alone, but you're not. I'm going to help you through this. You didn't kill your husband. I believe that."

"But the police might not. Especially if they find out about our financial troubles and the fight. There were people at Tea Totalers when we fought. Mr. di Sali was there. Customers, too. There's no way people didn't hear us argue."

I knew Sheriff Clark knew about the financial troubles. I knew it because even if nobody else had said anything, I had. All the more reason to help Genevieve get past this.

"I want you to listen to me. Something else happened on that trip to Los Angeles. Can you give me a list of what he was getting for you?"

She nodded. "I keep all of my shopping lists on the computer at the store. I can print you a copy tomorrow."

"You're going to open the shop tomorrow?"

"Maybe I shouldn't. I don't know what to do. If I don't open for business, I won't be able to pay my bills, and now that Phil's gone—" Her voice caught in her throat and she stopped talking.

I had an idea. "Wait here. I have something to show you."

I left Genevieve sitting on the stepstool and I went to the sewing station in the corner, where I'd been working on the secret French-themed makeover for her café. I carried the pile of completed items back to where she sat, hoping to temporarily distract her from her troubles.

"I've been working on a surprise for your tea shop. A French renovation with fabric." I held up a partially finished apron made of blue-and-cream toile. "I've only been working with fabrics that my aunt and uncle bought in France. I have tablecloths, seat cushions, aprons, placemats, and curtains." I held up the cuttings of fabric with the rooster. "I haven't had time to frame these yet, but I thought they'd be nice to decorate the walls with."

Genevieve's smile was small but genuine. "When did you have the time to do this?"

"I started it after we first met. I haven't been able to sleep much now that the grand opening is getting close. This relaxes me. And it was fun." I leaned against the wrap stand and refolded the apron. "Here's what I'm thinking."

I outlined my idea. Genevieve would hang a sign announcing that Tea Totalers was under renovation. With the store closed, I could easily come and go under the guise of measurement taking. And hopefully, by the time Tea Totalers was the French paradise she'd always dreamed it would be, Genevieve would be experiencing *La Liberté* and not become one of *Les Miserables*.

"It sounds perfect. I hope I'm around to see it when it's done," Genevieve said.

"Don't talk like that. You didn't do anything to bring this on yourself. Now come upstairs with me." I held out a hand and pulled her to her feet. Her blond curls had turned frizzy and moved in wisps around her face. She blew at the strands that fell in front of her eyes and kept the blanket tightly wrapped around her like a protective shell. We marched up the stairs to the living room. "Lie down and try to relax."

I brought Genevieve a fluffy pillow from the hall closet. It was encased in a cotton pillowcase printed with tiny pink rosebuds. A ruffle of pale green that matched the leaves and stems in the pattern framed out the pillow. I tucked the pillow under her head and covered her with a soft, white crocheted afghan. She closed her eyes. Even breathing followed. I retrieved the empty brandy glass from downstairs and carried it into the kitchen.

Charlie called at nine thirty. "How's Frenchy?" she asked.

"She's passed out on my sofa. Either too much brandy or sheer exhaustion. Probably both. I think we have a plan. She's going to close the tea shop for renovations. I'll handle them. That'll give her a reason not to interact with the general public, at least for a while."

"Did you find anything out from her?"

"There's a food distributor who wants to buy her tea recipes, and Phil was pushing her to sell. They had a big fight before he left and a bunch of people saw."

"Anything else?

"She said the driver of the delivery van knew Phil. I want to talk to him. I think there's something fishy about the fact that he didn't know his 'friend' was dead in the back of the truck. He must know something. Did Clark mention him?"

"I said I was going to detain him. I didn't say we discussed the case."

"How'd you detain him?"

"He's been pestering me about looking at his radiator. Clark wants to talk to Frenchy, but I get the feeling he knows something he's not saying. We have to keep her out of sight. Tell her to come to my auto shop tomorrow morning around six."

"Why are you helping her?" I asked.

There was a pause on the other end of the phone. "Maybe I'm trying to broaden my social circle," she said. "Six A.M. Don't forget." She hung up.

The alarm went off at five thirty. I was already awake, thanks to the sunlight streaming through the windows that faced Bonita Avenue. I liked waking up with the sun and kept the curtains open for that very reason. I shifted to the middle of the bed and stretched my arms out on either side.

Most of the apartment had been decorated with Victorian antiques that matched the style of the building, but the bedroom had, at one point, benefited from Aunt Millie's taste and talent in the form of her own glamorous fabric makeover. When I wasn't sleeping in the queen sleigh bed, it was dressed in a white-on-white jacquard duvet cover, accented with an ivory velvet throw blanket lined in washed silk. The headboard was an elaborate piece of inlaid walnut and chestnut. The armoire matched the headboard and the two nightstands that flanked the bed. Smaller accent pillows trimmed in marabou, ostrich feathers, and fringe, decorated with vintage pins, were stacked on the chaise.

Aunt Millie had taught me that glamour didn't need to be relegated to the closet, and the same ideas of personal decoration that women had relied on in the first half of the last century could be applied to home décor. I believed it was why she and Marius each had standing valets to hang their garments on. Their clothes acted as part of the room design.

I kicked my feet against the cool cotton sheets. Pins and Needles were curled up by the foot of the bed, their fur pressed against each other. Pins had his gray paw wrapped around Needles's tawny head. I liked seeing them so close. Even with the great expanse of the queen-sized bed, they wanted reassurance that they still had each other, like they did the day Vaughn McMichael had found them in the Dumpster behind the fabric shop.

The first time I met Vaughn, he helped me get through a very narrow window. Along with the unexpected push from behind, I popped through the window and crashed into him, knocking us both onto the floor. Since then he'd brought me dinner, given me answers about my family, and seen me in my underwear. I didn't have him figured out yet, but I'd seen more to him than what was on the surface. And because of the underwear thing, he could say the same about me.

The sheets were cool and soft against my skin, and still smelled of the clean fresh air that had dried them after I'd hung them out back. And even though I was learning to sleep in the middle, sometime during the night I gravitated to the right, the side I'd usually slept on when I had shared a bed with my now-ex-boyfriend in Los Angeles.

Waking in this apartment felt like waking in a different era. It was one of the reasons most of my belongings were still occupying a storage unit in Burbank by my parents' house instead of here. I didn't want traces of my old life to creep into my new one. Breaking up with my boyfriend, quitting my job, and moving to San Ladrón were all part of my future. I hadn't even been looking for a new life, but when it had found me, I couldn't deny it.

I tossed the covers back and sat up. In addition to the scent of the fresh air that clung to the sheets, I detected something new. Coffee. And sugar. I stood up and slid my feet into plush slippers. I gathered my nightgown in my hands and scampered across the hallway to the living room, where Genevieve had fallen asleep on the sofa. The covers were folded in a neat pile.

"Genevieve?" I called out.

"In the kitchen," she replied. I followed the aroma and found her dredging slices of bread in an egg bath. "Did I wake you?" she asked.

"No, the sun woke me. What's this?"

"I couldn't sleep. Preparing food calms me." She poured a mug of coffee and handed it to me. "After what I told you, I figured you wouldn't want tea," she said.

"I'll drink your tea any time you want to make it for me." I took a sip of coffee. She turned her back on me and pulled two slices of bread out of a skillet. She picked up a piece of paper that had been formed into a cone shape along one end, tipped it, and a dusting of sugar sprinkled onto the toast. She set the plate on the table in front of me.

"I didn't see any powdered sugar, but I prefer granulated sugar with French toast."

"What's that paper thing?"

"Makeshift shaker. I used toothpicks to poke holes in the end of the paper, and I turned the other side into a cone. I pour the dry sugar into the cone and shake it out on top of the toast. When it's all done I pour the sugar back into the bag and throw the paper out. Sanitary and effective."

I sliced into the toast with the side of the fork and bit into it. "Mmmmm. This isn't like any French toast I've had before," I said with my mouth full.

She rinsed the bowl and the pan and slipped them both into the dishwasher. "I added a little cinnamon, nutmeg, and vanilla extract to the egg wash. It adds something special."

"Aren't you eating?"

"I can't eat when I'm nervous."

Genevieve's lack of appetite worked out well for me. I finished off a second helping of French toast, transferred my coffee into a to-go cup, and set my dirty dish and mug into the sink. Somehow, even though Genevieve had whipped up the most delicious breakfast I'd had in months, she managed to clean up as she went. My dirty dish was the only thing left out.

"Everything's going to be okay," I said to her.

"I can't take a chance on that being true." She fidgeted with her sleeves for a second. "I'm going to call Mr. di Sali about selling one of my recipes. That's the only way I can see paying the bills now."

"I don't think you should make any rash decisions. Charlie said you can stay with her temporarily, until we figure things out. Give me a couple of minutes to get ready and we'll leave."

I selected what amounted to my daily uniform: a composite of black, black, and black. My old job in the garment district of Los Angeles had taught me that a working fashion institute graduate was a dirty fashion institute graduate, at least at first. Black hid stains from the grease on sewing machines and drips from glue guns. It was utilitarian in a non-army sort of way. My former boss, Giovanni, had made it his business to corner the market on cheap, gaudy pageant-slash-prom dresses in colors intended for shock value. Cornflower blue, saffron yellow, hibiscus red, and bright green were fine for floral arrangements and tropical fish, but if I never saw another electric prom dress, it would be too soon.

I traded my nightgown for a clean bra and panty set and pulled on black sailor pants and a close-fitting black boat-neck T-shirt. I slipped my feet into white deck shoes and ran down the stairs. Genevieve played with the cats in the living room. She pulled a hat down low over her blond hair and wrapped her jacket tightly around her shoulders. Out front, a police car sat in traffic. We gave him ample time to reach the light at the end of the street before running across the street to Charlie's Automotive.

Five

Charlie met us on the sidewalk and ushered us into her shop. She looked up and down the street before pulling the door shut behind her.

"Go into my office. We'll talk there."

I headed past the pit, pausing for a few seconds when I recognized Vaughn's black Mercedes. It was a coupe version of the S Class Sedan his father drove and was two feet off the ground. Tools I didn't recognize were scattered underneath. I turned around when I reached the office and saw Genevieve standing in the middle of the garage, staring at the calendar of scantily clad firemen that hung on the wall. I doubled back, grabbed her by her elbow, and pulled her along after me.

I'd been inside Charlie's Automotive before, but never in her office. It was a small room, about four feet by six feet. A two-foot shelf attached to one wall served as a desk. It held a monitor, a keyboard, a clock, and a set of bobblehead

Pep Boys. Pegboard hung on the far wall, holding half a dozen sets of keys, each marked with a small white tag. The desk was covered in invoices, as was a shelf above the computer monitor. A few colorful folders were sideways, on top of catalogs as thick as the yellow pages that advertised car parts I'd never heard of.

The door to the office shut behind us. I turned around and saw Charlie watching Genevieve. Gen was holding a five-by-seven frame that she'd picked up from the shelf. The photo showed a pinup girl in a short white sailor outfit. She saluted the camera, her smile as radiant as the sunlight captured in the background.

"Is that you?" Genevieve asked Charlie.

Charlie shrugged. "I used to do some modeling." She took the frame from Genevieve's hands and set it face side down on the shelf. "So, what's the plan?"

"Tea Totalers is going to be closed for the week. Renovations. I'm going to handle that. Did you mean it when you said Genevieve could stay here?"

"Why can't I stay with you?" Genevieve asked me, confusion clouding her expression.

"It would be too easy for the Garden sisters or Tiki Tom to notice, and you can't take that chance."

"But I can't stay here," Genevieve said.

"Yes, you can. There's a guesthouse out back," Charlie said.

"What am I supposed to do all day?" Genevieve asked.

"File your nails. Play solitaire on the computer. Practice how to say 'I didn't kill my husband' in French." Genevieve glared at Charlie. "Sorry, that was in poor taste, even for me." She put her hand on Genevieve's shoulder. "Most people leave me alone to do my thing. Use that to your benefit. Nobody's going to come looking for you here."

"But—"

Charlie looked at me. "A little help here?"

"Charlie's right. This place is safer for you than anywhere

else. We both know you didn't hurt Phil, but that means someone else did. Until we know who or why, we don't know if you're in danger. You can trust Charlie. I can vouch for that."

Genevieve looked back and forth between our faces. "So that's it?"

"For now," I said. I waited a few seconds. "Charlie, can I talk to you for a second? Out front?" I asked.

We left Genevieve sitting in Charlie's black leather swivel chair, staring at the blank monitor. I closed the office door behind me.

"Did you find out anything else from Sheriff Clark?" I asked.

"Nope. He's waiting for a report from the medical examiner. He's being tight-lipped on this one."

"Did he talk to the van driver?"

"He didn't say. He's still bent on talking to Frenchy, I know that. What's her plan?"

"She's not thinking rationally. She's so scared of losing everything, she's actually considering selling her tea recipes."

"Probably not a good idea for her to sell out the day after her husband was murdered."

"I know. She's terrified. You heard her last night; she thinks she killed Phil."

"How exactly does she think she killed him? She was here and he was there."

"She sent him off with a picnic basket of food and tea from the shop. The tea was made from catnip mixed with other spices and she's afraid that's what did him in. She doesn't want to talk to Clark because she thinks he's out to get her."

"Leave Clark to me. I'll make sure he stays out of her hair."

"I don't think ignoring the police is a good idea," I said.

"Oh yeah? And what if word gets out that he's testing the tea at her store? I'm guessing that won't be good for business."

I didn't answer her, because I'd already thought through what she was hinting at. Even a hint of scandal involving Genevieve's tea would destroy Tea Totalers, and probably any offers to buy her product would be pulled from the table.

I turned my head away from her and stared at the car up on the rack. "That's Vaughn's car, isn't it?"

"Sure is."

"He's been here recently?"

"No. He dropped off the keys last week. He said he was heading out of town and wanted me to check it out. Something about an oil leak."

Vaughn McMichael was the son of the richest developer in San Ladrón, which also made him Charlie's brother. Mr. McMichael owned half of the town and had tried to buy the fabric store out from under me when I first inherited it. He'd used aggressive tactics that led me to believe he was a dangerous man. One day, teetering on the edge of independence, I showed up at his office and let him know I was not only capable of running the store, but intended to do so.

Since then I'd written up a business plan and applied for a bank loan. The loan had come back approved, cosigned by Mr. McMichael. I didn't know if a thank-you was in order for a favor I hadn't requested, so I continued with my plans. On one hand, it was nice to know the businessman believed in my abilities. On the other, I knew if I failed, the store belonged to him.

When I first met Vaughn, I was on my guard. Rich boy with a fancy college degree who thinks he can buy his way through life. Turns out I was so far off base I was like an outfielder in the minors two blocks away from the game.

"He asked about you," Charlie said.

"What did he say?"

"What is this, fifth grade?"

"Sorry. Doesn't matter; I really don't care."

"Which is it? Does it not matter, or don't you care?"

"Forget it," I said.

"Forget what? I'm the one who brought it up."

"So what did you tell him?"

"I told him some things don't change and some things do, and if he really wants to know how you're doing he should ask you himself." She picked up a wrench and tossed it into a pile with other tools. Metal clanged against metal and resonated against the walls. "He's supposed to pick up his car this morning, but it's not done yet. I'd expect a visit if I were you."

I turned away from her so she couldn't see my expression. When I turned back, she had one eye narrowed and her head was tipped to the side. I felt scrutinized like a specimen in a Petri dish.

I left the auto shop and returned to Material Girl to pick up the completed items for the French fabric makeover, and then drove the short distance to Tea Totalers.

A cluster of people surrounded the front doors to the café. I parked around back, left the fabric in the car, and joined the crowd. I recognized a few local patrons. "Excuse me, pardon me, excuse me," I said. I taped a handwritten sign that said *Closed for Renovations* to the front door. "Tea Totalers is going to be closed for the week. It's getting a face-lift."

Amongst cries of "You're kidding," and "Figures," I politely asked people to find another place for their morning tea and croissant fix. Several people left. One lady commented, "Renovations at a time like this! Her husband just died, poor thing. I bet she can't even think straight."

"She has a point," said a voice to my left. I turned and faced Vaughn while the crowd of annoyed customers left in search of another breakfast option.

"Do you make a habit of popping up unexpectedly?" I asked.

"Only when I want the element of surprise to work in my favor."

"I'm not *that* surprised. Charlie said I might see you today."

"You asked Charlie about me?" he asked. A half smile crept into the corners of his mouth.

"Not exactly." I blushed.

His expression grew serious. "I heard about Phil Girard on the news this morning. How's Genevieve?"

"She's fine." I studied Vaughn's expression and told the truth. "That's a lie. She's not fine. She's a mess. I told her to take a few days away from the shop and let me do something nice for her while she deals with what happened." I knew I was editing the events of the last twenty-four hours into a sanitized version of why I was there, but it was all true. It was a good place to start.

"So . . . renovations?" he asked. He pointed to the sign I'd taped on the front door. "Do you have time for a project this size, considering you're opening your store this weekend?"

"I didn't realize you were keeping track."

"I saw your ad in the paper and the flyers you left at Charlie's and at Lopez Donuts. I have to admit, you advertise at all the right places."

I unlocked the front door and went inside. "Grand opening is under control. This is something I've been working on for Genevieve for a while. I wasn't going to tell her until it was done, but in light of everything, I think it makes for good timing. If you're not busy, I could use some help."

Vaughn followed me inside. Without the scent of brewing tea and pastries baking, the café lacked the warmth I'd come to expect from the usually cozy interior. The lights were off, and the mismatched faded floral curtains blocked most of the natural light. Dust had settled on the chairs that were upside down on the tables scattered around at random. I flipped the pass-through up and walked behind the counter, pushed aside the floor-to-ceiling curtains that separated the counter from the kitchen/office, and unlocked the back door. I transferred the pile of fabrics from my car into a wooden crate and carried it inside. When I reentered the kitchen, Vaughn stood by the desk with a glass of tea in his hand.

"Don't drink that!" I dropped the crate and rushed across the kitchen. I slapped the glass out of his hand, and it crashed to the floor and shattered into a thousand tiny, wet glass shards.

"What did you do that for?" he asked.

"I'm sorry. I don't know what came over me." I turned around and looked for a broom and dustpan. I expected Vaughn to press me to explain my odd behavior. He didn't. He stooped down and picked up a few of the bigger pieces of glass and tossed them into a plastic trash bag, then mopped the spill up with a wad of paper towels and threw that into the plastic bag as well. He carried the bag out to the trash while I swept up the floor. His face was drawn into confusion, like he was trying to rationalize my actions but, short of declaring me unstable, couldn't explain why I'd done what I'd done.

When he returned, I was in the front of the café taking the curtain rods down from the walls. Another couple walked up to the front door and tried to open it. The woman pressed her face up to the glass and cupped her hands around her eyes. I climbed down from the bunker where I'd been standing and walked over to the door. I tapped on the glass behind the sign and said, "Renovations." She said something to the man she was with and they left.

"I don't want to tell you how to do what you're doing, but if you want the renovations to be a surprise, maybe you should block out the windows so people can't see inside."

"Block them out with what? I only brought the fabric I'm going to use. Once the curtains are up, people are going to see them."

"I can get you a roll of butcher paper from the hardware store and help you hang it. It'll take most of the morning, but it'll give you a bigger reveal once you're done."

I studied Vaughn's face. As far as renovations went, he had a point. And blocking out the windows might not be a bad idea if anybody came snooping around the shop looking for Genevieve. Win-win.

"Thanks. Do you want some money?" I asked before remembering Vaughn's wealth.

"That's the nicest thing you've ever asked me," he said. "But no, thanks. I think I can cover it."

He left out the back door. I didn't know how long it would take him to return, so I had to act quickly.

I went to the back office. Genevieve's inbox was overflowing with invoices. I flipped past half a dozen and got distracted by a flyer announcing a party at the Waverly House.

The Waverly House was a restored Victorian mansion that housed an exhibit of photos and local memorabilia from the town's early days as a citrus supplier. The staff held a monthly murder mystery party and boasted one of the best restaurants around. Vaughn McMichael's seventy-year-old mother, Adelaide, ran the landmark-turned-museum.

Below the flyer were shopping lists and recipes. The piece of paper Kim had dropped still sat by the keyboard. In light of everything else going on, I wondered if there was another reason she showed up when she did.

I abandoned the inbox and jiggled the mouse. The files that had been left open were now closed. I launched an Internet browser and searched for a listing for "Special Delivery trucking company." I couldn't find a website, but a handful of favorable reviews showed up on Yelp. As I scrolled through the reviews of Rick's delivery service, I heard a knock on the front door. I waited a few seconds, expecting the person to go away. The knocking became more insistent. I powered off Genevieve's monitor and went to open the door. A squat man in a navy blue jog suit that zipped up the front stood outside. He had short black hair worn in a Julius Caesar style.

"The shop is closed for renovations," I said, pointing at

the sign. "Jitterbug is across the street and Lopez Donuts is about a mile down Bonita."

He held his hand out. "I'm here to talk to Genevieve Girard about her tea," he said in a voice that sounded like rusted pipes.

"She's not here."

"And you are . . . ?"

"I'm Poly Monroe. Like I said, Genevieve's not here." I stepped back and started to close the door, but he put a hand out and held it open.

"Are you in business with Mrs. Girard?"

"I'm managing her renovations."

"You're a decorator?"

"No. I own a fabric shop. What do you do, Mr. . . ." My voice trailed off as I realized I hadn't caught the gentleman's name.

"Topo di Sali." He handed me a business card with a flourish. "I work in Italian food distribution. I find products that are produced on a small scale like your friend's tea and I increase the demand to grocery stores throughout California. Ever hear of Presto Pesto? That was me. I took it from a grandmother's kitchen and now it's in a hundred and forty grocery stores up and down the coast."

"But Genevieve's whole theme is French. How did you find out about her tea?"

"Her husband told me about it. Met him on one of my trips. When he learned what I do for a living, he suggested I branch out and get in touch with her."

"Genevieve has a lot on her plate and I don't think the timing is right for her to consider expansion."

He stepped forward. "She's got troubles with money. I can solve those troubles."

"What's your take?"

"Half." He bent over and coughed a few times. When he spoke again, his voice was as raspy as before. "She doesn't even have to make the stuff. She can sell me her recipe and I'll make it happen. Or sell me her name and let me work up the recipe. The girl's got options."

I looked at the business card again. There was no address on the card, only a phone number. His name, Topo di Sali, was above the phrase "The Italian Scallion," and along the bottom it said, "Serving the Greater Los Angeles Area." The back of the card asked the question, "Who says you can't buy good taste?"

"Like I said, I don't think she's interested in selling out."

He put his hands in his pockets and rocked back on his feet. "You might want to let her make that decision. From what I'm hearing on the street, she might not have much of a choice."

Six

I didn't like the insinuation. "The next time I see Genevieve, I'll tell her you were here."

"I'm on my way to San Fran for business. If I don't hear from her by the time I return, I'll be back." He stared at me with eyes the color of glass cleaner. "You tell your friend to remember it's a two-way street." He held my stare for another second and then left.

I didn't doubt that, in Genevieve's current vulnerable state, she'd agree to just about anything Mr. di Sali offered her. I needed to get her back on solid footing before she made a very bad decision. And what exactly did he mean by that "two-way street" comment?

I called Sheriff Clark. "Hi, Sheriff, this is Poly Monroe. Have you found anything else out about Phil Girard's death?"

"Hold on," he said. I heard a click. A couple of seconds later, Clark returned. "Why are you so interested?"

I thought it best to keep Genevieve's name out of my

conversation. "I feel somewhat responsible. Phil went to Los Angeles to pick up fabric for me. I know they say there's no such thing as bad publicity, but I'd rather the fabric store not be linked to another homicide."

"It won't be. Is that all?"

"How did he die? Was he shot? Knocked out? Drugged?"

"I'm still waiting on some information from the medical examiner."

"Like what?"

"Tox screen."

"Why are you running that? Did you check my fabric for the death mask like I suggested?"

"Call it a hunch, Ms. Monroe." He sniffed, like he had a cold and no tissues handy. "I'm still trying to reach Mrs. Girard. You wouldn't happen to know where I can find her, do you?"

"Sorry, Sheriff. She arranged for me to handle renovations at the tea shop this week. I don't know where she's going to be while I'm here."

I said good-bye and hung up. The only new information I'd learned wasn't good. The medical examiner was running a tox screen. If Genevieve had accidentally poisoned Phil, Clark would discover it.

I'd assumed that Phil had been suffocated, but had he been alive when someone buried him? And if so, had he ingested something to keep him from fighting back? I shuddered. If Clark wasn't going to talk, then I needed to track down the van driver, Rick. He'd been in Los Angeles with Phil. He had to know something.

That led me to thought number two. Phil Girard wasn't a small man. He was easily six inches taller than Genevieve, and he carried enough weight on his frame to put him in "beefy" territory. He'd lost weight recently—vanity weight, I guessed, now that I knew about his affair with Babs—but still, the man wasn't a pushover. Unless the push came from a very strong force.

So how had someone gone about getting him under my velvet?

If he'd been sedated, he wouldn't have had the energy to fight back. Again, my mind trailed back to the tea. What would Clark find on that report from the medical examiner? I remember hearing somewhere that the lab tests would only show certain chemicals, unless the medical examiner had a reason to look for something suspicious.

I looked in the fridge. The something suspicious they would be looking for might be inside. I could dump all the tea, eliminating anything they could use to draw a connection between Genevieve and her husband's murder. Or should I leave it and assume her innocence?

Knuckles wrapped on the back door. I jumped and slammed the refrigerator door shut. Kim stood on the landing. She looked different today. Nervous. She fidgeted with her hands, moving them from the front pockets of her jeans to the back pockets. She then crossed them in front of the Care Bear on her T-shirt, and instantly uncrossed them and let them dangle.

"Hi, Kim, come on in," I said.

"Hi, Poly. I saw the sign out front. Genevieve didn't say anything about renovations. Is she here today?"

I studied the young girl. "Kim, do you watch the news? Read the paper?"

"Not really," she said. "Sometimes I watch TMZ," she added.

"Do you know what happened in San Ladrón yesterday?"

The color drained from her face. "I left San Ladrón right after we talked."

I didn't understand her response. "Have a seat."

Kim sat in Genevieve's chair, and I turned a wooden crate upside down and used it as a stool. The crate was lower than the chair, but I was five nine and she was barely over five feet tall, so we ended up eye to eye.

"Genevieve's husband died yesterday." I paused. "Somebody killed him." I focused on keeping my voice steady, even though the phrase "somebody killed him" left me shaken.

"Genevieve is going to take a few days away from Tea Totalers. I'm going to spend as much time here as I can, but I can't be here all the time. My store opens this week, and I have to take care of that, too. You said you took this job so you could learn about the restaurant business, and I don't think you're going to learn much about that from me."

Kim looked as if someone had knocked the wind out of her. "I need this job," she said. "There are people who are expecting me to be working here. I can't risk them knowing I'm not." Her face went from already pale to ashen and dark circles appeared under her eyes.

Whatever reason Kim had for working at Tea Totalers, it seemed to me that restaurant experience had little to do with it.

"Tell you what. This job at Tea Totalers is bigger than I originally thought. Can I count on you to help with the renovation here? Technically it's still working at Tea Totalers, even if the café is closed. If you're game, you can help me until Genevieve comes back."

She exhaled, making an *O* with her lips. Her cheeks puffed out like a blowfish. "That would work," she said after all the air was exhaled. She set her pink backpack on the floor under the desk. "Are we starting today? What do you want me to do?"

"Start by carrying the chairs from the front yard to the back. Then you can work on getting them ready for a new coat of paint."

"I thought I'd be working inside the store," she said. She spun the chair around and put her hands on the desk to stand up. The folded piece of paper she'd dropped fell to the floor. She squatted and picked it up. "I've been looking all over for this. What's it doing here?"

"You dropped it yesterday when you were leaving. I called out after you but you didn't seem to hear me. I figured you'd be back and this would be as safe a place as any."

"Did anybody see it?"

"I don't think anybody's been here since we left. Except for Vaughn, but I doubt he looked at it."

"Who's Vaughn?" she asked.

It took me a second to decide how to answer. "Vaughn's a regular of the tea shop. He's also a friend of Genevieve."

"Is he here?" She looked over my shoulder like she expected to see a third person in the small room.

"No. He went to the hardware store. Don't worry about him. If we want to get anything done today we should get started."

"Okay," she said. She folded the paper in half again and slid it into the outside pocket of her backpack, zipping it shut when she was done.

I had all of the curtains removed from the windows and the furniture pushed to the center of the tea shop by the time Vaughn returned with the butcher paper. He carried four rolls of the brown paper inside and laid them on the floor by the counter.

"I see you picked up a helper while I was gone. Didn't think I was coming back?"

"I don't know you well enough to know what you're going to do," I said with a smile. "That's Kim. She's supposed to be working here. I told her the shop is going to be closed for at least a week and she said she wants to stick around and help with the renovations. I'm not sure what Genevieve's going to say when she finds out she has to pay an extra salary on a week when she has no business."

"Are you going to tell her when you see her tonight?"

"Who said I'm going to see her tonight?"

"I figured, with you spending the day here, that you might report in to her when we're done."

"I don't think there's any need for reporting. She needs

some time and space to deal with what happened. I'm giving her time."

"And space, apparently."

My skin prickled with Vaughn's implications, true as they may be. I didn't think it was a good idea for anybody to know where Genevieve was, at least until we knew what the police would find from the tox screen.

"Have you been working nonstop since I left?"

I thought about the food distributor and the conversation with Sheriff Clark, but I wasn't ready to talk about either of them to Vaughn. "Pretty much."

"I don't know what's fueling you, but I thought you might like lunch."

"Lunch? I guess we could root around in the kitchen for some leftover croissants and jam," I said.

"Why eat leftovers?" He pointed to a picnic basket that I hadn't seen him carry inside. "Fresh from the Waverly House. My mother suggested it."

"How is Adelaide?" I asked.

"She's good. She misses you," he said. "She told me to tell you to visit sometime."

When I'd first returned to San Ladrón, I'd made Adelaide Brooks's acquaintance, but in the months that passed, as I separated myself from my life in Los Angeles and slowly prepared for a life in San Ladrón, I hadn't taken the time to return to see her.

"I will. I should." I thought about the fact that she had been friends with my aunt and uncle. "I will," I repeated. "So things at the Waverly House are fine?"

"Mostly. She's been planning Midnight in the Garden, the annual Waverly House spring party."

"I saw a flyer about that on Genevieve's desk. It's a pretty big deal, isn't it?"

"It used to be. It's a fund-raiser. The Waverly House opens

their gardens for a night. The admission fee goes directly to the annual operating expenses. Everything else is donated: music, food, drinks, decorations. But there's been a complication this year. Someone high up on the city council is saying the Waverly House is in no condition to hold the kind of party they used to. Now they're sending over a building inspector to determine whether she has to cancel it or not. Mom's not happy. She's been fighting city council for months while making plans. The party planning should be in full swing, but now it's on indefinite hold."

"Isn't your father on the city council?" I asked. Vaughn nodded. "Can't he do something?"

Vaughn looked down at the toes of his Stan Smiths for a few seconds, and then back at me. "He's the one who's holding things up." He picked up a rubber stress ball from the desk, tossed it about eight inches in the air, and caught it. The second time he did it, I shifted my eyes from the ball to his face and watched him concentrate on the path of the rubber blob. He clearly didn't want to talk about it.

After the third toss and catch he set the ball back on the desk and looked at me. "So . . . lunch?"

"Sounds great."

We carried two large picnic baskets into the center of the store and lined the floor with butcher paper. I found Kim in the front yard and asked if she wanted to join us. She declined, saying she'd packed her own lunch and preferred to keep working. There was something odd about her behavior, but I couldn't figure out what it was. I left an open invitation for her to come inside if she changed her mind.

Vaughn flipped the top of the first basket open and pulled out two glass bottles of Perrier. He set them between us and extracted several clear food containers with snap-on lids. I found glasses, silverware, and napkins in the kitchen and joined him on the floor.

"Today's special from the Waverly House: peanut butter and jelly sandwiches." He unsnapped one of the lids.

"You're kidding!"

"I'm kidding. How's rosemary sourdough, an assortment of cheeses, smoked salmon, and fresh fruit?"

"It's no peanut butter and jelly, but it'll do."

"Next time. It's on the children's menu."

I sliced a sliver of brie and layered it with apple on a piece of bread. "Is the Waverly House kitchen always so available to you?"

"To tell the truth, I waited until the chef wasn't looking and I snitched from the fridge."

Vaughn poured sparkling water into the glasses and handed me one. I speared a piece of salmon, added a sprig of grapes and a slice of rosemary sourdough, and handed the plate to him. He added a wedge of blue cheese. For the next couple of minutes, we ate in silence.

"Are you all moved in?" Vaughn asked.

"Not really. For now I'm making do with what my aunt and uncle left in the apartment."

"I guess your boyfriend will be bringing your stuff when he moves in."

"Carson's not moving in."

"Oh. I figured he'd move to San Ladrón with you, but I guess it's not that far of a commute from Los Angeles," he said.

"We broke up."

Vaughn layered a slice of cheddar on a piece of bread and set it on the plate in front of him. "Are you sad about that?"

"Not as much as I thought I'd be. I guess I have too much to look forward to to be sad. Does that make sense?"

He grinned. "It does to me."

We munched through a fair amount of the food he'd brought. It tasted so good that I ate more than I needed and felt the waistband of my sailor pants digging into my midsection. Soon enough, I had to stand up to relieve the pressure.

"Okay, break time's over. Back to work," I said.

"Yes, ma'am." Vaughn packed up the empty containers and set the basket in the kitchen. I folded up the butcher paper and shoved it into the trash can by Genevieve's desk. Within ten minutes, we had a plan for covering the windows. We started with the west-facing windows. Vaughn tore a piece of paper from the roll and held it in place with his hands on the upper corner. I ducked under his raised arms and secured the edges with tape. Vaughn tore off the next piece of paper and we repeated.

When we reached the front door, I looked outside. A shiny black pickup truck pulled into the parking lot to Jitterbug. The logo for Special Delivery was on the side, and Rick Penwald was the driver. I whipped the door open. Vaughn was unprepared and the door whacked him on the forehead.

"Ow!"

"What?"

He rubbed his hand over the red spot. "Nothing. Why'd you open the door?"

"I saw someone I have to talk to." I darted to the kitchen and threw a handful of ice into a towel, ran back, and thrust it at Vaughn. "Put this on your head. I'll be right back." Before he could stop me, I was out the door and across the street.

Seven

"Rick!" I called.

He looked around the lot, his expression of confusion changing to recognition when he spied me. I jogged to where he was standing.

"Rick, hi. I don't know if you remember me from yesterday—"

"You're the fabric lady, right?"

"Yes. Poly Monroe." I glanced down at the cup he held. It was the largest cup of coffee I could imagine, putting a Starbucks Venti to shame. "Is the coffee here any good?"

"I think it's an acquired taste. Keeps me awake on long drives." He peeled back the plastic tab on top of the cup and raised it to his lips. I got a contact jolt of energy from the bitter scent. "Good seeing you," he said.

"Wait!" I said. I put my hand on his forearm to keep him from leaving. "I wanted to ask you about yesterday."

He squinted his eyes and the creases that were already etched onto his face deepened. "What about yesterday?"

"Can you tell me again how Phil arranged for you to make that delivery?"

"Phil called me up and asked if I could take care of it for him. He said he had something cooking in Los Angeles and he didn't want to blow it by leaving too early."

"Were you already in LA?"

"What's with all the questions? I was here, at a poker game."

I smiled, hoping to gain his trust. "Rick, Genevieve Girard is one of my friends. The police think she might have had something to do with Phil's murder, and I don't. I'm trying to figure out what happened so I can help her. I'm not trying to insinuate anything."

He took another pull on his coffee and coughed twice. He set it in the back of his truck. Not only was it the only thing back there, but the black plastic liner of the bed of the truck was brand-new, much like the rest of the vehicle. It was a serious upgrade from the van he borrowed from Phil from time to time.

Rick shielded his eyes from the sun. The squinting lessened. "Phil called me early Monday morning and asked if I could make his delivery. He offered to pay me a thousand dollars. He told me where I could find the van. I made some bad bets Sunday night, so I figured if the van was there, great, I'd make up the loss. Phil said he'd leave the keys and the money with the manager of the motel where he parked. When I got there, the van was there, the keys were in the ignition, and there was a bank envelope on the driver's seat with my name on it and ten hundreds inside. I grabbed a cup of coffee at the diner next door and drove back."

"You didn't look in the back of the van to make sure it was loaded?"

"I didn't even know what I was delivering."

"Seems a little shady."

"A thousand bucks under the table isn't a bad offer for a guy who lost more than that the night before. Sure, it was shady. Sometimes delivery jobs are like that. Phil told me I was picking up food and fabric. He said the van would be loaded when I got there. No reason to get involved."

"Did you tell this to Sheriff Clark?"

"He knows what happened."

I sensed that Rick was holding back something. Otherwise, how could it be that he'd driven the van with a murdered man in the back and he wasn't in custody, or at least being watched carefully as the main person of interest?

"If you're done with the interrogation, I really have to get going," he said. His choice of words made it clear what he thought of me peppering him with questions about what happened.

"Sure." I stepped back and let him get to his pickup. I waited in the lot while he threw the truck into reverse, backed out of the space, and peeled away, the temporary paper license plate on the truck barely legible. His tires screeched from accelerating too quickly. Why was he in such a hurry to get away from me? Was he late for a job, or had I been sniffing around for information that he'd rather keep to himself?

I returned to Tea Totalers and was pleasantly surprised that Vaughn's work ethic had kept him busy while I was gone. I rejoined him, and we finished. The interior of the café grew darker with each window we covered, until eventually, it felt like midnight.

"Do you know what time it is?" I asked Vaughn.

He checked his watch. "A little after four."

That couldn't be. I walked past him into the kitchen and looked up at the clock. "When did it get to be four? Where's Kim?"

"I told her to leave. She's been at it as much as you have.

When I saw her bicycle outside, I offered her a ride home. She turned me down."

"There's something odd about her," I said.

"Because she turned me down? Nah, that's happened once or twice before."

I laughed without thinking. "You can be done for the day, too, if you want," I said.

"Do *you* want a ride home?" he asked.

I pretended to consider the question. "No, I don't think so. A precedent's been set for today. Maybe tomorrow."

"I can't be here to help tomorrow. My father's expecting me in the office."

"Sure, of course. I didn't expect you to show up every day just because I am," I said.

"So you'll be here all week?"

"I don't know. I have to take care of things at the fabric store, too."

"Did anybody ever tell you the side effects of all work and no play?"

"Maybe."

"I have a suggestion. Tomorrow's Wednesday, and the Villamere Theater shows movies from the thirties on the third Wednesday of every month."

The hair on the back of my neck stood up. That was where Babs performed her burlesque show.

"This week it's a Mae West movie," he continued.

"I love Mae West!" I said.

"I thought you might. The movie starts at eight. How about I pick you up at Material Girl at seven?"

I was so distracted by the mention of the theater that it took me longer than it should have to realize Vaughn was asking me out on a date. "Will your car be done by then?" I asked. "If not, I can drive."

"My car?"

"I saw it at Charlie's shop."

"I have more than one car," he said.

"Of course you do." Maybe I should stop talking. Not talking seemed like a good idea.

"So . . . seven?" he asked again. This time he seemed less sure of himself.

"Seven sounds great."

"Great. See you then." He let himself out the front door.

A date with Vaughn. I caught myself smiling. I hadn't expected him to ask me out, especially not on the same day that I'd knocked him on the head with the door. It was a good sign that he didn't hold that against me. I think that's why I was smiling.

And then there was the movie: Mae West on the big screen. I took inspiration for the dresses I designed in my old job from the glamour of the thirties: Mae West, Jean Harlow, Myrna Loy, Ginger Rogers. Neither my ex-boss nor my ex-boyfriend had understood, though for different reasons. Giovanni was too cheap to produce dresses trimmed with feathers, fur, or exquisite beadwork. Carson simply lacked imagination.

I called Charlie. "Quick question. You said you found a flyer from the Villamere in Phil Girard's car, right? Do you still have it?"

"No. Why? What do you need to know?"

"It's about Babs. Do you know when her next show is?"

"Two shows every Sunday. You planning on going to one?"

"I thought I'd check her out. I want to know if she figures into this whole thing."

"If Phil was in Los Angeles on Sunday, then she probably doesn't figure in at all. She's got shows at ten and twelve."

"That doesn't mean she couldn't have taken off after her second show and gone to LA."

"To do what? Murder her current squeeze? For all we know, he was the one keeping her in ostrich feathers and pasties."

"That's what she wears?"

"That's pretty much what's left by the time her show's done."

I had second thoughts about booking tickets if the show ended in ostrich feathers and pasties. I said good-bye to Charlie and locked up the tea shop.

I left out the back. Rush hour was full-on, and it would have taken longer for me to drive the four blocks to the fabric store than to walk them. Thanks to the renovation, I was beginning to feel pains in muscles I didn't know I had, and all I wanted was to go home and take a long bath.

I made it back to the fabric store in twenty minutes and went straight upstairs. Pins and Needles were asleep on the middle of the bed. I opted for a shower instead of a bath, changed into a pair of men's black silk pajamas, and poured food into the cats' bowl. After refreshing their water, I went downstairs to check things out at the fabric store.

The sewing machine sat idle in the corner of the store, surrounded by bolts of fabric that I'd been using at Tea Totalers. Two placemats were complete on the right-hand side of the machine, and the materials needed for another eighteen were on the left. I didn't have the energy to work on them tonight. My body was exhausted, but my mind whirred like a hundred sewing machines manned by workers on a deadline.

It was nice, working on the French fabric renovation for Genevieve, but it had put me a day behind on my own goals of opening the store. I consulted my list of things I'd hoped to accomplish this week: Replace the sign. Stock special velvet. Set up sewing area. Plan craft projects. Phil Girard's murder had derailed me from half of what I had left to do.

I opened a file that I'd started with craft projects for weekends. I liked to think that once I had the store up and running, I could set up an area where people could spend their afternoon learning how they could change their life with fabric. It was the kind of environment I'd grown up in, and I wanted to create it for others. So far, the list was far from complete. Dog coats, tote bags, pillows, curtains, hats.

I sat at the computer and pulled up my graphic files. In front of me was the sign I'd designed for out front. Material Girl, it said, the letters printed in a patchwork of fabrics that highlighted the offerings in my inventory. I'd had the logo painted onto a milky white plastic sign that was backlit with white tube lighting. After I'd gone through what had been left behind in the store and determined the fabrics with the highest worth, I'd photographed each of them and reprinted them in a flyer that I distributed around town. I used the same logo on my business cards and the promotional coupons I'd made up for the weekend. I wasn't happy with the *M* in *Material* so I searched for my phone so I could try out other options. When the photos came up, I scrolled to the most recent pictures. The second-to-last photo was the interior of the van with Phil's body alongside of the bolts of fabric.

I hadn't thought much about my fabric, but if it was in the truck with Phil's body, there was a chance someone at the fabric wholesaler knew something about the murder. It wasn't outside the realm of normal for me to call the fabric warehouse and follow up on the delivery.

I checked the time. It was a few minutes before six. I might still catch someone. I rooted around through scraps of notes and business cards on the desk until I found one for Mack's Fabrics. I called the number and got a recorded message.

"Hi, this is Polyester Monroe. I arranged to have twelve bolts of velvet picked up from you yesterday. I'd like to talk to someone about that delivery." I was halfway through leaving my number when a voice came on the line.

"Hold on, gotta turn off the machine. Okay. I'm here. I close in seven minutes. You coming or what?"

"Is this Mack's Fabrics?"

"Yeah, this is Mack. Listen, you gotta get this fabric outta here. It's takin' up too much room."

"I don't think you understand."

"What don't I understand? You're Polyester. You ordered twelve bolts of velvet made up of ninety percent silk and ten percent polyester, like your name. You paid in advance, and you were supposed to get this stuff outta here yesterday. Am I warm?"

"Okay, maybe *I'm* the one who doesn't understand. I thought that fabric was already picked up."

"Lady, I'm looking at twelve bolts of velvet. They have your name on them. If you don't pick them up by noon tomorrow, I'm selling 'em off to the highest bidder."

Eight

"There must have been some kind of a mix-up," I said. "Didn't someone pick up the velvet from you on Monday morning? Someone from Special Delivery? Or Girard Trucking Company?" I pushed the papers around on the top of the desk, looking for the pink form Rick had given me, and then remembered it was in the pocket of the pants I wore yesterday. "I don't have the paperwork here. The driver's name was Rick Penwald. He said the fabric was already loaded in the van when he picked it up. Does any of this sound familiar?"

"Whaddaya think, fabric reproduces like rabbits? I just said the velvet's here. Been sittin' here since Friday."

"So nobody came to pick it up on Monday?"

"Jeez, this is like talkin' to my wife."

"Don't sell off the fabric. I want it."

"Noon tomorrow."

"I'll do my best."

He hung up.

It didn't make any sense. How was it possible that Mack had my fabric—and since it was tagged with my name and had the specific fiber content that I'd ordered, it sure sounded like my fabric—when Phil had been buried under the very same fabric in the truck?

This new information raised a whole different set of questions, not the least of which was why Mack was acting like nobody had been to his warehouse. Because if nobody had, then where exactly had the twelve bolts from the back of the van come from? And how did they connect back to Phil?

If someone wanted to kill Phil when he was in Los Angeles, they might have followed him to the fabric district and jumped him while he was loading the van. Stacking the fabric on top of him would have served to hide his presence, but why would they have used the *wrong* fabric? Why would they have bothered with the fabric at all?

The fact that Phil's body was buried under fabric told me one thing: whoever killed Phil knew that he was going to show up at the fabric distributor. I already knew that Rick knew. He'd told me this afternoon. He could have murdered Phil and staged the van to fit his story.

For every detail that I didn't know about, there was one thing that I did. Fabric. I needed to see the fabric that had been in the van and find out for myself if it was what I'd expected to arrive in San Ladrón.

Depending on how close the weave was to what I'd requested, I would figure out in no time if it wasn't what I'd ordered. That was one of the benefits to growing up around material. My aunt and uncle had taught me the difference between weaves by the touch of my fingers. At first it was a simple identification game: close my eyes and name the fabric content. I mastered that at five years old. My mom thought it was cute, but Millie decided to cultivate my talent. We moved to the difference between pure fabrics and blends, and, when I mastered those, she challenged me to break down the fabric content by percentage. That's how I knew the ten percent polyester in my velvet would increase the drape and help the material hold its color.

If given the chance to inspect the fabric that Sheriff Clark was holding, I could determine if it was what I ordered or not, but that wasn't what concerned me. What concerned me was whether or not there was an identifier like a warehouse name or a factory that would lead me to where exactly the fabric had originated, or whose hands it had passed through.

Everything I'd learned about the murder of Phil Girard was scattered around me in a patchwork of information, like pattern pieces that needed to be assembled into a garment. It was up to me to figure out how they all fit together.

I changed back into my sailor pants, top, and sneakers and found the kitties, who were far more interested in the sock they swatted back and forth in the living room than in my theories about Phil's murder. I got down on my hands and knees and gave each of them a kiss between their ears, told them where I was going in case of emergency, and locked up behind me.

Outside, I turned left, walked the length of the sidewalk past the gas station on the corner, and turned left again. Two blocks later I was at the sheriff's mobile unit. Sheriff Clark sat at his desk eating a Snickers bar. When he saw me, he let the uneaten portion slide back into the wrapper and neatly tucked the plastic around the candy. He couldn't have shown more care if he was a vampire looking to conceal evidence of his bite marks.

"Ms. Monroe. What brings you to my doorstep?"

"Do you still have my fabric?" I asked.

"Like I told you, your fabric is currently part of my homicide investigation. I'm sorry for the inconvenience, but I can't let you have it."

"Would it be possible for me to examine it? Just a swatch?"

"While I appreciate the gesture, I think our technicians can handle that."

I detected a note of sarcasm. I lowered myself into the chair across from him and folded my hands on the desk in front of me.

"I spoke to the man who runs the fabric warehouse where I was to pick up my fabric. His name is Mack. He said my velvet is still in Los Angeles. He described it well enough for me to know it's what I ordered, which means what Rick delivered here *isn't.* So I'm trying to figure out how that's possible, that my fabric is there when we all think my fabric is with you."

Clark picked up a pen and wrote something on the corner of his desk calendar. He moved the Snickers bar on top of his notes so I couldn't read them.

"Don't you find any of this suspicious?" I asked.

"When you hired Phil to make this pickup, did you arrange it through his company? Fill out an invoice? Pay by credit card or check?"

"I hired him with a verbal agreement and paid him in cash. That's what he wanted. Why?"

"Seems to me this story about your fabric, if it's true, has nothing to do with Mrs. Girard."

"Yes! Exactly." I sat back and placed my forearms on the chair, my hands wrapped around the end of the armrests. "I'm glad you understand."

"What I understand is that you've brought me a story intended to throw suspicion away from Mrs. Girard. You have no proof that this story is anything other than that—a story."

"That's why I want to see the fabric, Sheriff. If you let me see it, I can tell you if it's really mine or not. If it's not, I can try to figure out where it came from."

"Ms. Monroe, I can assure you we're looking into every lead we have, and that includes your fabric."

"Does it include the fabric distributor where the fabric was picked up? Because I personally think it's a little weird that somebody let twelve bolts of fabric show up here and it turns out they're not the right ones. Those people are opportunistic. If they knew what happened, they wouldn't admit to the error. They'd sell off my fabric to someone else and wash their hands of the mix-up."

"So you're saying you conducted business with shady businessmen."

"There are people in the fabric industry who are less than honest, yes. I happen to know this because I worked for one of them. Until I get my store up and running, I have to rely on the contacts that I have."

Clark glared at me.

"There were crates of food in the back of the van, which means someone picked up a delivery. Did you look through the food? Was any of it suspicious? Maybe the food suppliers were the ones who did this. Did you know there's a food distributor named Topo di Sali who's pressuring Genevieve to sell out? Maybe Phil met with him. Maybe negotiations got out of hand. Have you talked to him?"

"Ms. Monroe, are you finished?"

"And what about Rick Penwald, the driver? He should be your main person of interest. He drove the van that had Phil's body in it. He must know something."

"I can assure you we have a list of suspects and we're pursuing each of them."

"Does that list include Babs Green?"

Clark leaned forward. "What does Babs Green have to do with this?"

"She was having an affair with Phil Girard."

"Did Mrs. Girard know about it?"

"I don't know. Why?"

"I imagine a wife might get angry when she finds out her husband is having an affair."

"I hope you see there's more to this murder investigation than a case of 'angry wife offs husband.'"

"And I hope you were paying attention when I said I wasn't going to discuss the case with you."

I felt a sneeze coming on, and I pinched the bridge of my nose to stop it. "As long as I'm here, why don't you let me take a close-up picture of the velvet so I can use it in my promotional materials?"

"Why would you want a close-up of velvet that wasn't your velvet?"

Drat. He was going to shut me out of his investigation. "Good night, Sheriff." I headed to the door, and then turned back around. "One more thing. When you finish up with the velvet that isn't my velvet, feel free to give me a call. Maybe I'll be willing to take it off your hands, since I have a fabric store and you don't."

Sheriff Clark had his elbows on his desk calendar and his fingers steepled in front of him. Before he had a chance to say anything else, I added, "Maybe this investigation is none of my business, but fabric is. So before you say anything, *that's* what I'm minding." I turned around and stormed out.

The streets were almost empty. I walked quickly to Charlie's Automotive and tapped a rhythm of beats on the glass door, followed up with a phone call and a text. The text was answered first. *We're around back.*

Charlie's Automotive was exactly what you'd expect an auto shop to be: an austere, exposed brick and concrete area with three pits for getting under cars, and two walls of tools to do whatever it was that needed to be done. Calendars of half-naked firemen shared wall space with images of Rosie the Riveter and Eddie Van Halen.

What most of San Ladrón didn't know was that Charlie kept a small oasis behind her auto shop. It was the size of a gardening shed, about eight feet by ten feet, whitewashed on the interior and outfitted with wooden benches that lined the walls. Decorative wicker baskets filled with plush Egyptian cotton towels, shower gels, and moisturizers sat below the benches, and framed pages from a 1970s mechanic's calendar featuring pastel drawings of women posing behind blankets, towels, and nightgowns hung on the walls. What Charlie exposed to the world in the form of don't-mess-with-me toughness was countered by what she kept in the back, her place to get away from it all when she needed to.

The only reason I knew about her private quarters in the back was because she'd offered me use of them when I first showed up in San Ladrón. My unpopularity at the time had inspired the destruction of her property. Until tonight, I didn't know what she'd done about it. I rounded the corner and saw the door of her shed propped open with one of her combat boots.

"In here," she called.

Inside the shed, Genevieve sat in a chair with her hair wrapped in a turban of plastic. She faced the wall. Charlie stood by a small sink, running her hands under water. A pair of clear plastic gloves sat on the edge of the sink. A small boom box sat on the floor, playing The Stray Cats.

I pointed at the boom box, at Genevieve, and at Charlie. "Do I want to know what's going on?" I asked.

"Charlie convinced me I need a new look," Genevieve said. "She's giving me a cut and color for the low price of organizing her invoices. Plus she let me pick the makeover music."

Charlie rolled her eyes. "Until ten minutes ago I didn't know rockabilly was French."

"What?" Genevieve asked, turning her head toward Charlie.

"Nothing." Charlie picked up a white plastic kitchen timer from the bench next to the sink and twisted the dial as far as it would go. "You can relax now. We rinse in fifteen."

"What?" Genevieve asked again. A ratty, faded towel was draped over her from neck to thigh. She reached a hand out from under the towel to the plastic that covered her ear and Charlie swatted her hand back down.

"Sit. Relax. Wait. Got it?"

"Yes, ma'am," Genevieve said with a salute.

Charlie turned to me. "Is this a social call?" she asked, her voice low.

"Not exactly. How's she doing?" I asked, pointing at Gen. Her head was tipped back against the top of the chair and her eyes were closed.

"Better. She stopped crying around noon. I gave her a couple projects in the office and told her to lay low. I expected her to be a real pain in the butt, but she didn't bother me once."

"Did she talk about Phil?"

"Nah. Every time she came close to bringing him up, the sniffles started. I put a moratorium on four-letter words that start with P. That seemed to help."

"Good, I think. There's definitely more going on than I originally thought. Can we talk outside?"

"Frenchy—yo!" Charlie called across the room. Genevieve rolled her head to the side and opened one eye. "Stay put. We'll be right back."

Genevieve nodded and closed her eye.

I followed Charlie through the door to the yard outside. The sun had dropped, but streetlights illuminated the stretch of Bonita that ran between the auto shop and the fabric store.

"I don't want to leave her alone for long," she said. "Is that cool with you?"

"Sure." If I was going by the timer Charlie had set for Genevieve's hair, I figured we had about ten minutes, max, before we had to head back. I cut to the chase and told Charlie about my phone call with Mack, the fabric distributor and how he claimed to still have my velvet order.

"I thought your velvet was in the back of the van on top of Frenchy's husband?"

"That's what I thought, too. That's what we all thought. But this guy described the fabric he has in Los Angeles, and it's mine, right down to the content."

"So what does Clark have?"

I shrugged. "For all I know the factory produced a double order. Clark won't let me see it, so I'm in the dark."

"So you told him about it?"

"I just came from there. He won't tell me anything." I kicked the toe of my boot against the ground.

"Do factories really produce double orders? Seems like a stretch."

"Rarely. The only other thing I can think of is that someone knew Phil was going to pick up twelve bolts of velvet but didn't know that it was a specific twelve bolts. So they killed him and buried the body under twelve bolts. It's possible the murderer never thought anybody would pay attention to the velvet."

"What do you think it means?"

"I don't know. Here's what I thought I knew: Phil went to Los Angeles on Sunday. Allegedly, he made arrangements for Rick Penwald—the other driver—to come to Los Angeles and make the delivery to San Ladrón. Only somehow the wrong fabric got loaded in the van—on top of Phil. I don't know when, how, or why."

"Why 'allegedly'?"

"Because that information came from Rick. He must know more than he's admitting. All he said was that Phil told him he wasn't leaving LA just yet. Maybe Rick made the whole thing up and killed Phil. A dead man can't contradict his story."

"That would be pretty gutsy: killing a guy, putting him in the back of his van, and making his scheduled deliveries."

"I know, but otherwise I can't figure it out. How did someone put Phil's body in the back of the van under my fabric without the driver knowing? The only answer I can come up with is that the driver knew. But what doesn't make sense is that Genevieve knows Rick. She said he and Phil were friends, that Rick borrowed Phil's van when Phil was on his taxi route. He just slapped a logo on the side and conducted business."

"Maybe that makes a lot of sense. He could have done all kinds of shady things. If anybody got suspicious he could have covered Phil's logo, or uncovered Phil's logo."

"Genevieve said if the tea shop ever took off, Phil was planning on leaving his delivery route to Rick. But Rick wasn't all that happy when I caught up with him and started asking questions. If he really was Phil's friend, wouldn't he want to help?"

Genevieve popped her plastic-wrapped head out the door of the shed. "Charlie? The timer went off," she called. "I don't want my hair to fall out."

"I'll be right there," said Charlie. She turned back to me. "Call me tomorrow," she said, and jogged back to the shed.

I ran across the street to Material Girl, unlocked the front door, and went to the bedroom. My clothes from yesterday were still on the fainting sofa. I went through the pockets until I found the pink page Rick had made me sign. I hadn't pressed hard enough and now my signature was little more than a smudge. Across the center of the page it said, "12 rolls velvet. Prepaid. Signature for delivery confirmation only." The carefully printed words were the only clear thing that had been added to the preprinted form.

I unlocked my phone and dialed 411. When the operator prompted me for city and listing, I said, "Los Angeles, Special Delivery. They're a delivery service out of Los Angeles," I added.

Keys tapped in the background. "You sure they're in Los Angeles?"

"I thought they were. Why? Do you have them listed somewhere else?"

"Nope. Hold on," she said and switched me over to a ringing number. One ring, two, three, four . . . After seven rings, three piercing tones came on the line. "I'm sorry, the number you have dialed has been disconnected. Please check the number and try again." The piercing tones repeated.

I called information again. "I just called for a number but I'm getting a not-in-service message. Can you double-check it for me? And this time don't connect me. I'll write the number down and call it later."

She asked for the city and listing again and clicked on her keyboard. "I got nothing," she said. "Hold on. That's interesting. Special Delivery, you said?"

"Yes. Twenty-four-hour delivery service. Did you find them?"

"No, and I don't think you're going to find them, either."

"Why's that?"

"Because I'm staring at a listing for a temporary number designated to that business. No address, no website, no e-mail." She chuckled. "I hope you haven't hired them yet, because it looks to me like Special Delivery was a fly-by-night operation."

Nine

I thanked the operator and hung up. My hand was shaking. I smoothed out the creases of the invoice and looked at the label that had been affixed to the upper left-hand corner of the form. Special Delivery, with an address, phone number, and website.

But Special Delivery didn't exist. Which meant not only was Rick not exactly telling the truth, but he'd gone out of his way to create invoices to back up his lie. Everything I knew about his story started to fall apart: the last-minute arrangement to make the delivery, the thousand dollars in an envelope on the front seat, the statement that he'd never looked into the back of the van. Even the sign on the side of the van had been temporary, and the fact that he'd been driving around this morning with that same sign on what appeared to be a brand-new truck told me he was trying to mislead someone. He could have known exactly what Phil was picking up in Los Angeles. I still didn't know what his motive might have been, but now I had evidence that he was lying to me.

I went downstairs to the computer, plugged my phone into the USB jack, and cued up the pictures from the back of the van. I enlarged the images, trying to make out the information on the tags. The screen was pixilated and all I saw for my efforts was a sequence of beige squares. I moved the photo from my phone to the hard drive of the computer and opened it in Photoshop. After fiddling with the contrast, resolution, and increasing the sharpness, I was able to read the writing on the tags. One word, the same on each of them. *100% Polyester.* No wonder someone thought it was my fabric.

My fabric wasn't 100 percent polyester, but someone who didn't know who I was might have heard the word *polyester* and mistaken it for the fabric and not the person who ordered it.

Fabric warehouses were some of the most overwhelming buildings I'd ever experienced. Rolls of material were stocked on deep shelves that went from floor to ceiling—and warehouse ceilings were sometimes twenty to thirty feet high. The owners knew their stock like the backs of their hands, but it would take even an experienced fabric connoisseur several hours to map out the rhyme or reason that an owner might use. According to Mack, my fabric had been left untouched, but that didn't mean Phil hadn't made the pickup he was hired to make. Velvet would be stocked with other velvet, and if twelve rolls were together, tagged *100% Polyester*, it was plausible that Phil would have made an erroneous assumption.

But if all of that was true, then I was saying that Phil Girard was murdered because he picked up the wrong twelve rolls of velvet. And I couldn't imagine circumstances where someone would commit murder over twelve rolls of fabric. Not even me.

So, who else would have found my fabric to be worth

killing over? It wasn't like I was under suspicion for Phil's murder. I wasn't anywhere near Los Angeles between Sunday night and Monday morning. I had a construction crew and a broken sidewalk as my alibi.

But so did Genevieve. She was right beside me when the van pulled up. I wondered why she hadn't been ruled out as a suspect because of that.

I zoomed out on the photo and took in the composition. The heavy rolls of fabric were on the right. Phil's body was on the left. Crates of dry goods sat by his head. Crumbs scattered about with plastic zip ties. And the empty jug of Genevieve's tea on its side.

But what was that under the tea jug?

Again I zoomed the photo, this time by the jug. The carpet under the jug was a darker color than the rest of the interior floor. The darkness spread in an irregular pattern around the lid of the container. It was a stain.

The tea had spilled onto the interior of the van. Which meant there was a chance Phil didn't drink it! Even if I couldn't find out who had murdered Phil Girard, I could prove that Genevieve hadn't poisoned him if I could prove it had spilled before he had a chance to drink it.

Genevieve kept shelves of those jugs at Tea Totalers. I had no idea how much tea one contained, but I watched enough true crime television to know that I could find out by re-creating the scene. What I needed was a carpet and a jug and a distance of six feet or so, to mimic the distance I'd stood when I took the photo.

Tomorrow morning, before going to Tea Totalers, I would swing by Get Hammered, the local hardware store, and buy a cheap carpet. I'd stage the spill. And once I had my proof, I'd take it to Sheriff Clark. I could have the whole thing wrapped up by lunchtime.

Which left me with one problem: How could I conduct

the experiment here and still manage to get my fabric from Mack by noon?

Even if I had the time to drive to Los Angeles tomorrow, twelve bolts of velvet wouldn't fit in the back of my VW Bug. I was going to have to call in a favor. And since this was a fabric-related favor, I knew exactly who I was going to call. If only I could predict what my former boss was going to ask in return.

I didn't bother calling the showroom. Giovanni closed up at six, if not earlier. He worked his staff far harder than other design studios, but the one thing that made the job bearable was that he was borderline religious about quitting time. Six months into my job with him, he'd put me on salary. I thought it demonstrated my value. I soon learned it meant he expected me to keep working from home when the showroom closed.

For all the hard work I'd put in at To The Nines, it was Giovanni who owed me something, not the other way around, but a certain devil-occupied condominium at the earth's core would freeze over before he'd acknowledge it. I braced myself for the inevitable hard time I was about to receive and called Giovanni's home number.

"Hi, Giovanni. It's Poly Monroe. I need a favor."

"It's about time you came to your senses. I'll take you back, but you're not getting more money."

So nice to know I was missed. "That's not why I'm calling. I'm in a bind and I was hoping you could help me out."

"That's rich. You leave me in the lurch during the holidays and you want a favor from me?"

"Giovanni, I left in early November. And I not only finished the sketches and the design direction for the workroom, but I left you concepts and sketches for Valentine's Day and prom. I did six months' worth of work for you in my last two weeks. I would hardly call that 'the lurch.'"

"We had to scrap your plans. Too much detail work. Too much fabric needed. I bought four hundred yards of pink netting. We're going with a princess theme, but the girls are having a hard time with the bodices."

I bit my lower lip and cringed, imagining the high schools of Los Angeles filled with wannabe princesses in poufy gowns of pink netting. Add in fairy wings from the dollar store and it would look like a clone army of Glinda the Good Witch. I wondered if Giovanni had been knocked in the head before his taste level had finished developing.

"By *girls*, you mean the women in the workroom, right?"

He grunted. "Why aren't they using boning?"

"Boning costs too much. I told them to figure out an alternative."

Boning is a thin strip of plastic encased in a sleeve of fabric. It is sewn inside a bodice to create a cage-like shape. These days, it's most commonly used in wedding dresses and the occasional Renaissance Faire costume, but judging from the stash I found when I took inventory of the store, it was fairly popular at one time. A lightbulb went off over my head and I knew my way in with Giovanni.

"You know I own a fabric store now?"

He grunted again.

"I've been going through the inventory, and I found a pretty sizeable supply of boning. It's yours if you'll help me out with my favor."

"What do you want?"

"It's minor, really. I ordered twelve bolts of velvet and they were delivered to Mack's Fabrics two blocks south of Santee Alley. There was a mix-up and Mack wants me to pick up the fabric tomorrow by noon. I can't get there."

"Why'd you use Mack? We never use him."

I didn't want to tell Giovanni that was one of the reasons. "I'm in a pinch here. Seriously. I prepaid for the fabric, and I can't afford to write it off."

"Pick up twelve bolts of velvet by tomorrow noon in exchange for—how much boning do you have?"

I'd counted sixty-three rolls. At twelve yards per roll, that was over seven hundred fifty yards of boning, way more than he'd ever need to produce pink net princess gowns.

"Twenty rolls," I said quickly. "Give or take a few," I added.

"Twenty rolls and you deliver complete patterns and instructions on how the girls should use it to minimize cost."

"You'll pick up my fabric? By noon tomorrow?"

"Yeah, fine, I'll get your fabric. What is it, anyway?"

"Thirty-dollar-a-yard velvet. Poly-silk blend. It's a custom weave and it has my name on it."

"You always went for those pie-in-the-sky fabrics. You got a buyer?"

"I *am* the buyer," I said.

"The world has changed, Poly. You're going to have to learn to function the way I do. Cut corners, quick turnaround."

"That's not my style," I said. "Can I count on you?"

He grunted a third time.

We said good-bye and hung up. As risky as it had been to ask Giovanni for help, I knew he'd come through for me. Ever since he learned I was reopening the store he knew I represented a channel for him to get supplies. Today's negotiation would serve to whet his appetite. He'd show up with my fabric, of that I was certain.

If only I was as certain of my efforts on Genevieve's behalf.

The next morning, I woke at six and took a quick shower. The scent of lemon verbena from the soap invigorated me, and I lingered a little too long under the hot spray. When I finally turned the water off, steam covered the mirror and left a film of moisture on the sink. I cracked the door and let the steam escape while I towel-dried my short auburn hair and finished the rest of my bathroom routine.

My black sweater and sailor pants were draped over the

foot of the sleigh bed, covering the dark cherrywood. Pins was curled up under the neckline of the sweater, his head tipped against his paw. I left the clothes where they were so as not to wake him and rummaged around in the large armoire for something to wear today.

I dressed in narrow black jeans, a black T-shirt, and a black zip-front hoodie. The arm of the sweatshirt had *Polyester* written down it in cheap rhinestones I'd found in the trash of a craft store next to To The Nines. When Giovanni learned I could embellish by hand he cleaned out the trash and demanded I teach the workroom my technique so we could hide flaws in the cheap fabrics he bought. That had been a particularly blingy season.

I pulled on my favorite riding boots, fed the cats, ate a bowl of raisin bran cereal, and left. It was just going on seven and I wanted to stop off at Charlie's before I headed to Tea Totalers.

I crossed the street and jogged between cars that were stuck at the light. The bays to her shop were already open, and sounds of Van Halen trickled out of the office. Vaughn's car was up on the lift, same as yesterday.

I went to the office and knocked on the door frame. Charlie spun her chair around and checked me out.

"She's a whiz kid, you know that?"

"Who?

"Frenchy. I told her to figure out a way to make herself useful. She set up some kind of accounting tool for me and inputted all of the receipts and invoices I've been meaning to get to. She filed the closed invoices from my desk. She flipped the calendar to April."

"It is April," I said.

"March was hot. I liked him. I wasn't ready to turn the page."

I glanced at the calendar hanging on the wall. "Do you have a problem with April?"

"The only problem I have with him is that he's going to make me forget about March."

"So yesterday was okay, right? You two didn't kill each other, nobody found out she was here, and some work got done."

"Sure, yesterday was fine, all the way up to last night. Her hair turned out better than I expected. Once she gets over that putz of a husband, she's going to be a real heartbreaker."

"So what's the problem?"

"I'm not so sure how today's going to go."

"Seems to me she likes the work. Give her a couple of projects and she'll stay busy."

"That's just it. I can't give her any projects because I can't find her." She crossed her arms over her chest. "Everything was fine when I did her hair. She said she was tired and turned in. I went out. When I got up this morning, she was gone."

Ten

There was one obvious reason Genevieve would leave, but I wasn't willing to accept it. "She's not guilty. She has no reason to leave town. Why is she acting like she's on the run?"

"What time was she with you at your store on Monday?" Charlie asked.

"It was around lunch. The workers took a break after the sign fell, and I asked her if she could make lunch."

"Did she?"

"Yes. The van showed up at the same time we returned with the sandwiches. She took one look inside and vanished. I didn't see her again until she came back to Material Girl on Monday night."

"All things considered, I'm surprised Frenchy turned back up as soon as she did. You have to admit that's a heck of a way to start a Monday."

"Maybe she's at the tea shop. Maybe she got up early so she could get a few things and not be seen."

"You like to believe the best about people, don't you?" Charlie asked.

"Not everybody," I said. "But with Genevieve, I do. I don't think she has a hidden agenda."

"For the sake of my newly organized business files, I hope you're right."

I left Charlie's Automotive. The morning air was chilly. I walked to Lopez Donuts. The small shop was run by Big Joe and Maria Lopez, two friendly and welcoming residents who had helped me out of a jam when I first came to San Ladrón. Today there was a line out the door. Two young boys, no more than ten, made their way through the line. Carlos, the taller of the two, offered small paper cups of coffee. Antonio, his younger brother, held a tray with donut pieces resting on white napkins.

"Want a sample?" Carlos asked each person in front of me. When he reached me, my place in line had crossed the barrier from the outside to in. "Hey, I know you, you're the material lady," he said.

"Yes, that's me. Polyester."

"Do you want a sample?" Antonio asked. He seemed pleased to have beaten his brother to the punch.

"Sure," I said. I took a small piece of donut and a paper cup of coffee. When I reached the front counter, Big Joe leaned across it and gave me a bear hug. He turned around and shouted into the kitchen.

"Maria! Guess who came to see us!"

"Not now, Joe," she yelled back. I craned my neck and saw her bustle back and forth between tall metal racks.

"Busy morning?" I asked.

"Nonstop. Something about the French tea shop being closed. Good for us, bad for her, I'd say. We ran out of tea bags half an hour ago. Never bothered much with tea before, and we lost some business because we weren't ready. Maria ran out and bought a box of Lipton. You should have seen the expression on the lady who got that!" He laughed long and loud. Several patrons looked up, startled at the boom of his laughter, but smiled once they saw him. There was no denying the joy of the moment when you were around Big Joe. His laughter was as contagious as poison ivy at a campground of sixth-graders.

"I see Maria brought in the power team to keep the line calm."

He shook his head. "She doesn't care about child labor laws, that's for sure. Now, what can I get you?"

To keep things simple, I went with coffee and a cruller. I waved to Maria when she turned around. She had a smudge of glaze on her forehead and chocolate down the front of her white shirt. I knew better than to hold her up. She was a woman on a mission.

I finished the donut by the time I was out the door. Across the street, an older gentleman in a plaid flannel shirt and jeans was unlocking the door to Get Hammered. I jogged through traffic and followed him inside. He headed toward the lumber and I headed toward the home décor section. I grabbed the top rug from a stack of clearance carpets and carried it to the front register. I thought about what else we might need to work at Genevieve's. The fabric would take care of my part of things, but if Kim was going to get that outdoor furniture looking new again, she was going to have to sand it, prime it, and paint it.

I balanced the carpet on my left hip and grabbed a small mouse sander from the power tool display. I tucked a few packages of refill sandpaper under my arm and proceeded to the checkout line.

After paying, I readjusted the carpet against my hip and started my walk. I approached the fabric store and looked at the front. Ten years ago my aunt had been murdered inside. Uncle Marius had covered the insides of the windows with thick matte black paint and closed the doors for business. It had taken me days to scrape the black paint from the glass with a small razor, but once I had, I knew the windows would be perfect for showcasing displays that enticed people into the store. I even considered setting my sewing machine in the window so people could watch me construct items. Once I had a staff to man the registers inside the store, that is.

Distracted, I tripped. The carpet fell to the ground and broke my fall. My coffee flew in front of me and splashed over the concrete. The cup rolled toward the curb.

The door to the right of the fabric shop opened and Tiki Tom came out. He wore a red short-sleeved shirt printed with the names and maps of various Polynesian islands, and he held a mug shaped like a coconut. "You're running out of time on the sign, aren't you?" he asked.

"The store opens on Sunday. The sign will be up by then."

"You sure about that? Looked like your construction crew at the Senior Center yesterday. I heard they were gutting the old workout room so they could add a bingo hall."

I stood up with no help from Tom. I corralled the cup and lid and tossed them into the public trash bin, then dusted myself off.

"I don't know anything about the Senior Center job. The foreman promised me I'd have my sign this week."

Tom looked at the crack in the sidewalk and scowled. "Better not cost me any more business," he said. He went back inside his store.

I had four days left before I was supposed to open my doors. On top of everything else, I had to get the contractors to finish the sign job. I didn't want to be known as the woman with the ugly storefront. I also knew I had my own financial responsibilities to take care of. The business plan I'd presented to the bank had secured me a modest loan that allowed me to pay the taxes and place an order for inventory that was more up-to-date than the store had been left with.

The clock was ticking on my opening, and I couldn't afford to default on the loan and lose the store altogether.

I picked up the carpet. It was proving to be cumbersome. I had four blocks to go and it was going to be a battle. I was somewhat uncoordinated, the unfortunate end result of being five foot nine with size-seven feet. What I lacked in balance I made up for in flexibility. Good for mat-based Pilates. Bad for ballroom dancing.

I reached into my messenger bag for my keys and unlocked the gate and door to the fabric store. In the corner of the shop was a small red wagon I'd purchased several months ago. San Ladrón had proven itself to be a small enough town that I could walk most places I wanted to go, but when I found myself loaded down with food, drink, fabric, or carpets and sandpaper, the child's toy was the perfect solution. I put the sander and paper in the wagon, added a portable steamer and a basket of emergency sewing supplies, and balanced the carpet along the top. I pulled it out the front door and locked the shop behind me. Taking great care not to trip over any additional cracks or exposed tree roots in the sidewalk, I made my way to Tea Totalers.

I carried the carpet behind the shop and set it on the landing next to the iron furniture Kim had moved around back. I went to the back door and was surprised that the knob turned easily in my grip. Had I forgotten to lock the back door?

I crept inside the kitchen and looked around. Everything was as I'd left it. In the café portion of the building, the windows were still blocked out by brown paper and the furniture was pushed into the center of the room. I doubled back to the office. The computer was off and the desk was neat. I looked at the counters behind me.

Clean. The bowl of fruit sat on the shelf and the brown paper bag of avocados was tucked next to it. Just like I'd left it two days ago. Still, something felt off.

I stepped back into the main portion of the shop and slowly turned around in a circle. The room was dark, and it was hard for me to see details. I couldn't figure out what had changed except for the rearranging required for the renovation.

I opened the front door and looked across the street at Jitterbug. As long as I knew Rick Penwald's routine, it seemed a good idea to keep an eye out for him. There were no black trucks in sight. I closed the door and headed back through the kitchen and the back door and unrolled the carpet. Time for my experiment.

I stood several feet away from the carpet and took pictures of it, establishing the appearance before I dumped tea on it. I went back inside and filled an empty container from the cupboard with water from the tap. An old bottle of green food coloring sat on a shelf with colorful sugar crystals and spices. If I was going far enough to conduct the experiment, I might as well make sure the results were easy to identify. I poured a small amount into the container and tendrils of emerald green bloomed in the water. I swirled the container until it was an even shade of St. Patrick's Day.

Outside, I poured half of the water on the carpet, set the container down so you could see it was still half-full, stood back, and took a picture. The stain wasn't nearly as big as the stain in the back of the van. I dumped the rest of the green liquid on the carpet, set the container down, and resumed the photo shoot. I heard the latch on the gate out front as I took the last of the pictures.

I didn't want to have to answer questions about what I was doing. I shoved my phone back into my jeans and doubled the carpet over itself twice just as Kim pushed her bicycle around the side of the building.

She seemed surprised to see me. "I didn't expect you to be here already."

"I wanted to get an early start."

"If you want me to show up earlier, I can."

Considering we'd moved from can-Genevieve-still-afford-to-pay-her to will-Genevieve-turn-up-by-payday, I didn't think it was in my best interest to extend the new employee's hours.

"You should stick to whatever you and Genevieve agreed to."

"Okay," she said. "What are you doing with that carpet?"

"It had a stain on it, so I'm throwing it out."

"Want help?" she asked and made a move to grab the end.

"No!" I yanked it out of her reach. "I can handle it. I bought some sanding supplies, so you can work on the furniture."

"Okay. There's one thing I have to do first." She headed inside while I used determination and a good hard shove to move the carpet from the ground to inside the Dumpster. It stood on end, the bound edge jutting out above the rim. I rested the black rubber lid on top of the edge of the carpet. An opening of about six inches would allow us to fit in anything else we needed to toss.

I scanned the area for traces of my experiment. Some of the green water had seeped through the carpet and left a splotch on the back sidewalk. I ran the bottom of my boot over it, but nothing happened. Maybe it was fresh enough for me to douse with water. I headed to the back door with the empty pitcher, prepared to fill it with tap water to flush the sidewalk clean.

Only, I couldn't get to the faucet. Kim stood hunched over the white double bowl sink, emptying all of the pitchers of tea from the refrigerator down the drain.

Eleven

I ran to the sink. "What are you doing?" I asked.

Kim pushed me out of the way. "I'm emptying out the fridge."

"Who told you to do that?"

"The shop's been closed for a few days and everything is probably bad. There's no reason to have it sitting around."

I'd had the very same idea, dumping the tea that might have poisoned Phil. I hadn't done it because I wanted to believe in Genevieve's innocence. And now that the tea was down the drain, it didn't really matter. If it was evidence of something against her, it was gone. Still, Kim's actions bothered me. Why was she inside dumping the tea when her task was to sand and prep the iron furniture out back?

I looked around the kitchen. "Did you throw away anything else?"

"No, there wasn't anything else to throw out. I figured you took care of that."

"What do you mean?"

"Yesterday there was a big plastic bin with wax envelopes of tea. Croissants, too. Now they're gone."

I turned my head to the right, and then to the left, scanning for traces of Genevieve's tea. That's what was wrong. The tea and the pastries that Genevieve moved from the front of the café to the kitchen each night when she closed were all gone.

When I had first started coming to Tea Totalers, I watched Genevieve flip through a small repurposed French armoire filled with parchment-paper envelopes of loose tea. She sprinkled the contents of an envelope onto a square of cheesecloth, clamped it shut, and steeped it in hot water. She kept larger quantities of the dried tea leaves in rubber bins behind the counter and brewed them in batches to serve as the daily special. That's what had been in the refrigerator. But today, the drawers of the armoire were empty and the rubber containers were gone. I opened the refrigerator and checked the plastic bins for the herbs that had been there on Monday. They were empty, too.

I had an uneasy feeling that someone had been inside Tea Totalers between last night and this morning. Maybe Topo di Sali had broken in and stolen Genevieve's tea when she refused his offer to buy. Or maybe Kim had thrown out more than she'd admitted to. If so, was she playing me to see how I'd react?

"Vaughn and I cleaned up after you left yesterday. We carried out bags and bags of garbage. I wonder if we accidentally threw it away. I'll have to ask him when I see him."

"Is he going to help us again today?"

"No, today we're on our own."

"Oh." She stood by the sink, her back pressed up against the counter. Today her pink T-shirt had a picture of a kitten in the middle of it. Her ill-fitting pink jeans sat low on her hips, this time exposing the waistband of floral cotton panties.

Being enamored of the fashions of the twenties and

thirties as I was, I'd never been much of a fan of the whole show-your-underwear trend. It was so prevalent on the streets of downtown LA that I'd come to identify strangers by the brand they wore. White Cotton Boxer, Navy Blue Jockey. Little Red Devil was the only nickname I used to someone's face. The guy who worked at the convenience store by the corner of my old apartment building gained notoriety—and the nickname—when his jeans fell down around his ankles while he was making change. From that day on he wore a belt, but the nickname stuck.

"We should get started. I'm going to be in here working on installing the fabric I brought. Are you okay out back with the sanding?"

"Sure."

Kim assembled the sander and found an extension cord. She ran it through the back door, which meant I couldn't shut her out from inside. When I heard the buzz of the handheld device, I filled the steamer with water and plugged it in. I checked the photos of my experiment on my phone while the steamer warmed up.

First I cued up the photo from inside the van and used my fingers in a reverse pinching action to blow up the detail of the tipped tea pitcher. Next I moved to the photos I took out back in my spilled tea experiment. It was obvious that the second photo, with the entire container of tea spilled on the carpet, was the stain that matched the inside of the van. It wasn't much, but it was something.

I looked out the window. Kim had her blond hair up in a ponytail on top of her head. She wore a pair of clear safety glasses over her eyes and used the small sander to scrub away at the finish on the iron table. By the looks of it, she was absorbed in her project. I pushed a chair against the back door, making sure it didn't blow open any farther than it was, and used Genevieve's phone to call the sheriff's mobile unit.

"Sheriff's office," said a familiar voice.

"Deputy Sheriff Clark, this is Poly Monroe. I have something I think you need to see."

"You're calling from Tea Totalers?"

"Yes. Can you come to the tea shop?"

"Is Mrs. Girard with you?"

"No."

"How long are you going to be there?"

"Most of the day."

"I'll be there after noon."

After I hung up, I copied the photos to Genevieve's hard drive and e-mailed them to myself as backup. I closed down the Internet window and turned off the monitor. It was slightly after ten. Time to get to work.

I moved into the store and flipped through the curtain panels I'd made. At the time, it had been little more than a project to take my mind off bigger problems, but it had gotten me back in touch with my love of combining textiles, creating a warm, cozy world with fibers, fabrics, and imagination.

The fabric colors and prints that I'd chosen for Tea Totalers complemented each other nicely. I used three different *toiles de jouy*: a pretty yellow, blue, and cream pattern; a cream and white; and a blue and white. I added a soft blue chambray and a cream jacquard. To add dimension to the color palette, I finished with a multicolored Provençal that captured the lush florals of France. Images of yellow roses and pink ribbons danced across a white background with green leaves. The curtain panels were all lined in a yellow-and-white gingham, which I also planned to use inside the store on the seat cushions and napkins.

I measured the circumference of the existing curtain rods, folded the fabric toward the front, and pinned along the fabric, creating a pocket through which to thread the curtain rod. When I finished pinning, I stitched the fabric into place, threaded the rod through the pocket, and set the curtain rod back on the wall-mounted supports. I stepped down from the chair and stood back. Aside from the wrinkles, the curtain was close to perfect.

I debated on whether or not it would be better to hang all of the curtains and then steam them, or hang and steam one at a time. I decided on the latter, impatient as I was to see how the curtains would look when finished. It took me longer to get from one window to the next, but by the time I had the west-facing wall complete, I could see how well my fabric choice complemented the butter color Genevieve had painted the shop when she first moved in. Alternating complementary fabrics created the effect that Tea Totalers had been here for generations. The mismatched fabrics worked together to give the interior warmth and timelessness, like a French cottage. I lost myself in the project and didn't hear Kim enter the room.

"It's like another world in here," she said.

I was steaming out the last of the curtains and turned to look at her. The steam shot onto the back of my hand and I dropped the steamer. Water sprayed the bottom of the curtain.

Kim rushed forward. "Are you okay?" she asked.

"I'm fine, just clumsy." I stepped down from the chair and moved the steamer from the floor to the windowsill. "That's probably a sign that it's time for a break. What do you think? Do you want to stop and get some lunch?"

"I'm kind of on a roll outside. But you can go get something if you want. I'll stay here."

Before I had a chance to answer, I heard a knock on the front door. I crossed the room and opened it, finding Deputy Sheriff Clark out front.

"Ms. Monroe," he said. "May I come in and talk to you?"

I glanced over my shoulder at Kim, but she wasn't there. To keep things confidential, I stepped outside and pulled the door shut behind me. "Let's talk out here. The windows are all covered inside and it's pretty dark."

I followed Clark down three concrete stairs. Like the morning, I scanned the lot across the street, looking for Rick's truck. It wasn't there. Clark looked around my head at the store and back at me. "Tell me again what you're doing here?"

"Renovations."

"I don't see any paint cans."

"It's not that kind of renovation." At his confusion, I continued. "I'm making over the interior of the tea shop with fabric. Curtains, seat cushions, napkins, placemats. Serving trays, wall hangings."

"Is Mrs. Girard paying you for the fabric? Or for your time?"

"I'm donating both."

"Seems like a costly donation."

"Genevieve is my friend, and this will help me out as much as it helps her. My store opens on Sunday." I pulled a coupon out of my back pocket. "Maybe you want to stop by and check it out?"

He glanced at the coupon. I kept it out in front of me until he finally took it. "This," I said, gesturing to the curtains, "is advertising. It's a perfect way to show people how important fabric is in decorating. When the store opens, I plan to run classes to teach people how to start with a concept and build a mood board and make it into a reality. Fabric is inspiring."

"What happened to her outdoor furniture?" he asked, looking at the bare yard. "Are you going to sew her a couple of tables and chairs?"

I ignored his sarcasm. "It's out back. It seemed as though it could use a freshening up to match the interior."

He nodded his head as though he agreed, but the slight crease in his forehead and the distant look in his eyes told me he hadn't been paying much attention to our conversation. He appeared to be looking for evidence that Genevieve was there, or had been there, or was going to be there.

"Sheriff, I have something to show you." I cued up the

photos on my iPhone and blew up the detail of the photo from the back of the van. "See this? It's from the back of the van the morning Phil Girard was found."

A shadow crossed Clark's face, probably because he didn't like that I'd taken that picture. "Is this about your fabric again?"

"No, it's not." I slid the photo to the side with my index finger and enlarged the image of the tea container. "That's one of Genevieve's tea containers."

"I know."

"Okay, good. See this stain? That's spilled tea. See the size of it?" He nodded. I flipped to the photos I took that morning. "I ran an experiment this morning. This is a carpet with half a jug of water spilled on it. And this next one is with all of the water on it. Notice anything?"

I handed my phone to him. He stared at the phone and used his fingers in the same reverse pinch, blowing up the detail. I held my breath, waiting for him to reach the same conclusion I had. "Why's it green?"

"Food coloring."

After he'd flipped back and forth between the two pictures, he handed my phone back to me.

"Ms. Monroe, what are you trying to prove here?"

"That the tea in the container spilled into the back of the van. If Phil didn't drink the tea, he couldn't have been poisoned by it."

His expression changed with a flash of excitement, like a contestant on Final Jeopardy who is an expert on the category. "I thought you wanted me to check your fabric for a death mask. Why do you think poison was the cause of death?"

"You said you were going to run a tox screen."

"Phil Girard's stomach was empty, so I already know he didn't drink the tea. That doesn't interest me nearly as much as you suspecting that the tea Mrs. Girard made for her husband was poisoned."

"No! I didn't say that. I was just saying if *you* thought he was poisoned, it couldn't have been the tea, because he didn't drink the tea. So you shouldn't be concerned by the tea."

"The tea isn't my concern. I already know it wasn't poisoned. What concerns me is the fact that I have five witnesses who can place Genevieve Girard in Los Angeles on Sunday night."

Twelve

It couldn't be. Genevieve had told me she was afraid she poisoned Phil, but she'd never mentioned anything about following Phil to Los Angeles. Why would she confess to an accidental murder and not confess to any surrounding actions that placed her directly in the scope of means, motive, and opportunity?

Clark pointed at my phone. "Ms. Monroe, those pictures indicate that you intend to disregard my request to stay out of my investigation in order to try to help your friend. If you want to help Mrs. Girard, tell her to talk to me. The longer she waits, the worse things are going to be for her."

I stood as straight as I could, which, at five foot nine plus the heels on my boots, put me eye to eye with Clark. "If I see her, I'll tell her."

We stood in a Mexican standoff for a few seconds. "I mean it, Ms. Monroe: stay out of this, for your own safety."

I expected Clark to punctuate his command with an abrupt turn and departure, but instead he approached the building and opened the door. He leaned inside and scanned the interior. After a few seconds, he closed the door, descended the concrete stairs, and walked around the side of the building. I followed a few steps behind.

When I caught up with him, he was running his open palm over the iron table. The mouse sander sat on the sidewalk. Kim wasn't there. Clark looked at the fine white dust that covered his hand, and then smacked both of his hands together. Tiny particles of sanded-off paint exploded from his hands and filled the air. It smelled like chalk. It caught in my throat and I coughed.

"Are you working on this renovation by yourself?"

"No, I have a couple of helpers," I answered.

"Anybody I know?"

I figured it was as good a time as any to name-drop. "Vaughn McMichael," I said.

He nodded. "That's right, he mentioned that yesterday. Anybody else?"

"You saw Vaughn yesterday? When?" He held my stare but didn't answer me. "Yes, there is somebody else. Kim Matheson. *M-A-T-H-E-S-O-N*," I spelled.

He pulled a notepad out of his pocket and jotted the name down. "He? She?"

"She."

"Is she here?"

"She was. I don't know where she went." I considered things for a second. And then lowered my voice. "Sheriff, Kim showed up the morning Phil was murdered. When I told her she should try to find other work, she got very insistent that people expected her to be working here. And I don't know if this means anything or not, but she has a parole officer."

"She told you this?"

"Not exactly."

He stared at me for a couple of beats. "Ms. Monroe, remember what I said. Stay out of this investigation. If Ms. Matheson returns, have her call me. I'd like to talk to her, too." Clark pulled a card from his wallet and handed it to me. It had numbers for the mobile sheriff's office and Clark's direct cell.

I took the card. "I'll give her the message."

I followed Clark around the back of the shop to the other side, and then to the front. He stood back and looked up at the façade. "Place looks different with that brown paper in the windows. Dark. Sad. Be a shame for San Ladrón to lose its tea shop."

"San Ladrón's not losing anything. Once you catch Phil Girard's murderer, everything will go back to normal."

Clark left out the front gate, and I locked it shut behind him. He wanted something to investigate? Let's see what he found out when he started digging into Kim's past.

I worked well into the afternoon. By the time I called it quits, my neck was sore, my shoulders were in a knot, and my stomach was empty. Kim hadn't returned. I wondered if I'd ever see her again. I swept the unfinished hardwood floor and thought about what Clark had said.

Five witnesses placed Genevieve in Los Angeles on Sunday night. If that was true, why hadn't she said anything? And what had she been doing in Los Angeles in the first place? If she'd asked Phil to go to pick up dry goods, then clearly she hadn't been planning to make the trip herself. So what was she doing there?

She didn't trust him.

I'd assumed Genevieve didn't know about Phil's affair, but if she suspected something, she might have tailed him to get confirmation. And if that was the case, things wouldn't look good for her. A lawyer could easily build an argument that the scorned wife murdered the cheating husband in a jealous rage. Genevieve might be able to claim temporary insanity, but for a woman who was innocent, insanity was a far cry from a desirable outcome.

After I finished sweeping, I locked up the shop. I double-checked the front door, the back door, and all of the windows, remembering how the knob had turned easily in my hand that morning. I still didn't know who had unlocked the door, but the contents of the refrigerator and the small bag of leftover croissants were missing. I looked up in the direction of Sheriff Clark. Had he been into the store before any of us were there, bagging and tagging Genevieve's supplies, looking for evidence against her?

I left the red wagon locked up inside Tea Totalers and drove back to the fabric store. There were three hours before Vaughn was due to pick me up for the movie, and since I didn't know if Vaughn's invitation included dinner, I thought it best to take Scarlett O'Hara's lead and eat a little something before the date. I also thought it best to eat before getting dressed so I avoided any unfortunate spills.

I made a quick salad from romaine and radishes, blended olive oil, Dijon mustard, lemon juice, salt, pepper, and oregano in a small cruet, and poured it on. I topped it with a handful of sunflower seeds and freshly grated mozzarella.

It took longer to make the salad than it did to eat it. When I was finished, I stacked the dirty dishes in the sink. Then, feeling guilty, I rinsed them and moved them to the dishwasher. Still not enough for a full load, but the kitchen looked better. Now to transition from my current mental state into something more calm before I could begin to relax in his company. *Calm* meant sewing.

I went downstairs to the sewing workstation and worked on the placemats. First I cut eighteen-by-twelve-inch rectangles from the fabric. I sandwiched batting between mismatched but coordinating pieces, pinned them together along all four sides, and free motion quilted the layers together by moving them in a random pattern while running the needle. I finished the edges with yellow seam binding. I had a stack of twenty by the time I was finished. I turned off all of the equipment and draped a long length of faded pink taffeta over the sewing machine.

I headed upstairs to the apartment and found the kitties in the kitchen. Needles was swatting a crumpled piece of paper back and forth. Pins was hunched down, his head swinging from side to side, following the path of the paper. Even though he was still young, his face was contorted into one of concentration. Needles knocked the paper out of range with his small orange paw and Pins pounced. I turned around and found the trash can tipped over, leaving behind a banana peel, an empty orange juice container, coffee grounds, and the takeout bag from The Earl of Sandwich. I righted the bin and collected the trash, leaving the small wad of paper on the floor for the kitties to play with.

As I watched them swat the ball back and forth, my mind wandered to tonight.

For the last three years I'd been in a relationship with Carson Cole, a financial analyst in Los Angeles. We'd gone from having drinks with friends, to hanging out, to living together. Soon after that, conversation turned to getting married. I guess that's what life was like for a financial analyst. You project into the future and do what you need to do to stay on track with your expectations.

Carson was a nice enough guy, and if I were judging in terms of previous generations, I'd go so far as to call him a good provider. He had a steady job and a steadier lifestyle. We fell into a routine dictated by the days of the week: Tacos on Tuesday, Wash on Wednesday. If Carson had anything to do with the Villamere Theater, he'd show movies from the thirties on the third *Thursday* of the month. I was glad he didn't, because just thinking all of those TH sounds made me feel like Elmer Fudd.

The truth was, I stayed with Carson longer than I should have because our relationship, like the rest of my life, was comfortable. Other friends who had wrestled with the same "what do we want out of life?" questions had either pursued promotions or marriage. I'd climbed to the top of the ladder at To The Nines looking for some kind of job satisfaction that I never found.

I chalked my general dissatisfaction up to the fact that Carson and I were dealing with the realities of our lives now that we were officially among the working class. But while Carson embraced his professional life and emulated the senior advisors at his company, I was the opposite. I was restless, as if caught in a temporary world. There had to be more out there for me than designing cheap pageant dresses for a slightly shady shop in the heart of Santee Court in downtown Los Angeles. It was after I learned Great-Uncle Marius had left me the fabric store in San Ladrón that I saw things in a new light. I didn't need the fast pace and urgent buzz of Los Angeles to feel alive. I needed something that felt uniquely me, something I could own.

Once I decided I was going to move to San Ladrón, everything else in my life fell into place. I broke up with Carson, gave notice to Giovanni, and spent my first unemployed week moving my meager belongings into storage. It wasn't until I packed up everything of mine from that shared apartment that I realized how little of "our" life was "me." I said goodbye to Los Angeles, loaded what was truly important into my Bug, and drove to San Ladrón.

Thinking of Giovanni reminded me that I hadn't heard from him today. I didn't know if it was good news or bad news. What I did know was that the surefire way to get on his bad side was to nag him about something he said he'd do. We'd struck a deal, and I knew I'd sweetened my end enough that he'd want to uphold his.

I moved from the kitchen to the bedroom, stripped down and tossed my dirty clothes in the hamper, took a quick shower, and wrapped myself in a black dressing gown. When the steam cleared from the mirror in the bathroom, I studied my reflection. My fair complexion held a tinge of pink from the hot shower. I smoothed tinted moisturizer over my face and squeezed a blob of styling crème onto my palm. After rubbing my hands together, I raked the product through my hair and combed it away from my face with a wide-tooth comb. I pushed the back forward, found a deep part on the left, and tucked the left side behind my ear, shaping the ends into a curl below my ear. I swept the long front to the right side with my fingers and left it to air-dry in place.

I used a sharpened pencil to define my thin brows, and I dabbed a dark cherry lip stain onto my lips. I finished with an eyelash curler and a coat of mascara. Needles wandered into the bathroom and meowed at me. I closed the lid to the toilet and he jumped up and nosed the belt to my dressing gown.

"I'm going on a date with Vaughn McMichael," I said in response to his meow. "You remember him, don't you? He's the one who found you in the Dumpster."

Needles meowed again. Three months ago I stopped worrying about becoming one of those people who talks to her pets. Now I worried about the kind of people who didn't.

I moved to the closet and rolled the doors to the side, exposing feathers, velvet, beads, and silk. Most of the clothes in the closet had belonged to my aunt. It was she who first taught me the importance of learning to make patterns by deconstructing vintage clothes. She'd been a collector herself in the fifties. She taught me that there was always a decade that went out of fashion, and that's when you could get the best prices. She also taught me that fashion draws inspiration from the past, so what was out today would be in tomorrow.

Among the truly important things I'd packed into my car and moved with me from Los Angeles to San Ladrón was my own collection of vintage clothes from the thirties. I scoured eBay, estate sales, and movie studio wardrobe liquidations for items in my price range. Once I accepted my working wardrobe of black, black, and black, I spent less on regular clothes and more on my collection. I told Carson they were inspiration for my job, but there was a reason I only bought ones in my size. I'd never had an opportunity to wear any of them, but tonight felt like the perfect opportunity.

I selected a sheer black blouse with tiny white polka dots. It tied in a full bow at the neck, and had a series of pleats across the back. I tucked it into a black satin pencil skirt that fell three inches below my knees, a length that only worked with heels. Carson had complained when I wore heels because they made me taller than him. Vaughn was over six feet tall, so that wouldn't be a problem. I added the diamond stud earrings my parents gave me when I graduated from design school and a simple tennis bracelet I'd found in Aunt Millie's jewelry box.

I slid the closet doors shut and the door caught on something black velvet. A cape. It was about twenty-four inches long and lined in a brilliant turquoise silk. A rhinestone clasp by the neckline kept it closed so it wouldn't fall from the hanger. I undid the clasp and slipped the cape around my shoulders. The A-line cut swirled around me. I slipped on my black pumps—a comfortable style despite their pointy toe and three-inch heel—and looked in the mirror. I was only starting to get to know the glamorous stranger who looked back, and that's how I liked it.

Downstairs, there was a knock on the back door. Needles jumped down from the toilet seat and ran into the hallway. I followed. It was six thirty, too early for Vaughn to arrive. I moved to the kitchen and looked out the window above the parking lot. There were no cars other than mine. I took off the cape and left it on the kitchen table, then scampered downstairs as the knocking grew louder. I unlocked the door and pulled it open. Genevieve stood on the other side.

Thirteen

Her newly cut and colored honey-blond hair was plastered to her face and her clothes were damp. I looked at the lot behind her and up at the sky to see if I'd missed a sudden shower. There was no evidence of rain.

"I know you're probably wondering why I wasn't at Charlie's this morning. I appreciate everything you did for me, but I can't stay there. Not now. Not after what I saw," she said.

"Come in. You're wet. Why are you wet?"

She ushered past me. "I was trying to sneak down the alley next to the Waverly House and I got caught in their sprinklers." She used her index finger and thumbs to pinch the fabric of her shirt and pull it away from her body. A bubble of air filled the space between the material and her skin. When she let go, it looked like her shirt had been inflated. "I'm sorry I dragged you into this, Poly."

"Never mind that. Let's get you upstairs and into some dry clothes."

"I don't think I'll fit in your clothes."

"Trust me. I have clothes you'll fit in."

She followed me to the stairs. The kitties had followed me down. I scooped up Pins and she scooped up Needles. When she held him close to her, he wriggled around to get away from her wet shirt. She held him out in front of her, his body curling forward like a *C*.

We went to the bedroom. I found a clean rose-pink towel and handed it to her, along with a white terry-cloth robe that had puffy moons and stars appliquéd onto it. "Take the wet clothes off. I'll wait out here."

She went into the bathroom and shut the door, but kept talking. "If Charlie asks if you saw me, you can't tell her anything."

"What happened with Charlie?" I asked. Last I'd heard, Charlie was as concerned with Genevieve's disappearance as I was.

"After she finished with my hair, she said we should go out. When I said no, she said she was going anyway, and she'd be at The Broadside Tavern if I changed my mind."

"The Broadside's a rough bar, Gen. I don't know if it's a good idea for you to make it your new hangout."

"The owner is one of my regulars. I thought I'd say hello."

"Charlie didn't tell me you two went out last night," I said.

"She never saw me. I went inside and saw her talking to that cop. I left before they saw me."

"Charlie was talking to Sheriff Clark last night?"

Genevieve cracked the door. "Yes. I thought I could trust her, but not after that."

I set up a collapsible drying rack from the closet and draped Genevieve's wet clothes over it. Charlie hadn't mentioned anything about talking to Clark, and that made me suspicious. I believed Charlie was a good person, but she had her own agenda, and in this case, there was a very good chance her agenda was at odds with Genevieve's.

"Let's get you something to wear," I said.

"This is fine." She fingered the ends of the terry-cloth robe.

I turned to face her. "What time is it?"

"Almost quarter to seven."

"Vaughn McMichael is due here in fifteen minutes. I hardly think it's in anybody's best interest for you to be sitting around in a bathrobe when he arrives."

"Why is he coming here?"

"We're going out." At her confused look, I continued. "On a date."

"You and Vaughn? Poly, that's great."

"It might be great, but we don't have time to sit around talking about it. You're about a size eight or ten, right?"

"Twelve. I'm curvy."

"Curvy is good." I reached into the back of the closet, where I'd discovered a pocket of clothes Aunt Millie had made in the fifties when she went through her Brigitte Bardot phase. "Try this," I said, and handed her a black wool jersey tunic and cropped pants.

"I can't wear that," she said.

"Why not?"

"It would get stretched."

"It's jersey. It's meant to be stretched. And here it is, hanging in a closet. Take it." I pushed the hanger at her. "And then you have to get out of here."

She slipped the pants over her legs and closed the side zip, and then turned around and pulled the tunic over her head. I handed her a length of fabric to belt it. "It fits," she said, surprised.

"Of course it fits. It looks great on you, too. One of these days, when this is all over, you can come over and we can play dress-up."

Genevieve's eyes dropped to the floor. She tugged at the hem of the tunic, and then dropped her hands to her sides. Both fists balled up and released twice before she spoke.

She seemed to be fighting with something inside her, an impulse to confide in me or an impulse to run away.

"Gen, the sheriff wants to talk to you. It's routine. There are things he already knows about that you need to explain. I know you're scared, but he knows you didn't poison Phil. Avoiding him is only making matters worse."

"Poly, I was there, in Los Angeles. When Phil said he was going to head out Sunday night so he could get a head start, I was so mad. But then I started thinking about what it was he wanted from me, and I got a crazy idea. I thought if I could do something spontaneous like surprise him at the motel, we wouldn't fight. He'd realize we could have what we used to have. You know, put the spark back into the relationship or something."

I waited for her to go on.

"I found the name of the motel on our online bank statement. I rented a car and drove to Los Angeles. I even bought champagne with a credit card and stopped in the lobby of the motel and told the man at the front desk who I was and that I wanted to surprise my husband. How stupid could I be?"

"What did you do?" I asked quietly.

"I tapped on the door to his room. He said it was open. When I went inside, it was obvious he wasn't expecting me."

"Obvious?"

"He was already naked and he had one of those premade Christmas bows . . . down there."

As much as I wanted to know what happened, I wished she hadn't put that visual in my head. Phil had a more than generous amount of body hair. And what kind of woman goes for a premade Christmas bow?

"What happened?"

"He accused me of spying on him. I freaked out. I said I might as well have been spying on him because he was obviously cheating. I threw the champagne at the wall and the bottle broke. It was loud. The people in the next room came out to see what was going on. I ran out of the room and left."

"You came home?"

"No. I was shaking so badly I couldn't drive. I booked a room at a Best Western and left early Monday morning—really early, before rush hour. I was on the road by six."

There was another knock downstairs, this time on the front door. I'd left the gate open because I knew Vaughn would be coming. The color drained from Genevieve's face.

"It's Vaughn. Now listen to me. I want to keep talking to you about this, but I can't now. You can stay here while I'm gone."

"Where is he taking you?"

"The Villamere Theater."

She smiled. "Thirties night. He's been paying attention."

Another knock sounded on the door. "I have to go, Gen, but I'll be back. Try to relax. Okay?"

"Have fun," she said. I ran down the stairs with my handbag in one hand and my cape in the other.

Vaughn stood on the sidewalk. He wore a dark gray suit with a white dress shirt, unbuttoned at the collar in lieu of a tie. A Black Watch plaid scarf was draped around his neck. The expression on his face was a mixture of concern and surprise. Behind him a row of parked cars lined the street. A shiny silver Porsche was sandwiched between a dirty blue coupe and a black VW Bug from the same era as my yellow one. It would be a challenge for the Porsche to get out of its space, as the VW Bug had parked it in.

"I'm sorry if I kept you waiting. I was upstairs and didn't hear the knock. Have you been here long?"

"Slow down, Poly. You didn't keep me waiting. I'm early. And even if you had kept me waiting, I'd say it was worth it." He smiled, erasing the concern and the surprise. "This is for you," he said, holding out a plant. "It's a gardenia," he added.

I buried my nose in the blossom, inhaling the richness of the soil, the freshness of the leaves, and the sweetness of the blossom.

"It's beautiful. Thank you," I said.

"I was going to bring you flowers, but I wanted you to have something that would last longer."

I looked up at Vaughn's face for a moment and caught him staring back at me. Embarrassed, I looked at the gardenia. This was stupid. I couldn't go all night carrying around a plant to avoid looking at the person I was with. I looked back at Vaughn. "Let me put this inside."

I crossed the room and set the plant on the wrap stand next to the register. A few months ago Vaughn and I had shared an impromptu candlelight dinner on that very wrap stand. I'd misunderstood his intentions—convinced he was using me—and had asked him to leave. I wondered if another man would have asked me out after that.

When I returned to the door, Vaughn was still standing on the sidewalk. He took my cape from my hand and held it open while I backed into it. His hands lingered on my shoulders for the briefest moment. I hooked the rhinestone clasp in the front and turned around to face him. His green eyes, rimmed with flecks of honey and amber, sparkled. "Too many people dress down these days. I'm glad you're not one of them."

"We should be going if we want to get good seats," I said.

"The Villamere allows reserved seating. I snagged us the best seats in the house when you said yes."

I closed the front door, locked it, and secured the gate across the front. Vaughn walked to the black VW Bug and opened the passenger-side door.

"*This* is your other car?" I asked.

"What did you expect?"

"Not this." I laughed.

"I already told you, we're not as different as you think,"

he said. He closed the door behind me and got into the driver's side.

We kept up a steady stream of small talk on the way to the theater, mostly about the renovation of Tea Totalers. I told him how much I'd gotten done and joked that I was more productive without him. Neither of us mentioned Genevieve or Phil. I'd expected him to bring it up and was on my guard, afraid to relax and accidentally spill the depth of my involvement.

When we reached the theater, Vaughn went to the Will Call counter while I lingered in the lobby, studying posters and ads for upcoming shows. The Villamere was an old movie house that had been converted with new equipment. Their schedule varied among movies, bands, and theatrical performances. The original poster for the Mae West movie we were about to see hung between a poster for a big-budget car-chases-and-explosions blockbuster and a sign advertising Babs Green's next burlesque show.

Beyond the wall of posters was an office. The door was ajar, and I heard voices. Soon, a striking redhead in a snug, fifties-style black-and-white houndstooth dress walked out, followed by a balding man in a brown corduroy suit. I pretended to study the posters one by one and inched closer to their conversation.

"My contract says I get paid whether or not I perform," she said. "I expect to be compensated at my regular rate."

"I put a lot of money into promoting your shows, Babs. Last-minute cancellations put a real dent in my cash take. I rely on that money to keep this theater running."

"My shows pay your bills. You're coming very close to telling me that maybe it's time for me to renegotiate my contract with the Villamere."

"You wouldn't!"

I hovered by the poster for *Diamond Lil*, showing next

Wednesday. I couldn't believe what I'd heard. Babs had canceled her show on Sunday? That meant she *didn't* have an alibi.

"Nice theater, isn't it?" said Vaughn from my right. I jumped. "Did I scare you?"

"My mind wandered, I guess." I looked up at the original elaborate gold ceiling. "This place is amazing."

"It's been restored from when it first opened. I worked here when I was in high school. I'd give you the history, but I don't think we have time. Would you like anything from the concession stand?"

"Sure." After some quick negotiations, we agreed on a bag of popcorn, a split of champagne, and a box of Goobers. I told Vaughn I wanted to look around a bit more. As soon as his back was turned, I turned around and studied the announcement of Babs Green's performance.

The date on the poster was for this past Sunday night. The show, billed as adult fare, started at ten and ran until eleven. A second show ran from midnight to one. If she'd performed both shows, she couldn't have murdered Phil in Los Angeles on Sunday night, but the conversation I'd just overheard led me to believe she'd canceled at least one show. And two shows on Sunday night didn't provide her an alibi for Monday morning.

The image on the poster showed Babs in profile, one hand up, tangled in her vibrant red hair, the other holding a thick green boa that draped over her shoulder. Her dress looked like it had been painted on her body, and she wore her expression like an invitation.

A man in a burgundy uniform approached from the left and secured a velvet rope by a staircase that led to an upper theater.

"Excuse me," I said. "Do you know when Babs Green is performing again?"

He looked me up and down and raised his eyebrows. I guess I didn't look the type to take in a burlesque show. "She's here every Sunday. One of our biggest draws."

"I guess it's a shame she had to cancel last week."

"What makes you think she canceled? Full house, as usual. Her second show was better than her first."

"I must have been misinformed," I said. I looked over his shoulder toward the office.

"People are going to remember that show. Things got a little wild. Ms. Green kept us here an hour after her second show ended. She wouldn't come out of her dressing room until the last of the audience members left the parking lot. She sat in there and hit the champagne. She kept saying she was afraid to drive home in case someone was waiting for her. We drew straws to see who got to drive her home. My buddy won," he said, looking wistful.

"Did she say who she was afraid of?"

"You didn't hear it from me, but she was having a thing with a married man. I think she was afraid of the wife finding out."

This didn't sound good. "So she left her car here and your friend drove her home?"

"Yeah, and apparently when she showed up Monday morning to get her car she was still tipsy. The manager didn't want to chance her not sticking around for the Monday walk-through, so he told her to sleep it off in her dressing room."

Vaughn waved from the concession stand. "Thank you." I hurried to the usher and pointed at Vaughn, who had one arm wrapped around the bucket of popcorn and the split of champagne and two plastic coupes in the other hand. The box of Goobers was tucked under his elbow. The usher let me through. I rescued the box of Goobers and the plastic glasses from Vaughn and we ducked into the darkened theater.

I'd always heard movies were meant to be viewed from the ninth row but was happy we sat in the twelfth, considering it came with an ample amount of legroom. I turned my phone off while Vaughn filled each of the plastic glasses with bubbly. Before he had a chance to make a toast, the rest of the lights went out. We clinked plastic and turned toward the screen.

We finished most of the popcorn and all of the Goobers during the trailers. When the movie started, Vaughn set the popcorn on the floor and we focused on the screen. It was a good thing I was familiar with the movie, because I had a hard time paying attention.

When Genevieve told me she went to Los Angeles and caught Phil dressed for a romantic interlude that didn't involve her, I was sure he'd been expecting his mistress Babs. But how would that have been possible? She'd been in San Ladrón. She'd performed two shows to a full house—two full houses—filled with witnesses. A theater employee had driven her home. A taxi had driven her back the next morning. She'd been too drunk to drive, so the manager had told her to sleep it off in her dressing room.

Not good for Genevieve's story.

After the movie, Vaughn and I strolled through the lobby. He pointed out details in the interior architecture I might not have noticed. Try as I did, I still couldn't focus. I feigned interest in a subject I would normally love to hear about, but I could tell from the expression on his face that he knew my mind was miles away.

"Is everything okay?" he finally asked.

He'd been nothing but nice all night, and while I wasn't comfortable telling him the whole truth, I felt I owed him something. "I'm sorry I'm so distracted. The truth is, I have a lot on my mind."

"Your store opens on Sunday. Are you ready?"

"No," I said. "I mean, yes. I mean, I'm ready to open the store. In some ways, I think I'm more ready for that than anything. But that's not what's worrying me. I can't stop thinking about Genevieve."

"That's why you're working so hard on the fabric renovation for her, isn't it? It's not just about the renovation. You're trying to do something nice for her to make up for what people are saying."

"What are people saying?"

"That she poisoned her husband."

"But she didn't. I proved as much today. When I tried to show Sheriff Clark how I knew Phil didn't drink the tea Genevieve gave him, he said he already knew that."

Vaughn's face froze. "How do you know about the tea?" he asked.

"Clark came to Tea Totalers today." I didn't want to tell Vaughn about my tea spill experiment or the photos I'd taken to prove Phil hadn't ingested the tea. Admitting to that would be too close to telling him that I was trying to figure out what happened, and that would be too close to admitting that I'd spoken to Genevieve.

"Can we go someplace to talk?" he asked.

I knew I couldn't invite him back to the fabric store because Genevieve might still be there. And I didn't want to suggest we went back to his place, because not only did I not know where his place was, I didn't want to seem forward. I opened my clutch handbag and stared at the keys inside. "Let's go to Tea Totalers. I have the keys. We can talk there."

Vaughn drove at a fast clip and parked behind the shop. I unlocked the back door and he followed me to the front. I unfolded a large piece of toile and laid it on the floor like a blanket. I unclipped the cape and draped it on the counter, then kicked off my shoes and lowered myself to the floor, tucking my feet in beside me. Vaughn sat across from me. I braced myself for his questions, questions that would force me to either admit I'd talked to Genevieve or to lie to Vaughn. Until he asked, I didn't know which direction I'd go.

"When you knocked that glass of tea out of my hands yesterday morning, I knew what you thought," he said. "You were afraid there was something in the tea that killed Phil and you didn't want me to drink it."

I neither confirmed nor denied his suspicion.

"I assume you were protecting Genevieve, and I can respect

that. And if there *was* something in the tea, you kept me from drinking it, so I guess I owe you a thank-you for that, too."

"Vaughn, I can't tell you why I reacted the way I did."

"I don't want your explanation. There's something I need to tell you." He sat Indian-style and looked down at his feet. His highly polished black wing tips crossed over each other. I noticed how the knots in his shoelaces weren't centered on top of his foot, but were closer to his instep, as though he'd crossed his foot over his knee to tie each shoe. His socks had a small chevron pattern in black and forest green.

I reached across the short distance between us and put my hand on his knee. "What is it? What's so important that you have to tell me?"

"After you cleaned up the spill, you put the paper towels and the broken glass in a bag and you put the bag out back. I took the bag to the police to analyze." He looked up. "*That's* how Sheriff Clark knows the tea wasn't poisoned."

Fourteen

Heat rushed into my head and my heartbeat thumped in my ears. I pulled my hand away from Vaughn, sat up straight, and looked around the interior of the shop for a way out. Even though I'd spent most of the day here, tonight I felt like an animal trapped in a cage.

"How could you do that to her? I thought you were Genevieve's friend."

"I am her friend. Poly, listen to me—"

"No, I won't listen to you." I cursed the narrow skirt that made it impossible to stand gracefully. Vaughn jumped up quickly, anticipating my flight. My right foot twisted around my left ankle and, halfway standing, I tipped and started to fall back down. Vaughn's hands shot out and caught me by the waist. He righted me but didn't let go. Our faces were inches apart.

"Yes, you *will* listen to me, because you asked me how I could do something like that to her. I did it because she asked me to."

I tried to pull away from the grip he had on my waist, but when his words sank in, I stopped. He must have sensed that the fight had left me, because his hands relaxed. His left hand reached up and he tucked his index finger under my chin and tipped my face so I was looking directly at him. "Did you hear what I said?" he asked softly.

"Genevieve asked you to take the tea to the police?"

"Genevieve asked me to find out if she'd put something in the tea that could have killed Phil."

"That's a pretty big risk, taking it to Clark to answer her question."

"If that's what I'd done, then yes, it would have been a big risk. I wasn't willing to take that chance. I took it to a private lab and had them run up a chemical panel on the contents. After I knew for sure she was in the clear, I took it to Clark."

I didn't know what to say. Here I was, trying to re-create the stain in the back of the truck while Vaughn had a private lab at his disposal. It was Trixie Belden vs. Bruce Wayne.

"I don't know what to say."

The side of his mouth raised into a shy smile. "I told you we're not all that different."

I stepped backward and this time his hands lost contact with me. "But we are different, Vaughn. I'm out here with carpet scraps and green food coloring trying to prove Genevieve's innocent and you've got private labs at your disposal." I hadn't told him about the carpet experiment and, judging from the expression on his face, he was confused. Humiliation warmed my cheeks and throat, restricting my breathing. I wanted to turn around and leave, bury my head in a pillow and try to pretend I hadn't said anything, but it was too late.

He'd used the resources he had to help Genevieve, just like I had. I was being irrational about the methods he'd used to get there, but I was too far gone to let it be.

Vaughn stepped toward me and I stepped backward. He stepped toward me again, and this time I stayed put. "This isn't about what I did for Genevieve, is it?" he asked in a soft voice.

"I don't think it is." I felt myself shaking.

Vaughn must have seen it, because he stepped closer. "Come here, Poly. Shhhh." He folded his arms around me. We stood like that until the shaking stopped. When I pulled away, Vaughn relaxed his embrace. "Do we need to talk about this?" he asked.

"No. I'm sorry I overreacted."

"You didn't overreact; you reacted the way that was natural for you to react. I can't say I understand it, but it was real and it was honest."

I reached out and took his hand and led him back to the toile floor covering. I sat down first and Vaughn followed.

"First things first," I started. "Genevieve asked me to help her. No, that's not true. She didn't ask for my help. She thought she accidentally poisoned Phil. I volunteered to help her, because I knew she needed it. I remember how it felt a few months ago, when I didn't know anybody and people were saying things about me."

Vaughn nodded and I continued.

"I told her to stay away from the store. The renovation with fabric, this whole project, was supposed to be a surprise for her. I got the idea a while ago, back when I first came to San Ladrón. The first time I sat in this tea shop after she told me how she wanted it to feel like a French café, I knew the fabrics at the store could make a world of difference. I started working on things a little bit here, a little bit there. In secret, between planning to reopen the fabric store and moving from Los Angeles." I shrugged. "After Phil's murder, we thought it was best for her to close the café for the week. We agreed to tell people it had been scheduled for a while. It was as good an excuse as any for her to stay a way while we figured this thing out."

"The morning I came here, you weren't expecting me."

"No, pretty much the opposite."

"But you didn't kick me out."

"Turns out you were a pretty good worker." I smiled as much of a smile as I could manage. I still felt stupid for my reaction, and I knew I was far from explaining how I felt.

"Maybe I enjoyed the company." He returned my smile, and I relaxed.

"This whole thing is a lot of work, more than I thought it would be. Truth is, I can't really afford to turn away any help, which is why Kim's still working here even though I don't completely trust her."

"Kim?" he asked.

"You know, the young blonde who was helping us yesterday?"

"That's right, there was someone else here yesterday. I barely noticed her."

It felt both awkward and comfortable, standing in the dark of Tea Totalers with Vaughn. If there'd been any food in the kitchen, I might have set out a late picnic to give us something to do, but there wasn't, so I didn't. The candles we'd lit when we came in were burning low. Soon we'd be in complete darkness. I didn't know what time it was, but it felt like it was after midnight.

"What did you tell Sheriff Clark when you gave him the tea?"

"That it came from the refrigerator at Tea Totalers."

"He didn't question the broken glass or the rags?"

"I'm sure he questioned them, he just kept those questions to himself. You said he knew Phil didn't die from drinking the tea."

I thought back about the conversation I'd had with the sheriff earlier that day. "It was more what I told him. I tried to show Clark the photos from my own experiment, but he said he'd already ruled out poisoned tea as the cause of death."

"Tell me more about this experiment."

"I took a picture of Phil's body when he was found in the back of the van. There was something that looked like a puddle in the back of the van next to the tea container, so I thought maybe the container spilled, and if so, Phil couldn't have drunk it. I ran a couple of scenarios here with a scrap of carpet and a container of colored water, to see the size of the spill and compare it to the stain in the back of the van. I thought if I could show how much tea might have spilled, I could make an argument against Phil having ingested enough to be poisoned even if there was something poisonous in it. Accidentally."

"That's genius."

"I don't think it's genius, but I was working with what I had. Just like you were."

"No, what you did was resourceful. I'm impressed."

Again a flash of embarrassment flushed my cheeks. Before Vaughn could say anything else, I changed the subject.

"You said Genevieve asked you to look into the tea. When was that?"

"Yesterday. I went by Charlie's to check on my car. I didn't know Genevieve was there. Charlie told me you were at Tea Totalers. When I asked how you got the keys to the store, Genevieve came out from inside Charlie's office and told me she'd made arrangements for you to work there."

"She's not supposed to be letting people know she's there."

"I'm not exactly 'people.'"

"I'm sorry. When I accepted this date, I thought you were human. Did I get that wrong?"

Vaughn laughed out loud. He reached for my hand and braided his fingers through mine. I expected his hands to be soft and smooth, but they weren't. I ran my thumb against his palm and felt rough calluses and small abrasions where his skin had been scraped or cut. I looked down and flipped his hands palm side up like I was a fortune-teller and was checking his lifeline.

"I bought an apartment on the outskirts of San Ladrón," he said. "It's a fixer-upper. I've been spending a lot of time working on it, and I've got the battle scars to prove it."

"Is that why I haven't seen you around much since I moved here?"

"It's one of the reasons. I was out of town for a month, too. Business for my dad."

I wondered if Vaughn knew his father had cosigned the loan on Material Girl for me. I didn't ask. Business was business, and that was mine. And as far as money went, I'd already acted stupid enough for one night.

"It's getting late. Maybe we should call it a night," I said.

"Already?"

"Now that you admitted you're not human, I don't know if it's safe to be around you after midnight," I joked.

We stood up and cleared the seating area from the floor. I shook the toile and folded it neatly. Vaughn blew out two of the three candles and carried the third—the only light inside the tea shop—to illuminate our path.

"What time is it, anyway?" I asked.

"Not sure." He opened the back door, blew out the third candle, and set it on the counter. He let me pass through the doorway first. Once he was out, I went behind him and locked the back door. We walked side by side to his car. He unlocked the passenger side door and held it open for me. I didn't get in right away.

"My family struggled," I said, turning to face him. "We weren't poor, but we were money aware. Both of my parents worked full-time jobs while I was in high school. I had a job during summers, which helped pay for my tuition to design school, and I worked part-time when I was in college. Aunt Millie was the one who got me into fabric and sewing, not because it was chic or cool, but because it was less expensive. She taught me to cut the buttons and zippers out of clothes that were worn-out. Together we'd search thrift stores and estate sales for dresses that were out of fashion, and look for ones that appeared to be damaged beyond saving. She taught me how to deconstruct them to make patterns for new clothes. I remember her as being so glamorous, but in junior high, the other kids made jokes about the clothes she wore."

"Poly, I might have money, but I don't have the kind of memories about family that you have. We struggled in different ways. I grew up knowing people wanted things from me. Friends expected me to pay for things because I could. My parents got divorced when I was young. I didn't even know I had a sister until after I graduated college. I went to private school. My dad wanted me to go to Harvard. I wanted to go to William and Mary. He said if I wanted it enough, I'd get there without his help."

"And you did," I said. He held up a hand to quiet me and continued.

"I took two years off and worked every job I could get. I qualified for a partial scholarship and paid for my first two years' tuition myself. I stayed in Virginia and got a job at an investment firm. It took his heart attack for me to realize that maybe I should come back here and help him out with the family business. Until then I was too busy trying to earn his approval. When I said you were resourceful, it was a compliment. Most people I've met see a problem and try to buy their way out of it. There's a part of me that thinks the only reason Genevieve asked for my help is because she thought my money could solve her problem. And in a way, it did. And Genevieve's a friend, so I'm glad I could help."

I leaned forward and gave Vaughn a soft, quick kiss. The impulse was spontaneous, as was the surprise on his face.

"Maybe we are more alike than I thought," I said. I climbed into the car and Vaughn shut the door behind me. I reached across the driver's seat and unlocked his door. He started the engine and pulled out of the lot, onto San Ladrón Avenue, and then right on Bonita.

"Would you like to do this again sometime?" he asked.

"Which part? The movie? Or the trespassing on private property?"

"Either. Both. I know a couple of nice, out-of-the-way buildings we can squat in—"

"Giovanni's van."

"You want to squat in somebody's van?"

"There." I leaned forward and pointed to the white van parked in front of the fabric store. "What's it doing here? Now?"

Vaughn pulled the Volkswagen over and I was out before the car came to a complete stop. I approached the van and looked in the window. The driver's-side seat was reclined, and a figure shifted. It was Giovanni. I knocked on the window several times. He shifted again, opened his eyes, and jumped when he saw me. He pulled the seat up and opened the door.

"Do you have any idea how long I've been sitting here waiting for you?" he asked. His forehead was bruised, and his lip was cut.

I came around the side of the van as he stepped out onto the gravel. His legs gave way beneath him and he fell to the ground.

Fifteen

"Vaughn," I called over my shoulder. "Help me get him inside the store."

I rooted through my handbag for my keys. Vaughn pulled Giovanni to his feet. I unlocked the gate, heaved it open, and unlocked the front door. I returned to where Vaughn stayed with Giovanni. I got on one side of him; Vaughn on the other. With Giovanni's arms draped over each of our shoulders like a scene from *Weekend at Bernie's*, we guided him inside.

"Can you make it up the stairs?" I asked Giovanni. A trickle of blood had dried on his cheek next to the cut.

"If that's where you keep the liquor, then yes, I can make it upstairs."

As we went up, Giovanni in the front with Vaughn and me behind him, I knew there was a possibility that we'd find Genevieve when we got there. I didn't know how I would explain it if we did, but I sensed whatever had happened to my former boss related back to Phil Girard's murder.

I guided Giovanni to the sofa. "Vaughn, there's a bottle of brandy on the kitchen counter. Can you pour him a glass?" Vaughn nodded and went to the kitchen.

"Is it the good stuff? Bring the whole bottle," Giovanni said.

I glared at him. "Are you really hurt or are you faking this?"

He sat up. "Would you like me to describe the thugs who jumped me over your fabric?"

"You were jumped over my fabric?" A chill swept over me like an X-ray machine at airport security. There were only three people who knew that my real order of fabric was still in Los Angeles. Two of them were in this room. The only good thing I could think of was that there was a new angle to Phil's murder.

"Yes. Which means you owe me. Which means I want your best brandy."

I found a terry cloth rag in the hall closet and ran it under the cold water tap in the bathroom. When I returned to the living room, I handed it to Giovanni. "We should call the police," I said.

Giovanni waved a hand back and forth in front of me. "I have enough problems of the not-legal variety. I don't need to be involved with the police over this little favor." He laid the wet rag across his forehead, tipped his head back, and closed his eyes. A few seconds later he opened one. "Is that your new guy? Not bad. He's rich, right? Bet that's driving the last guy crazy."

"Giovanni, here's the thing. I think it's best that you don't let Vaughn know what you told me about the fabric."

"Ah, the ever-popular building-a-relationship-on-secrets approach. Yes, I believe I've tried that once or twice. What's it worth to you?"

"We already made a deal! You're getting twenty rolls of boning and instructions on how to use it."

"That was before I was beat up. Now I want a children's collection inspired by trees. Twenty sketches."

"Have you lost your mind?"

"My niece is in a play. My sister wants costumes for the whole class, and I've decided to use it as an opportunity to enter the children's market."

Vaughn rounded the corner with a glass of brandy. He handed it to Giovanni, who took a long pull on the amber liquid. He closed his eyes and swirled the drink around in his mouth, then swallowed.

"I'll be right back," I said to Giovanni. I reached out for Vaughn's arm and gently pulled him into the hallway. "That man used to be my boss. I asked him to do a favor for me, which he did, but things are complicated now, so I think we're going to be renegotiating."

Vaughn's face looked serious. "What kind of renegotiating?" he asked. He looked over my shoulder into the living room.

I twisted around and looked at Giovanni. His head was tipped back, resting against the top of the sofa. His mouth was open. Three buttons had been undone down the front of his shirt and the empty brandy glass rested on the top of his stomach.

"Not *that* kind of negotiating," I said quickly. "Come with me. I'll walk you to the door."

I led the way down the stairs. I turned the knob of the front door and cracked it. "In spite of what happened with my boss, I had a nice time tonight."

Vaughn studied me. I felt nervous, having already kissed him in the parking lot outside Tea Totalers. In the span of fifteen minutes, we were worlds apart again.

"Good night, Poly," he said and let himself out.

"Good night, Vaughn," I said to the door as I locked it behind him. I went back up the stairs and found Giovanni asleep on the sofa, his ample stomach rising and falling in time with the buzz of his breathing. I tiptoed through the remaining rooms of the apartment like a bear looking for Goldilocks. She wasn't there.

The next morning I showered early and dressed in a long, thin black sweater over a black tank top and black leggings. I brewed a pot of coffee and put two slices of whole wheat bread in the toaster. Giovanni hadn't stirred despite the increasing noise level. Pins and Needles, who had been asleep on the bed when I woke up, swarmed around my ankles and meowed for food. I gave them fresh water and topped off their Cat Chow, then carried a mug of coffee into the living room.

"Rise and shine, sleepyhead," I announced. I set the mug onto the coffee table with a clunk and pulled the cord on the curtains so the room was flooded with natural light. "Time to wake up."

"What are you doing?" Giovanni said. He put his hands over his eyes and rolled into the back of the sofa.

"You're parked in a no-parking zone. You better move your car or you're going to get a ticket."

He blinked his eyes a few times and then closed them again. "Five more minutes."

I almost couldn't believe I'd worked for this man for seven whole years. "There's a mug of coffee on the table. You have thirty seconds to tell me what happened."

"You never talked like this when you worked for me."

"Actually, I did, but you threatened to dock my pay, so I stopped. I don't work for you anymore. So drink your coffee and start talking."

Giovanni sat up and rubbed his face a couple of times. He yawned, made a howling sound as he did so, and then stretched his arms in either direction.

"You got any donuts?"

"I'll get you donuts after you tell me what happened."

He held his hands up in front of him as if I'd won some kind of battle. "Okay, okay. Donuts later." He swallowed some coffee. "After you called me about your velvet, I called Mack and made arrangements for him to hold it until five."

"I told you noon."

"Turns out it wasn't a firm noon. I can't leave the workroom unattended now that you left. Those women lose all sense of productivity when I'm not there to crack the whip."

I shook my head at Giovanni's lack of sensitivity. He employed some of the best sewers in Los Angeles, all underpaid if you asked me. The newer ones were afraid to talk back for fear of losing their jobs. Those who had been in the workroom for longer, some for decades, knew what they could get away with. Even though it hadn't been part of my job requirements, I'd often acted as a representative for them, fighting on their behalf when his demands grew too unrealistic. The week I'd gotten Juanita Ramirez a raise so her husband didn't have to take a second job was one of the best I'd had. I could still taste the homemade tamales she'd brought me to say thank you.

"One of these days they're all going to leave you and find someone better to work for," I said.

"You always did fancy yourself to be their own little Norma Rae, didn't you? It's touching."

I rolled my eyes. "Back to my velvet. You made arrangements with Mack to pick it up at five. What happened?"

"He helped me carry it outside when I got there. I loaded it into the van. He locked up and left before I was done. Some guy came over and asked if I was making the delivery. I said yes."

"And?" I was getting impatient. Giovanni was drawing this out longer than necessary and I regretted not filling him with refined sugar first.

"He said 'make sure we get our money this time.' I told him the velvet was already paid for."

"That's right."

"Then he says, 'funny guy,' and punches me. I landed on the ground and hit my head." He touched the bruise on his forehead. It had already turned from dark red to a yellowish green with purple at the center. "Stupid Italian. He said the last guy tried to be funny, too, but that didn't work out so well for him."

"How do you know he was Italian?"

"He sounded like half my family."

"Giovanni, you reported the attack, right?"

"Are you kidding? The guy left and I drove here. If word gets out that I called the cops over a fabric delivery, I'm done. What's the big deal? I'm here, your velvet's here. No harm, no foul."

"Yes, harm! Yes, foul! This is not normal. Picking up fabric shouldn't be dangerous."

"You've watched me talk to these guys a hundred times. You know they're always looking for an angle. You're a pretty, young girl who ordered twelve bolts of custom fabric. Somebody got wind of your situation and thinks they can make a little money off you."

"Would you do something like this?"

"No, but I got morals."

Sure, Giovanni was the poster child for morals—not. But he had come through for me, and in light of the confrontation at Mack's, he could have walked away and washed his hands of my delivery problem.

"Listen to me. You might not have told the police in Los Angeles about what happened, but you have to talk to the sheriff here."

"When did you get so sensitive? Somebody tried to put a scare into you. You're lucky you had me on your side. Although this cut better not leave a scar—"

"Giovanni!" I clapped twice in front of his face to get his attention. "This isn't someone putting a scare into me. The last man who tried to pick up the fabric was murdered. There's a homicide investigation going on. The sheriff thinks the wife did it, but I don't. You have to tell him what happened so he knows I'm not making this up."

"Whoa!" He put his hands up in front of him. "Are you talking about that body they found in a van up here? That guy was your driver? I saw that on the news. They didn't say anything about any velvet."

"They're set on the wife as the murderer and I don't think they're spending a lot of time on the fabric angle except for the fact that it was in the van at the time."

"Fine. I'll talk to your sheriff. Can you do something about the donut situation first?"

I pulled on a pair of Reeboks and slung my messenger bag across my chest. "I have two cats. Leave them alone and they'll probably leave you alone. There's more coffee in the kitchen. Stay put and I'll be right back."

I hustled to Lopez Donuts. Unlike yesterday, the line was under control, but the interior of the shop was packed. Scents of cinnamon and spices mingled with the sugary donut smell into a multilayered olfactory experience. I closed my eyes and inhaled deeply. Someone bumped into me. I opened my eyes and saw Maria carrying a tray of tea and croissants to a table in the corner.

"Poly, wait there. You're not going to believe what happened," she said.

I stepped out of the way, or as out of the way as I could get, and scanned the rest of the tables while she emptied her tray at the table. Behind the counter were two of her sisters. I didn't see Big Joe or either of the boys.

When Maria returned, she grabbed my sleeve and pulled me with her. She flipped the hinged counter up and I followed her through the saloon-style doors that led to the kitchen. "Keep giving out samples," she said to the women. "I have to talk to Poly. I'll be right back."

She went to the back of the kitchen, opened the door to the outside, and waved at me to come with her.

"This is crazy!" She ran her hands over her thick curly black hair. "You would not believe it. Like little elves or something. *Ay dios mio!*"

"Slow down. What are you talking about?"

"You saw how busy it was yesterday, right? And everybody wants tea. So after we closed yesterday, Joe went out to buy tea so we were prepared."

"Looks like it worked."

"You don't even know the half of it! When he came home, he found a large box on our doorstep. It was filled with croissants and packets of tea. Like elves, I say."

I thought back to the empty shelves at Tea Totalers. Already I had a pretty good idea where the croissants and tea had come from, but I said nothing. "Was there anything else?"

"There was a note. It said, 'This might help.'" She shook her head and dropped her voice to a whisper. "I mean, between you and me, it's obvious that it came from the tea lady, but I'm sure she has a good reason for not signing that note. We're giving out samples of her croissants and any money we make from the sale of that tea is going into a special jar for her."

"Maria, you're amazing," I said. I gave her a big hug—having learned that hugs were like handshakes in the Lopez family.

"I told Joe nobody who murdered her husband would do a thing like that. You tell that pretty widow if she needs us, we're here for her. You got it?"

"I don't know what you mean," I said. "I haven't seen Genevieve in days."

"Sure. And Dunkin' Donuts called and offered a million dollars for Big Joe's cruller recipe. You keep your secrets and I'll keep mine."

"You have secrets?"

She turned her head away from me but looked at me from the corner of her eye. "You won't get anything out of me. That's the promise I made."

The back door pushed open and Maria's sister Marisela looked out. "We're out of glazed. When's Joe getting back?"

"Baker's rack to the left of the oven. Four dozen cooling. I'll be right in." She turned to me. "Honestly, you'd think these people never worked a donut shop before."

"Where is Big Joe?" I asked.

"I sent him and the boys on an errand. Now, what did you come for?"

"A dozen glazed."

Her expression changed to one of fear. "I can give you six. We better hurry."

I tucked the box under my hip and walked back to Material Girl. The white van was gone. Lilly Garden was wrestling a faded tin umbrella stand outside the doors of Flowers in the Attic. The narrow container held several faded floral umbrellas. At least two of them showed exposed metal frames and threadbare fabric. There was no call for rain in the forecast, so it was just as well.

"Hi, Lilly," I said. "Did you see a white van here?"

"Was that man a friend of yours?" She stood up straight and her hand toyed with the pearl buttons on her flowered maxi dress. "I didn't know what to make of him when he came out. Are you planning to have lots of men up to your apartment?"

I rolled my eyes. "He's my old boss. He made a delivery for me from Los Angeles and it was late, so he crashed on my sofa." Why was I explaining this to her? "Did you see where he went?"

"Poly, I'm not the type to sit around watching where people go and what they do." She bent down and adjusted the placement of the tin umbrella stand a few inches to the left. "By the way, did I see Genevieve Girard behind your shop last night?"

"I don't know what you saw last night. I was out on a date."

"So many men," she said, shaking her head. She turned around and went back into her shop.

A parking enforcement cart was parked at the curb. A woman in a white uniform stood behind the silver Porsche that had been there last night. "Did I hear you say you were looking for the man who drove a white van?"

"Yes. Did you see him?"

"About five minutes ago. He ran out of there." She pointed the pen to the door of Material Girl. "He threw a twenty at me and took off around the back."

"He might have a parking ticket situation in LA."

"Lucky I didn't run his plates. Sounds like it would have been worth more than twenty dollars."

I balanced the donut box on one hand and tried the knob of the store with the other. It was locked. I unlocked the gate and the door, juggled the donuts against one hip, and managed to turn the knob. Just as the door swung open, Charlie showed up.

"Nice juggling act. You need a hand?"

"Your timing is impeccable."

I handed her the pink bakery store box and went inside. "There are only six donuts in there and my old boss will probably take four. So if you're hoping for a donut, you'd better act quickly."

"Your old boss? The Italian guy who drove the van?"

"Yes."

"Real charmer. He offered to take me out for drinks if I could recommend a cheap happy hour."

"Classic Giovanni. Did you see where he went?"

"He said you were taking too long." She waved her hand. "He dumped your velvet out back and took off."

Sixteen

"You're serious?" I looked up and down the street. "How could he leave? He was going to talk to Clark. He knew I was getting him donuts."

"Yeah, I hear they don't have donuts in Los Angeles."

I headed to the back of the store, slowing only to take the donuts from Charlie and set them on the cash wrap. Charlie stayed behind and opened the box while I unlocked the back door. Twelve rolls of velvet, each bagged in heavy plastic and secured along one end with a plastic zip tie, were propped up against the exterior wall of the fabric store. I wrapped my arms around one and stepped backward, and then pushed it back toward the wall, where it knocked into two other rolls, crashing them to the ground like dominoes.

"Yo, Polyester, keep your pants on. Did you ever think of asking for help?"

"I thought I could handle it. When you get enough sugar coursing through your veins, will you help me with these?"

"Sure. But you're the fabric expert. Shouldn't you know how much a roll of velvet weighs?"

"It was heavier than I expected," I said. "Make sure your hands are clean first."

"Are you afraid I'm going to dirty up the plastic?"

She finished her second donut and wiped her hands on her jeans. I found a dull pair of scissors I'd been meaning to have sharpened and sliced through the plastic that covered the forest-green velvet. I fed my hand through a narrow opening and ran my fingertips over the nap. It was as soft as I'd anticipated. I reached a few inches in from the selvage edge and tugged gently on the material, testing the gauge. It had a little spring to it. I pulled my hand out of the opening and taped the plastic back together. A shot of excitement pulsed through me. This was my very first order of custom fabric. Rich, elegant, unusual. But the ten percent polyester gave it my personal stamp.

She studied me. "This is like Christmas for you, isn't it?"

"It's amazing, you know? This fabric represents the beginning of what I'm going to do here. And it represents what my aunt and uncle passed along to me. It's so much more than material. I can't wait to open for business and let people see how fabric can change their lives. Help me with the rest, will you?"

She followed me out back. I tipped the navy blue bolt toward me and took careful steps backward, until it was at a thirty-degree angle with the floor. Charlie wrapped her arms around the other end, dropped into a partial squat, and stood up. I walked backward into the store and tripped over the welcome mat. The end of the roll fell from my hands. Charlie anticipated my klutzy move and tried to overcompensate by lifting her end up high. She tripped over the same carpet and the roll dropped to the floor. She bent down, grabbed her ankle, and hopped around for a couple of seconds.

"Are you okay?" I asked.

"I'll live."

"Sit down. I'll get the rest myself."

"Sure, right after you down a can of spinach."

"Don't underestimate me. I've been carrying rolls of fabric practically my whole life." I headed outside and squatted in front of the burgundy, wrapped my arms around it like I was hugging a tree, and stood. I staggered backward for a few steps until I was able to hoist it onto my shoulder. I carried it inside and bent forward, letting the plastic slide over my shoulder onto the ground.

Charlie seemed to have no compunctions over sitting on the wrap stand playing with Pins and Needles while I made multiple trips outside and in. After seven trips I was out of breath and needed a break. I washed my hands, grabbed a donut, and sat on the concrete floor, my feet thrust out in front of me.

"I would have helped, but you seemed like you had it under control," she said.

"Sure, no problem. I could tell you didn't want to get your hands dirty."

She held her hand in front of her with her fingers splayed and looked at her fingernails, blackened around the cuticles from working on cars. "You're right. I might be due for a manicure." She laughed. "WD-40 works wonders for the skin, though. You should try it. I bet my hands are softer than any of those prima donnas who fill the salons around here."

"You have a real thing against the salon crowd, don't you?" I asked between bites.

"I just think it's silly that we have more salons than restaurants. What's the point? There are better ways to spend money."

"Like what?"

"Like oil changes and fabric." She ruffled Pins's fur from his neck to his nose, leaving it standing up in little spikes. "Have you seen Frenchy recently?"

I considered whether or not I should tell Charlie that I'd spoken to Genevieve last night and decided I should. "Yes. She's okay—she just had a few things she had to take care of."

"She could have told me."

"She said she saw you with Sheriff Clark at The Broadside. She got spooked."

Charlie looked surprised. "She knows about that?"

"She didn't know what it meant. I figure there's a perfectly good explanation. There is, isn't there?" I asked.

"I told you two to let me take care of Clark. I was taking care of Clark. She thought I was throwing her under the bus?"

"I don't know what she thinks. What I do know is that she's afraid to trust anybody right now, not just you."

I headed back outside for the next roll of velvet. Charlie hopped down from the wrap stand and joined me, and together, we carried the remaining rolls inside. When we finished, Giovanni's van pulled into the lot.

"I thought you went back to Los Angeles," I said.

He parked his van at an angle a few feet from the Dumpster. He rolled up the window and hopped out. "I changed my mind. I don't want to pass up the opportunity to check out this fabric store of yours." He aimed his remote at the van and then pocketed his keys. "The next time you need a favor, I'd like to know what to ask for in return."

I turned to Charlie and dropped my voice. "This is a limited window of opportunity. I don't care how you do it, but get Sheriff Clark here fast. Giovanni won't make a statement, so we have to use the element of surprise."

"I'm on it." Charlie wiggled her fingers at Giovanni and hiked out of the lot.

"Where's she going?" he asked. He leaned over backward and watched her walk away.

"She'll be back. Promise. She said something about thinking you were cute." I glanced at Giovanni's face and was vaguely surprised I didn't choke on my words.

"You could learn a thing or two from a woman like her," he said. "I bet she doesn't take orders from anybody."

I fought the urge to comment. What was the point? The

more important issue was keeping him occupied until Clark arrived.

"Come on inside."

Giovanni followed me inside. I opened the fuse box and turned on all of the lights, illuminating the entire interior of the store. Until I was open for business, I tried to use only the lights I needed in order to conserve electricity and keep the bills at a minimum. Today, I needed the distraction of my full inventory to keep my old boss from getting antsy and leaving before Sheriff Clark arrived.

Giovanni headed straight for the donuts and picked up one with each hand, the heels on his sea-foam-green oxfords clapping against the concrete floor. He owned the shoes in four colors: lavender, light blue, orange, and sea foam. They'd been a gift from the men's store at the end of our block, in exchange for the loan of two of our seamstresses. It had been classic Giovanni to not think twice about taking the garish pimp shoes as a thank-you.

He stopped in front of the silk charmeuse. When I'd started cleaning and organizing the store, I'd come across thirty-five bolts in various colors. They'd been on a shelf, stacked horizontally. The only thing you could see were the ends of the round cardboard tubes that the fabric was wound around. Because I was light on inventory and interested in maximum visual impact, I'd moved them to a wall of shallow bins and set them up like soldiers, vertically, mixing the shades. Now the colors popped against each other: acid green, poppy red, cornflower blue, lemon yellow, tangerine. Even the more subtle colors had their own muted intensity: olive green, navy blue, rich sienna, and maize. I could picture a one-shoulder Grecian goddess dress cut from one of these fabrics. It would be a simple enough pattern: drape the fabric from front to back over one shoulder, gathering it with a vintage brooch. Side seams to finish it off, and belt at the waist. The expense of the dress would be in the fabric, not in the workmanship. Giovanni would never go for it.

"I know what you're thinking," he said with his back to me. "You and the girls think I can't appreciate fine fabrics. You're wrong." He ran an open palm over the row of colors, stopping by the acid green, and felt the weight of the fabric between his thumb and forefingers. "How much are you charging for this?"

"Fifteen dollars a yard."

He dropped the corner of the fabric. "Call me when you mark it down ninety percent."

A car pulled up in front of the store. Sheriff Clark got out. It was ten minutes past the restricted parking hours, so I had no reason to ask him to park in the back other than my concerns that the businesses on either side of me were going to talk about the regular police presence in front of my store. I greeted him before he reached the door.

"Sheriff," I said.

"Ms. Monroe," he replied. "Charlie said you had urgent information."

"You know, I'm not going to report you to your superiors if you call me Poly." I stared at him and he crossed his arms. "Fine. I asked my old boss to go pick up my fabric from the warehouse in Los Angeles. He went last night and he was jumped in the parking lot."

"Is he here? Can I talk to him?"

From out back, I heard the sound of an engine starting. Curses! I raced across the interior and looked into the parking lot. His van was gone. I thought about Giovanni being knocked out when he picked up the fabric and what his attacker had said.

"Sheriff, how about we go sit down and talk this over?" I grabbed the box with the one remaining donut and headed upstairs. Sheriff Clark followed me. "You want some coffee? A donut?" I asked.

"He wants both," Charlie said, appearing behind Clark. "I'll get the coffee. Cream, two sugars, right?"

"Right."

She winked at him, he turned red, and she went into the kitchen. I set the donut box in the center of the coffee table.

"Maria and Joe got the situation under control today?" he asked, nodding at it. "Yesterday it seemed like the laws of supply and demand were a little out of whack."

"They're fine today. They're handing out samples of croissants to keep the patrons happy."

"Croissants?" He perked up. "Doesn't sound much like Maria to give away food."

"She's a smart businesswoman. She knows people will come back if they're treated well."

"Takes a different setup to make croissants than it does to make donuts."

"I don't think she's planning to branch out. Your donut supply is probably still safe. There's one left. Do you want it?" I asked.

"No, I think I'll head that way when I'm done here."

"Suit yourself." I told Sheriff Clark about the attack on Giovanni at the warehouse in Los Angeles. "He said they told him to make sure they got their money this time. He told them the fabric had already been paid for and the guy hit him."

"Probably wasn't smart for him to get involved."

"Giovanni's been in the garment business forever. He probably really thought someone was trying to get me to pay twice. When it comes to saving money and not getting swindled, it's second nature to him."

"Did he report the attack when it happened?" he asked.

"No."

Clark took off his hat and ran his hand over his hair. "Why not?"

"I get the feeling it's not the first time Giovanni's been

punched, and I'd be willing to bet it's not going to be the last." I'd had my own share of impulses to pop him one when I worked for him.

"So he picked up the fabric, got punched, and still drove the fabric here? Must have been some way you made it worth his while, considering what you just said about him. What'd you pay him?"

"He's still trying to replace me as senior concept designer for his store. I offered him some supplies and agreed to do a little freelance work for him in the meantime." I thought about his request for children's outfits inspired by trees.

Clark stared at me for a couple of seconds, but I didn't offer more information. Charlie rounded the corner and bumped Clark with her hip. He looked startled. She raised her eyebrows and handed him the mug.

"I'm going to want to talk to this Giovanni. Can you give me his contact information?"

"Sure." I went to the kitchen and found an index card and a Bic pen in the junk drawer. I scribbled the phone number for To The Nines on the card and carried it back to the living room.

"You'll have a better chance getting him at the shop than if you call his cell phone or home phone. Even better, ask for Eiko. She's the Korean lady who works there. She speaks the best English. Tell her you're my friend." I paused, thinking about the improbability of me and Clark actually being friends. "Tell her you need to talk to Giovanni. She'll get him on the phone without making him suspicious."

Clark tucked the index card into the pocket of his suit jacket. "Nothing you told me here changes the fact that Mrs. Girard is my number one person of interest."

"I know you think you have some kind of motive worked out for Genevieve killing her husband, but what possible reason could she have for wanting to take out my old boss?"

"Not sure. That's why I need to talk to him."

"There's no connection through Genevieve. It's something else."

"Money's tight at her store. Maybe she figured out a way to boost her bottom line. Who knows what she's moving along with tea."

"You already know Phil wasn't poisoned with her tea."

"He wasn't. He was suffocated."

"With the fabric?" I leaned forward. "Did you find the death mask?"

"No, not with your fabric. Phil Girard was suffocated with a fistful of croissants."

Seventeen

"How long have you known this?" I asked.

"I can't see how that's any of your business."

"The crumbs on the floor by Phil's hand? They were croissant crumbs? You knew all along that the tea had nothing to
do with his murder."

"Shocking, I know, that I wouldn't share important information regarding a murder investigation with you," he said.
He pressed a button on his phone and turned his back to me.
I heard him identify himself and request help. He recited my
address and added "the old fabric store on Bonita." I felt heat
crawl up the back of my neck. My fists balled up and released
twice.

"Pretty soon it's going to be the *new* fabric store on Bonita,"
I said under my breath.

I felt Charlie's hand on my upper arm. "If you want to keep
helping Frenchy, you two are going to have to learn to play

nice in the sandbox," she whispered. "Come on, Sheriff. I'll walk you downstairs." She looked at me. "Poly needs to change the litter." She led Clark downstairs. I shut the door behind them and put on the chain lock, even though I expected Charlie to come back.

Charlie hadn't been kidding about the litter box. I scooped it clean, bagged the refuse, and knotted it shut. When I unlocked the door and went downstairs, I found Charlie and Clark standing by the wrap stand. He said something to her, turned to look at me, and left out the back.

"You're not doing Frenchy any favors by getting him angry," she said.

"Since when are you the poster child for peace and togetherness?"

"You've had a positive influence on me. Now listen. Frenchy doesn't trust me, but she trusts you. You have to tell her what's going on. Whoever killed her husband wants it to look like she did it."

"I know that. I also know she's been her own worst enemy when it comes to the evidence."

We walked to the area of the store set up with rows of tables and chairs for a future sewing class. Charlie dropped into a chair in the back row, and I leaned against the cutting table behind her. I told Charlie about Genevieve going to Los Angeles to surprise her husband, discovering him in anticipation of someone else, and the paper trail she'd left that put her at the scene of the crime.

"Frenchy's in some deep *merde*," Charlie said.

"The sheriff has a laser-sharp focus on Genevieve right now. He's not even considering any of the other people who could have done it. I could do a lot better proving her innocence if he'd tell me about his evidence up front."

"How's the view up there in Fantasyland?"

"I'm missing something; I know it."

She leaned back in the chair and tucked her hands behind her head. "Who else do you like for the murder?"

"So far, I see a couple people who are acting suspicious."

"Walk me through your theories."

I moved into the chair next to Charlie and leaned forward, elbows on my knees. "Phil went to Los Angeles to pick up produce for Genevieve and velvet for me. There's no proof of either of those jobs. He asked me to pay him in cash."

"That's not all that suspicious. He wanted to make a little money under the table. That's just good business. "

"That's what Rick said. Something about a cash deal under the table being the type you don't turn down. Do you do jobs like that?"

She held up her hands in front of her. "My tax advisor recommended I don't answer questions like that. Better for all parties involved."

"Okay, back to Phil. He goes to Los Angeles a day early. Genevieve wants to surprise him but she finds him all primed and ready for a romantic interlude, which is weird because the woman he's having an affair with was in San Ladrón."

"We know this?"

"We know this. Apparently Babs kept the staff at the Villamere late because she was afraid to leave. One of the ushers drove her home. The next morning she took a taxi to the Villamere to get her car but the manager wouldn't let her drive because she was still drunk. She slept in her dressing room until she was sober."

"What was she afraid of?"

"According to the usher, she was having an affair with a married man and she was afraid of the wife."

"That's not good. What else do we know?"

"Genevieve and Phil had a fight on Sunday afternoon. Loud enough for several witnesses to catch on—including the man who's trying to buy out her tea recipe—and she stormed out. At that point, everything we know is hearsay. That Monday morning, Phil decided not to come home on time, then he called another driver and asked him to make the delivery. Except—"

"You have that 'aha' look in your eyes."

"If Rick drove Phil's van back here, how did he get there? He either left his car in Los Angeles, which is crazy because there's nowhere to park, or he had a partner. He said the truck was packed and locked. He said Phil told him he was staying in LA. And remember when I first tried to track him down? His trucking company was completely fake. Clark should be on him like white on rice. Why isn't he? There was a dead man in the back of the truck he drove. He's the one who says Phil hired him to pick up the fabric and Genevieve's shopping list."

"Genevieve's shopping list," Charlie repeated. She sat up and leaned forward. "What exactly was on that shopping list? Have you looked at it?"

"No, but she said she didn't need much. And the first day I went to Tea Totalers, Kim said there were crates of produce stacked up outside when she got there. She put the stuff away, but it was all in the wrong place. And she's the one who threw out the tea, too. She said she thought it had gone bad. Don't you think that's suspicious?"

"Maybe she was trying to be helpful."

"I don't think so. She showed up when Genevieve wasn't there. She doesn't seem to know a thing about working in a tea shop. What if someone planted her there? Like the Italian Scallion. Maybe he has her working on the inside to steal Genevieve's recipe?"

"Tell me more about him."

"His name is Topo di Sali. He showed up at Tea Totalers the morning I started working on the fabric renovation. He wants to buy Genevieve's proprietary tea recipe and distribute it to grocery stores up and down the coast. So far she's turned him down, but I think she's starting to consider his offer."

"You said he was at the tea shop when Genevieve and Phil fought?"

"That's what she said. He showed up on Tuesday, too. I get the feeling he's persistent."

"'*Italian* Scallion?' Why's he so hot for Frenchy's stuff?"

"I asked that, too. He said he was branching out. Something about not limiting his options. He knows about her money problems. I don't know how. And his take is half of the profits. He said Genevieve doesn't even have to make the tea. He'll package something and slap her logo on it."

"We can't let Frenchy agree to something like that. Have you seen him since Tuesday?"

"He said he was heading to San Francisco. Seems like an awfully suspicious time to skip town."

"Yes and no. Maybe you're right about that Kim girl working for him. She could be reporting in to him in code, you know, pretending to give di Sali Tomato the weather report."

"She could be. She was at Tea Totalers on Monday. When I told her Genevieve wasn't going to be opening the shop and suggested she find another job, she was very adamant that people were expecting her to be working at that particular restaurant. And she dropped something when she left. It was a notice from her parole officer."

"You read it?"

"I didn't mean to. It fell open and I couldn't help myself. I put it in the office so she could get it the next day."

"Is it still there?"

"No. She took it."

"That's too bad." Charlie twisted a thick silver ring around her left index finger. "Parole officer, you said. Not probation officer?"

"That's right. Why?"

"I don't know how much you know about the law, but she wouldn't have a parole officer unless she was on parole."

"Gee, thanks for thinking I couldn't figure that out on my own," I said.

"That's not what I'm saying. If she wasn't charged with anything, she'd have a probation officer. If it was a *parole* officer, then she's already been convicted of something. Too bad you didn't keep the piece of paper. If we knew who her parole officer was, we might be able to find out what she did."

I chewed my lower lip and stared at the toe of my boot. "I may have taken a picture of the document." Slowly, I brought my eyes up to meet Charlie's. She was staring at me with openmouthed surprise. "What? Genevieve's innocent and somebody has to help her."

"Fo shizzle," she said.

I pulled my phone out of my back pocket and flipped through my photos until I reached the one with the document. I handed it to Charlie, who used her fingertips to manipulate the screen of the phone until the image was large enough to read.

"It doesn't say much," she said. "There's an appointment listed and a courthouse. The name of the officer is handwritten and it's hard to read. Is that Medoza? Menendez? Is that even an *M*? Or is it an *N*?" She moved the image around on the phone with her fingertips some more, and then handed the phone back to me.

"I don't know. I wish it said what she did."

"They keep that information in her file. Do you know how old she is? Is she a minor or an adult?"

"She talked about college, so I'm pretty sure she's an adult. Another weird thing is that the first day I was there, she acted like she'd never met Genevieve. She said she answered an ad on Craigslist."

"Sounds suspicious. I'd keep an eye on her."

"I plan to, at least until I can find out more. What could she mean when she says people are expecting her to be working at Tea Totalers? If she's so interested in restaurant experience, she's not going to get it by helping with a renovation of the interior."

"What kind of experience does she want?"

"She said she wants to open her own restaurant someday."

"Well, Frenchy's place fits the bill, but she's not the only game in town," Charlie said. "There's The Earl of Sandwich, Antonio's Ristorante, The Broadside Tavern—"

"And there's Lopez Donuts," I said slowly. "I'll talk to Big Joe. If she wants experience, she'll get it there. But if what she really wants is to keep an eye on Genevieve's shop, she won't like it when I tell her I made other arrangements for her."

"What makes you think the Lopez's are going to make room for this Kim character in their operation? Between Maria's four sisters, Big Joe, and the two boys, I think they have plenty of help."

"Sure, but Maria and her sisters don't normally work at the donut shop. They run Neato Cleaning Service. This would help her out with an extra set of hands, and there's no risk. As soon as things are cleared up at Tea Totalers, Genevieve's going to want Kim back. If Kim's innocent, then she'll go with Gen."

"And if she's guilty, she can work in the prison cafeteria."

"Exactly. Now it's up to me to convince Maria."

"Don't you mean, convince Big Joe?"

I rolled my eyes at Charlie. "I'll start with Big Joe, but we both know who wears the pants in that family."

Charlie grinned. "Are you heading that way now? Trying to get there ahead of Clark?"

"No, I think it's better to let Clark do his job. Maria's going to tell him whatever she sees fit." I checked the time on my cell phone. "I didn't realize how late it is. Kim's probably already at Tea Totalers. Can you lock the place up?"

"Sure."

I was halfway to the back door when Charlie called out behind me. "Yo—Polyester! If you run into Frenchy, tell her I have more paperwork for her to file."

The familiar "I know something you don't" expression that usually defined Charlie's features was gone, and in its place was a look of concern and caring. I sensed she was hurt that Genevieve hadn't trusted her, but I knew Genevieve had done what she thought she had to do.

"If I see her, I'll give her the message." I smiled and left.

Kim wasn't at Tea Totalers when I arrived, but Vaughn was. He didn't see me at first. His back was turned to me, and he was standing over a table saw, cutting rectangles of wood. He wore a navy blue chamois shirt, khaki trousers, and white Stan Smiths. His hands were protected with work gloves, his face with clear plastic safety glasses like Kim had worn days before.

Not wanting to surprise him while he was operating a fairly sizeable power tool, I waited until he moved the saw to the upright position and turned it off before making my presence known.

"Good morning," I called out.

He turned around and lifted the glasses from his head. "'Good afternoon' is more like it. I wasn't sure if I'd be seeing you today." He set the glasses on the table and dusted a film of wood pulp from the front of his shirt. "Did you work everything out with your boss?" he asked.

I was confused for a second, until I remembered how much had happened since Vaughn had helped me get Giovanni up the stairs. He didn't know details about the attack, or that Clark knew that Phil had been suffocated with croissants, or that Genevieve had been at my place but wasn't anymore.

"Things got complicated," I said. "I honestly don't know if it's all going to work out."

"That's too bad. He seemed like a good guy." We looked at each other for a few seconds, then at the same time we both said, "No, he didn't," and laughed.

"What are you working on?" I asked, hoping he wouldn't

think too harshly of me for changing the subject in such a blatant manner.

"Serving trays," he said. He laid a rectangle of wood on the right-hand side of the saw and set smaller blocks of wood along the short and long edges of the rectangle. The shorter pieces of wood had oval-shaped openings cut into them already—handles for easy carrying. "I thought you could use pieces of fabric from the interior to line these so they'd coordinate with everything else."

"I could decoupage the fabric to the wood. That way the fabric won't stain and they can be cleaned with soap and water."

"Is that hard?"

"Not hard. Time-consuming. I'll need to get supplies. How many are you making?"

"How many do you think she'll need?"

"A dozen is a safe number. If there are more, they can be used to hold croi"—I caught myself from using the word *croissant*—"muffins and pastries."

"I have enough wood for two dozen, easy. If you make me a list, I'll get your supplies when I'm done with the preliminary cuts."

"A list . . . sure." I remembered Genevieve mentioning her shopping list. Maybe if I looked at it, if I checked her records and could see where she got her own supplies, I could get a lead on where Phil might have gone in Los Angeles. "I'll be inside," I said.

I went in the back door and beelined for the computer. It was in sleep mode. I jiggled the mouse impatiently until I realized the monitor had been turned off. When the whole system was awake and running, I opened Word and scanned the list of recent documents. The third one listed was titled "Shopping list." The date the document was saved corresponded with Sunday, the day Phil had left for Los Angeles.

I checked over my shoulder to see if Vaughn had followed

me inside. He hadn't. He was bent over the table saw, cutting another length of wood. I turned back to the computer and scanned the items on the screen. It was a short list, mainly composed of items I assumed couldn't be found locally or ordered online: "*fleur de sel*, *herbes de Provence*, leeks, shallots, lentils." And at the end of the list, one item had been added: "Croissants (6 doz)." Following it, almost as an afterthought, was an asterisk and the words "Highly confidential. Tell anybody about this and I'll kill you!"

Eighteen

My first instinct was to delete the entire last line. That, I knew, would change the date saved on the computer, and I knew if Clark was smart enough to come check the computer, he'd be smart enough to check the dates and times saved on any relevant files. Simply by searching her hard drive for the word *croissant* he'd find this. The fact that it had last been saved the day before Phil was killed with said baked goods was not going to help Genevieve's case.

In fact, just about everything Genevieve had said, done, and probably even thought about on the day Phil was murdered had not helped her case. I couldn't imagine a crooked prosecutor planting better evidence against her than she'd created on her own. I couldn't undo the damage Genevieve had done to herself. What I could do was find someone with a better motive.

Again my thoughts turned to Kim. She had access to the computer, the kitchen, and the tea. What had she and Genevieve talked about before she was hired? I didn't know. What *did* I really know about her? Nothing. I did a cursory search on the computer for applications but found nothing.

Movement from the backyard caught my eye, and I closed out of the files I had opened on the computer, turned off the monitor, and scrambled into the front room. It was as Vaughn and I had left it last night. I picked at the tape that secured the butcher paper to the window frame until I'd freed enough to pull it off. Sunlight flooded through the glass, warming my face and arms.

I let the curtain fabric fall through my fingers. The panel was heavy, thanks to the lining. Too heavy? I set the wooden rod on the finials mounted to either side of the window and stood back to consider how it looked. During the day, Genevieve might want to have natural sunlight flowing through the shop, and these panels would prohibit that. She needed something else, something sheer to tone down the sun's intensity but still allow the rays to filter inside. What I needed was voile.

Voile was a sheer delicate fabric sometimes with a small pattern woven into it in a repeat, and I knew it would be the perfect solution for filtering the sunlight into the tea shop. I could use a double-rod curtain system to allow the sheer panels to hang directly inside the window, and hang the thicker panels on a rod outside of them so they could easily be draped open during store hours. Genevieve could control the amount of light or dark by closing one or both sets of curtains.

There were a few bolts of voile at the fabric store. I'd relegated them to the should-be-discarded-but-I-can't-quite-throw-them-away pile after noting an unfortunate musty odor that clung to them. If I remembered correctly, more than one of them even had a fleur-de-lis pattern—perfect for the French theme I was going for. And because Giovanni had always been buying heavily discounted, somewhat

damaged fabrics for To The Nines, I already knew there was
a way to get rid of the musty odor: white vinegar. Lots and
lots of white vinegar.

I set the curtain panels down and went back to the computer, only to find Vaughn sitting at the desk where I'd been
minutes before.

"I didn't see you come in," I said.

"You looked like you were pondering deep questions
involving curtains. I didn't want to interrupt you."

"I'm not sure how I feel about the fact that curtains can
distract me from someone entering the building."

"Don't let it get to you. I've been told I can be highly
stealthy when I want."

I raised my eyebrows and glanced down at his Stan
Smiths, which had given him away on more than one occasion since I'd known him.

"Everybody isn't as observant as you are," he added. He
made no attempt to hide his feet under the chair. "Did you
need the computer?"

"It's nothing that can't wait. Actually, I was thinking of
getting some lunch." I hesitated for a moment. "Would you
like to join me?" I asked.

"I can't. I already have plans." He turned back to the
computer, closed out the window he had open, and stood
up. "Will you be here when I get back?" he asked.

"Not sure. I'm going to head to Material Girl to pick up
some voile. Did you finish the cuts on the trays?"

"The cuts are done. I'll assemble them with wood glue and
reinforce with the nail gun. Then they'll be all set for you."

I shook my head. "I should decoupage the fabric before
you put them together. I have to pick up some supplies, but
I can do it after lunch and you can assemble the trays when
the decoupage is dry."

"Sure, okay." He looked confused. "Did you make me a list?"

"I'll take care of it."

"It's no big deal, Poly. Where do I need to go—hardware store? Paint store?"

I hesitated. "Dollar store." His forehead creased. "You have been to a dollar store, haven't you?"

His expression said that he was losing patience with me. I held up my hands in surrender.

"I need white school glue. Lots of it. Paintbrushes, Popsicle sticks, and a plastic bucket. And I need white vinegar, too. As much as you can get." I looked up at the ceiling and thought for a second. "I will need some acrylic sealant, and they probably don't have that at the dollar store. I can get it from Get Hammered. If it's a bother, I can get everything. I don't want to interrupt your lunch date."

A smile toyed at the corners of his mouth. "It's with my mother. She says I've been neglecting her since you came back to town. I'd invite you to join us, but I'm pretty sure she invited me to see if I'm willing to go head-to-head with Dad on the garden party problem."

"I don't get why your dad is holding everything up. The Waverly House is her life."

"The Waverly House is the most valuable landmark in San Ladrón and my dad doesn't own it. That would be reason enough for him to want to acquire it, but the fact that my mom is the one who keeps saying no to his offers just makes him want it more."

I leaned back against the desk. The corner of it dug into the backs of my thighs. I stared at the exposed wood floor in the office, studying how well the planks fit together. After an uncomfortable pause, I looked at Vaughn and caught him staring at me.

"Money doesn't make things easier, Poly. It just makes them different."

I nodded slowly. "Are you going to do it? Go head-to-head with your dad?"

"I don't know. She hasn't asked yet, so maybe I'm wrong about her intentions."

"I hope for your sake you are."

Vaughn stood up and jiggled his keys in his hand. "Back to the business at hand. White school glue, white vinegar, brushes, popsicle sticks, and a bucket. Anything else?"

"Surprise me."

He left out the back door. I watched from a distance, waiting for him to start up the car and drive away. Once his black VW Bug was out of sight, I called Charlie and arranged to meet her at the fabric store. I locked up and took off.

I took advantage of my walk to the fabric store to stop off at The Earl of Sandwich for a cup of soup and a half veggie sub. The lunch crowd had passed and I was at Material Girl ten minutes later. I finished the soup, put the sandwich in the refrigerator, and went to the pile of musty fabric to see if the voile was salvageable. Both Pins and Needles followed.

Since I'd already determined that the fabric would require a vinegar wash to remove the odor, I figured a little grunge from the exposed concrete floors wouldn't do much more damage. I laid the bolt on the floor and walked the opposite direction with the end in my hands, unrolling several yards behind me. Needles thought we were playing, and he pounced on the fabric.

"No!" I said. I scooped him up under his belly and set him on the wrap stand. I had a plan to deal with the odor. Dealing with kitty claw marks? Working for Giovanni hadn't provided a solution for that.

I bent over him and shook my finger at him. "You have to stay up here while I work, or I'm going to take you back upstairs. Can you do that?" I asked. He meowed and swatted at my finger.

"Let me guess," Charlie said from the back entrance. "Van Halen, 1984. Hammer man."

I stood up and looked at her. "What are you talking about?"

"The logo from Western Exterminator Company in Los

Angeles. Big guy with a top hat holding a mallet and lecturing a mouse? That's what you looked like. Eddie and the boys used it as the backdrop for their eighty-four tour. Geez, we have got to work on your education."

"I'm a little more Jackson Five than Van Halen," I said.

"Nobody's perfect." She looked at the fabric rolled out on the floor and waved her hand in front of her nose. "Is that smell coming from the fabric?"

"Yes, but I'm pretty sure I can get rid of it. I need to cut this into panels that are three yards long. If I'm right about what's on the bolt, I think I can get eight panels and have some left over. Then we need to get them to the washing machine and—"

Charlie put her hands up. "Whoa. I have to get back to the shop. I have two oil changes and a tune-up coming in this afternoon. Once I close up at five, I can help you with whatever you want, but I can't afford to turn business away during the day. Sorry, Polyester, but I have to take care of myself first."

"Sure, I understand. Are you heading to your shop now?"

She looked at her watch. "I can give you five minutes."

"I can get a lot done in five minutes," I said. "Hand me the rotary cutter."

"The what?"

"That thing on the table that looks like a pizza cutter. It's a cutting tool. It cuts the fabric. Guess I'm not the only one who needs an education."

Charlie handed me the wheel and it turned out I was able to make all of the measurements and cuts before she left. She watched out of the corner of her eye, as though she was fascinated at the speed with which my rotary cutter sliced through the fabric but didn't want me to know it. She left out the front door as I started folding panels of voile. When I was finished, I went upstairs and got my sandwich out of the refrigerator. I unwrapped it and took a bite. My cell rang. I set the sandwich down and chewed as quickly as I could, and then answered on the last ring.

"Are you still at your store?" Charlie asked.

"I'm just finishing up."

"You better get over here. Fast. Clark just arrested Genevieve."

I left my sandwich on the counter and ran out the front door. I jogged through traffic and stormed into Charlie's Automotive.

Clark and Genevieve stood next to each other. Genevieve's blond hair was twisted up in a style that would have looked pretty on her under other circumstances. Her face was ashen, and wet streaks down her cheeks told of tears recently shed.

"What is going on here?" I asked.

"Ms. Monroe, you'd do best to stay out of this. You, too, Charlie."

"Does this have something to do with the croissants at the donut shop?" I asked. "Because I'm sure there's a perfectly rational explanation for them."

"No, Ms. Monroe, this doesn't have anything to do with croissants." Clark glared at me while Genevieve dabbed her nose with a red bandana. "It has to do with the life insurance policy we found that makes Mrs. Girard the sole beneficiary of her husband's estate."

Nineteen

"Where did you find an insurance policy?" I asked Sheriff Clark.

"Tea Totalers."

"You can't just search her cafe without permission."

"Poly," Genevieve interrupted. "I told him he could. I wanted to help."

"But why didn't you say anything about an insurance policy before now?"

"Because Phil and I don't have one."

Her use of the word *don't* told me something I'd suspected: she hadn't yet let herself believe that her husband was gone. My heart went out to her as she continued. "His brother is an insurance agent and tried to sell us one, but with money being tight, we didn't think it was worth it. Not while we were both still young and healthy." She raised the bandana to her face and sobbed openly.

"Sheriff Clark, did you hear that?"

"Ms. Monroe, please let me do my job."

I glared at him. "If your job is arresting innocent people, then by all means, go ahead."

Clark looked like he'd stubbed his toe and was trying not to show that it hurt. "I have enough on Mrs. Girard to get a conviction. Right now I'm taking her in to have a long talk. If it turns out you know anything about this investigation—if you're withholding information—I'm bringing you in next. I appreciate that she's your friend, Ms. Monroe, but if she murdered her husband, she deserves to be in jail."

"Charlie, do something!" Genevieve cried out.

I looked at Charlie. Her forehead was drawn, her eyebrows low over hooded eyes. Her anger was directed at Clark. For a moment we were frozen, him staring back at her as if he, like me, was waiting to see what it was Genevieve wanted her to do. After a few seconds Clark turned Genevieve around to face the door. With his hand on her arm, he guided her toward his car and directed her into the backseat.

Charlie cursed and kicked the tire of the car in the first bay of her auto shop. "This is bad. Really bad."

"You think I don't know that? Genevieve is a mess," I said. "Two days ago she told us she thought she murdered her husband. Now the cops have arrested her. She's produced more evidence against herself than anybody else could have. Who knows what she's going to tell Clark!"

"What about your other suspects. Did you find anything out about that Kim girl?"

"No. She wasn't there today."

"I thought she said there were people who expected her to be working there."

That bothered me, too. "There has to be a way for me to get in touch with her. I'm going back to the tea shop to look for contact info on her. If anything comes up—and I mean anything—call me."

"You got it."

I went back to the Material Girl and sat in my car. Before I pulled away from the curb, I called Lopez Donuts. Big Joe answered.

"Hi, Big Joe, it's Poly. How's business today?" I crossed my fingers that things hadn't changed.

"Poly, you're not going to believe what kind of a day it's been. Busy as all get out. And then that sheriff came in and asked about the croissant samples. I told him they were all gone and offered him a donut. He actually looked angry for a second! Have you ever heard anything so crazy?"

Relief settled in on my shoulders at the knowledge that Clark hadn't been able to get ahold of the croissants. The relief was followed by guilt when I realized the only reason for worrying was if he could prove they were the same croissants that Phil was suffocated with—and I was pretty sure that it would be hard to prove such a thing. I mean, a croissant was a croissant, right?

"Do you think maybe you could use another set of hands around there?" I asked.

"Sure, sure. Why? You looking for a part-time job?" He laughed.

"Not me." I hesitated. "Her name is Kim Matheson. She's a college student with an interest in running a restaurant. Genevieve hired her to work at Tea Totalers, but with the shop closed for renovations, she's not really getting the kind of experience she was looking for. I thought, what with the business boom you guys are having, that maybe you'd want to talk to her?"

"You know what Genevieve is paying her?"

"No idea."

"She's your friend?"

"Not exactly." I turned in my car seat and watched traffic zip by at the end of the alley. "I only just met her this week. She showed up at the tea shop the day Phil Girard was murdered. I think she has a secondary agenda and I need to do a little digging into her background."

"Send her my way. I'll tell Maria to keep the boys away from the shop and I'll keep an eye on her myself."

"I don't want to put you in any danger."

He laughed. "Don't worry about me. I'm a former marine who runs a tight kitchen. If this girl wants to learn, I'll teach her. If she wants something else, I'll find out."

"Thanks, Big Joe," I said and hung up.

I drove to Tea Totalers and pulled into the lot. Kim's bicycle was propped by the front entrance. No other cars were there. I parked in the farthest space, making sure to drive past the length of the back windows, giving Kim every opportunity to see me. I left the musty fabric in the back of the car and headed to the back door.

"Kim?" I called. She wasn't in the office or the kitchen. I went to the front of the café and looked around. The curtain panels were where I'd left them, in a general state of disarray. Behind me, I heard a toilet flush. Seconds later I heard a faucet, then smelled cookies. The door opened and Kim came out of the powder room, the scent of Genevieve's vanilla hand soap following her.

"Hi," she said. She wiped her palms against each other as if she were rolling a piece of clay into a ball between them. "I'm sorry I was late this morning. I would have called you but I don't have your number."

I forced a laugh as an opportunity presented itself. "I was thinking the same thing. I'm sure Genevieve has your contact information around here somewhere, but I don't know her filing system. Why don't I get your phone number and address? In case something pops up?"

"Sure." She looked over my shoulder. "Is Vaughn here, too?" she asked.

"He was this morning." I crossed the office to the desk and pulled a blank sheet of paper out of the printer. "Here, you can write on this." I picked up a pen and held it out to her.

She lowered herself into the chair in front of the computer

and pushed the keyboard aside to make room to write. Her handwriting tipped backward and her letters contained fat loops. I half expected her to dot the *i* in *Kim* with a circle. She didn't. After she'd written her name, e-mail, and cell phone number, she held out the paper.

"Do you have a home number, too?" I asked innocently. "In case of emergency," I said again. I wondered if she would ask what kind of tea emergency I anticipated.

She hunched over the paper again and hesitated before writing a second number. She put a *C* next to the first one and an *H* next to the second. "I always have my cell phone on me. Always. And I have a backup battery, too, so you really don't ever have to call that second number."

"I'm hoping I won't have to call either one," I said. I took the paper and set it in a metal tray on top of a stack of unpaid invoices. Her eyes followed the sheet of paper, as if she wanted to see exactly where I'd put it. I shifted to my right, blocking her view.

"Kim, I need to talk to you about something." I leaned back against the desk. "I'm friends with the couple who runs the donut shop at the other end of San Ladrón Avenue. Lopez Donuts? Have you been there?"

"No. I come straight here and go straight home."

"Here's the thing. You said you wanted restaurant experience, right? As great as it would have been for you to work with Genevieve, you're simply not going to get what you want by working with me. I know for a fact that the Lopezes could use an extra set of hands. You'll be able to see the business up close and personal. And when Genevieve reopens Tea Totalers, if you want, I'm sure you can come back and work for her."

I expected the same quiet nervousness that I'd seen on that first day to resurface. Instead she stood up straight and tugged the hem of her sweatshirt down to cover the waistband of her pink corduroy jeans.

"Can you excuse me while I make a phone call?" she asked.
"Sure."

I went into the front room of the tea shop, but apparently that wasn't enough distance for Kim. She gripped her phone in both hands and bounced her thumbs over the screen rapidly, and then looked up at me. I got the hint. I went out the front door and around the side of the building. When I glanced in the kitchen window at Kim, she was arguing with someone on the other end of the phone.

I raised my cell to my head like I was on a phone call of my own and crept toward the building until I could hear Kim's voice. "I didn't ask her to do anything. I'm telling you, she's trying to get rid of me. I don't know how much longer I can stick around here," she said. She had one finger plugged into the ear not against her phone, which worked out pretty well for me. I hovered by the window and leaned closer to the glass.

"I don't know what she knows or how she knows it," she said. She paced away from me and continued. "I can't do what we agreed to if she kicks me out of the tea shop." She reached the corner of the kitchen and turned around. I put my phone to my ear and pretended to be in the middle of a conversation of my own.

"Sure, okay. Yes. White vinegar. And school glue, just like I said. And if you think of it, something to drink. And tell your mother I said hello."

"Who are you talking to?" Vaughn asked from behind me.

I whirled around, my eyes wide with embarrassment over the fake conversation I was having with him. "I gotta go," I said to my phone. I didn't bother hanging up since there hadn't been a call to begin with. The charade had gone far enough.

Vaughn held an assortment of white plastic shopping bags bulging with the requested supplies. "Was that me on the other end of that conversation?"

"Um, yes?" I said, hoping he'd be willing to go along with me.

"Is that the first fake conversation we've had? Because if it isn't, I might need to see the transcripts so I can get caught up."

"I can explain everything, but not now. Can you give me a couple of minutes alone with Kim?"

"Sure. I have a feeling that explanation is going to be worth the wait." He turned toward the front of the building, shaking his head and laughing at me.

I looked back in the window. Vaughn and Kim were talking. A few seconds later I heard the back door shut. I walked around the side of the building and found Kim standing by Vaughn's wood-cutting station, dragging her fingers through a pile of wood shavings that had accumulated next to the blade.

"Kim, Joe Lopez is at the donut shop now. He wants you to stop by to discuss wages."

"I'm not—this isn't—Genevieve isn't paying me," she stammered. "I thought you knew that."

"But I thought you said you answered her ad. She wouldn't have placed an ad if she wasn't looking to hire someone."

"We worked out an arrangement. She agreed to keep it confidential."

"I've spoken to Genevieve several times since Monday and she hasn't mentioned you once. I'm starting to wonder if maybe there's a different reason you keep showing up other than wanting experience at her restaurant. In fact, I'm starting to wonder if Genevieve's ever even heard of you."

"What are you saying?" she asked. She put her hands on her hips, facing me directly. Gone was the shy girl who matched the kitten and Troll-doll T-shirts. If this was a showdown, she was an ace. Maybe it was time to play my hand.

"I'm saying I don't think you're here to learn how to run a restaurant. I think you're working for someone else, and maybe it has something to do with the reason you're on parole."

Twenty

Kim's face went red. "You couldn't know that unless you went through my things!" she said. "You had no right to do that."

"I didn't go through your things. You dropped a piece of paper. I tried to tell you, but you didn't hear me because you had on your bike helmet."

"I can't believe you're going to ruin this for me after everything I did to set it up." She threw her fists down next to her thighs and stormed inside through the back door.

"Kim! I don't know what you're hiding, but I'm going to find out," I called. Seconds later the front door slammed.

I entered the back door of Tea Totalers and went straight to the desk. Just as I figured, Kim's personal information was missing from the metal tray. I cursed myself for letting that happen and went back out front. She was already down the street on her bike.

"Did that have something to do with the conversation

you were having with me when I got here?" Vaughn asked, surprising me. He put his hands on my upper arms and I tensed. He gently rubbed his hands up and down my sleeves.

"She's hiding something," I said. A mix of frustration and anger left me in need of an outlet.

"Most people are hiding something."

I turned to face him. "Are you?"

"No."

I was aware of how close we were to each other, aware that he smelled like tanned leather and aged oak. Like I imagined a men's club would smell. His green eyes glowed as sunlight picked up the ring of gold around his irises.

"Well, maybe. Nothing serious, though."

I reached my hands up to his elbows and rested them for a second, then stepped backward. His hands fell from my arms and caught my fingertips. There was something comfortable about standing there with the California sun shining down on us as we stood in front of Tea Totalers. Something that made me feel like I was in the right place at the right time. I didn't know what Vaughn would say if he heard what my morning had been like, or why I'd been arguing with Kim. I didn't know if he'd judge me for getting involved. But for everything I didn't know about how he'd react, I knew—I could sense—that he'd understand whatever it was I felt I had to do. It was an unfamiliar feeling and I needed to test it, to see if it was real.

"Genevieve's in trouble. Sheriff Clark took her to the police station this morning. He said he has enough evidence to get a conviction."

"What does this have to do with Kim?"

"I think she knows something. She showed up the day Phil died. I think whatever she's hiding has to do with Phil's murder."

A breeze blew over our heads and ruffled Vaughn's hair. The front of my own hair blew, too, my long bangs coming loose from where they'd been tucked behind my ear, now obstructing my vision. Vaughn reached a finger up and pushed my hair back to the side of my face. He slipped his finger under my chin, tipped it up, and kissed me lightly.

"Genevieve's lucky to have you in her corner," he said. He rested his forehead against mine and I closed my eyes and relaxed for the first time that day. "Is there anything I can do to help?"

"I don't know yet."

"If there is, will you let me know?"

"Maybe," I said. "I wouldn't want you thinking that's the only reason I'm letting you stick around."

"Aha. So you admit you have ulterior motives."

I looked at the plastic bags he'd propped against the side of the house. "Sure I do. I need your vinegar." I crossed the yard to the back door.

He followed. "I guess my mother was wrong about catching flies with honey," he said with a grin.

"Depends if you want more flies or quality flies." I looped my index finger through the handles on one of the bags and slung it over my shoulder.

"Should I point out you're the fly in this particular metaphor?" he asked.

"Should I point out you're implying you're trying to catch me?"

"Maybe we should call this a draw."

I picked up the rest of the bags with my other hand and carried them to my car.

"Where are you going?" he asked.

"I'm taking the supplies to the fabric store to work there." After loading the vinegar bottles in the backseat, I put the rectangles of wood that Vaughn had cut into the trunk. It took several trips. When I went back inside and looked around, I assessed how much work there was to do. A lot. The project had started out as a reason for Tea Totalers to be closed for the week while I helped Genevieve get her life in order. We were four days into the week and not only was her life not in order, but it was about as far from orderly as it could get. And while I suspected the repetition of decoupaging fabric to the tray table components would take my mind off Phil's murder, I knew Genevieve didn't have time for me to sit around crafting.

And then there was the issue of the fabric store opening in three days. Thanks to the help of my parents, the store had been ready before any of this had happened. At least if you didn't count the sign fiasco. But in three days Material Girl would be open for business. The celebration of reopening the fabric store would be tarnished by sadness if Genevieve wasn't free by then.

I called Charlie. "Have you heard anything from Genevieve yet?"

"No. I can't believe that jerk had the nerve to take her in. He knows she didn't do it. I've half a mind to swipe his distributor cap."

"I don't think it's such a good idea to tamper with a police vehicle."

"Just joining you in Fantasyland," she said.

"Don't make me have to prove your innocence, too." I told her about my conversation with Big Joe and my argument with Kim. "I doubt she'll follow through on his offer, but if she does, he'll keep an eye on her."

"Good."

"Call me if you hear anything, okay?"

"Sure."

I hung up the phone and tapped my fingers against it. After all of the evidence that had turned up, it was the appearance of an insurance policy that had led Clark to arrest Genevieve. But she claimed they didn't have a policy, and if that was true, then where did this one come from?

Outside, Vaughn was stacking scraps of wood into neat piles. I suspected it was a made-up task to keep him occupied while I was on the phone.

"What do you know about life insurance?" I asked.

"A fair amount. Why?"

"That's what finally got to Clark. He had all this evidence against Genevieve, but when he found out Phil had a life insurance policy in her name, he took her in."

"She should have told him about that up front."

"She and Phil didn't have life insurance. His brother is an agent and kept trying to sell to them, but she said they always said no."

"Money's been tight for the Girards, but maybe they changed their minds."

"How do you know about their money problems?" I asked.

He looked embarrassed. "I'm sorry. It's confidential."

"But it has to do with Genevieve and Phil?"

"I don't think I should be talking to you about this," he said. "I'm sorry, Poly." He watched me for a few seconds and I stared back at him. I expected him to say *Just kidding*, or *On second thought*, but he didn't. Instead, he turned back to the workbench and covered it with a large gray tarp that had been sitting on the ground next to him.

I hadn't expected Vaughn to hold out on me after I'd confided in him. I went back inside, through the kitchen, to the front of the café and sat along the wall under the one window that didn't have brown butcher paper covering it. I wrapped my arms around my knees and tried to think. Outside, an engine started. Gravel kicked up. A car pulled out of the lot and drove away. I didn't bother looking to see if it was Vaughn. I already knew it was.

I couldn't just sit here. I had to do something. I went to the computer, cued up a search engine, and typed in "San Ladrón life insurance." Several possibilities showed up. I added the name *Girard* to the end of my search terms and found a Samuel Girard connected to a local branch of a major insurance carrier. I called the number and a woman answered.

"San Ladrón Insurance," she said.

"Hello. I'm trying to reach Samuel Girard about an appointment."

"Sure, let me get his calendar. How is next week? Tuesday?"

Tuesday was too late. I changed tactics. "You misunderstood me. I have an appointment today but I'm running late."

"That's not possible. Mr. Girard had a death in the family and I moved all of his appointments to next week. Unless you arranged to meet him at his home office?"

"I did, but I think I wrote the address down wrong. Can you confirm it?

"Sure." She rattled off an address. "Are you familiar with San Ladrón?"

"A little."

"Do you know where Gnarly Waves, the water park, is?"

"Vaguely."

"Head south on San Ladrón Avenue, cross the highway, and turn right at the first street. His office is on Thicket Road, your first left. It's a light green bungalow with white trim. Sam has a sign in the yard out front."

"Where does the water park come into play?"

"If you reach the water park, you've gone too far."

I thanked her and hung up before she could ask my name or offer more assistance. It was after four and I was about to pay a surprise visit to Genevieve's brother-in-law. I grabbed the address I'd scribbled down, locked up the front and back doors, and left.

On the way to Sam Girard's house, I stopped at Rosie's Posies. It was a freestanding florist located in a small shack by the side of the road. Sam Girard's brother had been murdered. I didn't know if they had been close or not, but family was family. Regardless of what I hoped to gain by talking to him, I wanted to show respect.

The structure, not more than ten feet square, had been painted a cheerful yellow with soft green trim. Tall forest-green buckets sat around the exterior of the building, holding cuttings of colorful long-stemmed flowers. A sign advertised *Message to Heaven* bouquets for five dollars, and a hand-painted arrow directed me to an entrance in the back. I followed the perimeter of the building and found a pretty woman in a straw hat and gardening gloves standing outside, trimming the branches on a small topiary.

"Hi," she said. "I'm Rosie. Are you looking for some flowers to brighten your day?"

"Not really. Something more somber, I'd say."

"Are you on your way to the Hi-Ho Cemetery?"

"The what?"

She looked embarrassed. "I meant no disrespect. The Hickman-Howard Memorial Park. It's about a quarter mile down the road, and a lot of people stop here to get a Message to Heaven bouquet on their way. Rumor has it Grumpy from *Snow White and the Seven Dwarfs* is buried there, or at least the person Grumpy was based on. He supposedly haunts the place, so people started calling it the Hi-Ho Cemetery. Is that where you're headed?"

"No, but I am here because of a death in the family."

"I'm sorry for your loss," she said quickly.

"It's not my family. I'm visiting someone whose brother recently died, and I wanted to take him a plant or something."

"You must mean Sam Girard," she said. "I heard about his brother Phil on the news. They say his wife killed him, but I don't believe it." She set her clippers on a concrete step. "Follow me."

The interior of the small building had been divided in half thanks to a counter that held her register, a helium tank, and an assortment of foil balloons with colorful expressions on them. The right side of the building included a wall of refrigerated cases that housed buckets of roses in peach, pink, yellow, red, magenta, and white. In front of the refrigerated cases were small potted plants. They all looked either too feminine or too familiar for me to buy a stranger.

"How well do you know Sam?" she asked.

"Not well. He's a business associate," I added quickly.

"How about a topiary?" She bent down behind the counter and stood up with a small tree shaped like a ball. There was a green ribbon tied around the trunk of the tree, which couldn't have been wider around than a D-cell battery.

"It's perfect," I said.

I paid her what seemed like too low of a price for such a pretty plant and drove to my destination.

Sam Girard's house was in a residential community of flat-roofed ranches in various pastel shades. I parked along the curb under a tree that was just starting to show signs of life thanks to the gradual temperature shift that comes to California every April. I checked my reflection in the rearview mirror, reapplied my lipstick, and tucked the loose hair that had blown around my face back behind my ears. I wished I'd worn something nicer than a sweater, leggings, and high-tops to work, but that couldn't be helped now.

A small rectangular sign mounted to a wooden stake announced Sam's business. The stake stood in the front yard a few feet back from the mailbox. The house was mint green with off-white trim. Delicate lilac flowers surrounded the base of the house, their pastel shade of purple complementing the mint green siding. In front of them, blooming groundcover in a deep purple alternated with thick fern-green leaves. The house looked warm and welcoming.

I approached the front door with the plant under one arm. As I pressed the doorbell, a series of chimes sounded on the other side of the door, followed by footsteps.

The door opened and I found myself face-to-face with Kim Matheson.

Twenty-one

The young blonde took one look at me and slammed the door in my face. Startled, I stepped back and readjusted the plant that was balanced on my hip. I pressed the doorbell again and waited. Her footsteps hadn't receded and I suspected she was still standing directly on the other side of the door. After thirty seconds of waiting, I rang the doorbell again. She yanked it open immediately.

"This is borderline harassment," she said. "How did you find this place? I didn't give you an address."

A man stepped into view at the end of the hallway. Although the light was dim, I could see a facial resemblance between him and Phil. This man's hair was darker than Phil's but had the same unruly curls.

"Kim, who is it?"

"Nobody." She slammed the door on me a second time.

On the other side of the door, footsteps approached. The man opened the door. "May I help you?" he asked.

"I'm here to speak to Sam Girard about an insurance matter," I said.

"I'm Sam Girard." He held out his hand. I readjusted the plant against my left hip again and shook his hand.

"I'm Poly Monroe. I'm sorry for your loss." I held out the plant. "This is for you."

"Thank you." He took the plant and set it on a table inside the front door. When he turned back, he looked confused. "Your name doesn't sound familiar, but I admit I'm off my game this week. Did we have an appointment?"

"No, we didn't. I'm sorry to show up like this, but I need to talk to you. May I come in?"

"Sure." He stepped to the side and I entered.

A formal dining room sat to my left, furnished with a dark wood table and a matching hutch filled with crystal stemware. To the right was a living room. An overstuffed beige chenille sofa lined one wall and faced a brick fireplace. Dark, polished hardwood floors anchored both rooms, along with the hallway. The interior of the house was colorful. The dining walls were lavender, the living room yellow. The hallway was taupe.

"I have to apologize for my niece," Sam said. "She's going through a phase."

"Your niece?" I was confused for a moment. "Kim is your niece? But Genevieve and Phil don't have a daughter."

"My other brother. Kim's been testing her boundaries lately." He looked surprised. "You know Genevieve and Phil?"

"I'm friends with Genevieve. In fact, that's what I wanted to talk to you about."

"Come with me to my office."

As we walked down the hallway to his office, I wondered why Kim had lied about her relationship with Genevieve. From the very first day that I'd met her at Tea Totalers, she had pretended that she was a new employee who hadn't met Gen. Turns out, they were related. Why the secret?

We reached a small room at the back of the house. The

walls were dark hunter green. A worn cognac leather sofa sat along the wall under a hunting painting. Behind the desk was a brick fireplace with a wooden mantel filled with framed photos, diplomas, and awards. Sam's desk sat to the left of the office and faced the sofa. An oriental rug in shades of green, white, red, and blue covered much of the hardwood floor.

"Can I get you a drink? Scotch, brandy"—he looked at his watch—"sherry?"

"How about water?"

"You sure you don't want something stronger? This has been a heck of a week."

"Water's fine for me," I said.

He emptied a small bottle of club soda into a glass and handed it to me, and then fixed himself a scotch and soda. "I can't begin to imagine what Genevieve's going through."

"You haven't talked to her?"

"She's not returning my calls. I know what people are saying and I—we—want to help. Kim said Genevieve hasn't been at work all week and that's not like her. We can't help her if she won't let us."

"Sam, the sheriff picked up Genevieve and took her to the mobile unit. I don't think he arrested her, but I think he's close. He said he has enough to get a conviction. I know she didn't have anything to do with your brother's murder, but there's a lot of evidence against her."

He shook his head. "Genevieve couldn't harm a fly. My brother was lucky to have her. I wish she would have listened to me about the insurance policy. Now she's got nothing except the shop, and she's probably going to lose that."

"See, that's just it. There *was* a policy, a recent one."

"There was? Who drew it up?"

"I don't know. The sheriff found it this morning. Genevieve says she didn't know anything about it. And if you've been trying to convince them to get one, why wouldn't they go through you? It doesn't make sense."

"No, it doesn't. Especially since *I* have a policy all drawn up for them. All it needs is their signatures."

"Where is it?"

"I keep it in the safe." He downed his scotch and soda and stood up. I thought he was going to make himself another, but instead he walked to the hunting painting and removed it from the wall. Behind it was a safe. He spun the lock back and forth a few times and opened the door. I watched his back as he rooted through a small stack of papers. "Here it is," he said. He pulled a manila folder out of a stack. He flipped past the top pages to the back. "Wait a minute—that can't be." He flipped to the top page again and looked at the writing. "This isn't possible."

"What is it?"

He sat back down at the desk and laid the document in front of him. Starting slowly, he flipped through the pages one by one, scanning the text. When he reached the last page, he slowly shook his head back and forth.

"What is it? What's wrong?"

"This document is signed, that's what's wrong."

"How could the document be signed and put into your wall safe without you knowing? Who else knows your combination?"

"My wife knows. It's our anniversary date. Same as the alarm code on the house."

"Who else knows that code?" I asked, already suspecting the answer.

"Mostly family."

"Did Genevieve know it?"

"She might have. Phil did. I know I should change it more frequently, but it's easier this way. One of the kids house-sits for us when we go out of town, and they know it, too. I lock the office, so the safe's never been an issue."

"When's the last time you went out of town?"

"We were supposed to go a couple of weeks ago, but a

family situation came up and it didn't seem like a good idea to leave. It was just as well that we canceled."

I didn't miss how his eyes cut to the door. "Does Kim ever house-sit for you?"

"She has," he said.

"Tell me again how Kim is related to you."

"She's my niece. My other brother, Jim, is a traveling salesman. He's on the road fairly frequently. Has been since Kim was a girl."

"What can you tell me about her?"

He looked at me sharply. "Kim's family and she's had some hard times. I told you she's going through a phase, but that's all I'll mention."

I understood where Sam was coming from. Family was important to me, too. As an only child, I didn't have a large circle of relatives around me. I had my mom and dad. When I came to San Ladrón after inheriting the fabric store, I'd gotten into some trouble, and my parents had been there for me. I knew no matter what happened, I could count on them.

"Did Kim have access to your safe?" I asked softly.

He nodded. "My business involves a fair amount of confidentiality. I'm going to have to talk to the sheriff about this, tell him what I found. I don't know what it means."

There was a tap on the door to the office. "Uncle Sam?" said Kim's voice from the other side of the door. "I need to talk to you."

"Come in," he called.

The door opened and she came inside. She was dwarfed by the darkness of the green walls and the heaviness of the wood beam ceiling. She shoved her hands into the kangaroo pocket of her pale pink sweatshirt. Her shoulders were slouched and her eyes were red.

I stood up. "Thank you for your time, Sam. I can show myself out."

"Don't leave, Poly. I want to talk to you, too," Kim said.

I sat back down. Kim walked over to the desk and played with a clear globe paperweight on the corner. "I heard you two talking. I know what you think," she said to me.

"Kim, I haven't broken any confidences here," Sam said. "You don't need to tell Poly anything if you don't want to."

"But, Uncle Sam, I did something really bad," she said. Her eyes grew wide and bloodshot. "I forged Aunt Genevieve's and Uncle Phil's signatures on that insurance policy. I'm the reason the police are after her!"

Twenty-two

I wasn't sure which one of us was more surprised: Sam or me. After a pulse of shock, a cloud of darkness came over Sam's face. "You what?"

"She's been so nice to me with my problem that when Uncle Phil was murdered I wanted to help her. I knew you had a policy drawn up for them and I knew you kept it in the safe. I figured if it was signed, you could have your company pay on it and she'd have money." Tears streamed down Kim's face. Her fair cheeks were blotchy and her eyes, already bloodshot, were now puffy and red. Her breathing was erratic and her pink sweatshirt convulsed in spasms every time she took a breath.

Sam opened the manila folder and held up a form. "Kim, did you make a copy of this policy?"

She sniffled and nodded. "I put a copy in Aunt Genevieve's office. I didn't mean for anything bad to happen, I swear it!"

He stood up and shooed us out of his office. "Wait in the living room. I'm calling your father."

Kim turned to the door and I followed her down the hallway. She sat on the chenille sofa in the living room, her hands in her lap, her ankles crossed. She was slouched down, staring at her hands. Her fingers were threaded together, and she chipped at the polish on the thumbnail of her left hand with the thumbnail of her right.

"Kim, that very first day at Tea Totalers you acted like you didn't know Genevieve. Why'd you lie about her being your aunt?"

"We thought it would be better if we pretended we didn't know each other. I didn't want anybody to figure out why I was working there, and she promised not to say anything."

"But that first day—that was the day your uncle was murdered."

She sniffled. "I didn't know about that when I got there. I was running late just like I told you, and I knew I'd be in lots of trouble if anybody found out, so as soon as I got there, I found the key and went inside and started working."

"You said there were people who were counting on you to be working there. Who were you talking about?"

"My family."

"Kim, Genevieve is a member of your family, and she's in real trouble. You said you wanted to help her. If that's true, you need to tell me the truth. The whole truth."

Kim continued to stare at her hands. She was so involved in what she was doing that I wondered if she'd even heard me.

"Kim?"

She took a deep breath and exhaled. "I got a DUI last month. It was my second one. My license was revoked and I was suspended from school. I needed a letter of recommendation to lift the suspension. I have community service on Saturdays, so I can't work weekends. And I can't drive—it would violate the terms of my parole."

"And Genevieve's your aunt, so she gave you a job at the tea shop. And she's not paying you, but she can verify where you're at. That's why you said you had to work *there*."

Kim nodded.

"But I don't understand why you threw out the produce and the tea."

"I only did what Aunt Genevieve told me to do. She said we always used fresh ingredients. She said the deliveries came on Mondays, so by the end of Monday night, we threw out everything that wasn't fresh. That was supposed to be one of my job responsibilities, to look at what we had a surplus of and suggest recipes so we wouldn't be so wasteful."

"So you threw out everything? The vegetables and the fruit? And the croissants?"

"The vegetables and fruit, yes. I didn't find any croissants."

That made sense. Genevieve had made lunch for the construction crew at my shop, and she'd asked Phil to pick up six dozen croissants on his trip. There shouldn't have been any croissants to throw out except for the small bag I'd found in the kitchen.

The door to Sam's office opened and shut. Kim looked up. I followed her gaze. Sam appeared and stood under the dark wooden trim above the doorway.

"I've contacted your dad. We think it's best for you to tell the police what you did."

"But you said yourself it didn't work. Can't you just tear up the policy and pretend I didn't do it?"

Sam looked at me. "Do you want to tell her what happened?"

I turned from Sam to Kim. "When the police found the copy of the insurance policy on Genevieve's desk, they figured they had her motive."

Kim balled her fists up and put them to her eyes.

"You have to take responsibility for your actions," Sam said.

"But the police will look up my history."

"Yes, they will. And they might not believe you based on your past. But you need to tell them the truth and accept whatever punishment comes along with it," Sam said.

"Uncle Sam, I'm only nineteen!"

"Yes. You're an adult and it's time you started acting like one." He crossed his arms over his green shirt. "You can use the phone in my office."

"Are you going to listen in?"

"No, I'll give you privacy. I want to talk to Poly for a second."

Kim shot me a look that I couldn't read. Embarrassment? Humiliation? Anger? She stood up and shuffled past Sam and headed toward his office. I heard his office door shut.

I stood up. "Do you really think you can trust her to tell the truth?"

"She has to be given boundaries. It'll be easy enough to find out if she doesn't make the call." He ran his finger back and forth across the base of his nose and sniffed in sharply like he was trying to stifle a sneeze.

"She told me about the DUI," I said.

"Kim's had a troubled childhood. Her mother passed away when she was thirteen. And with her father on the road so much, she went unsupervised. She fell in with a bad crowd and has been in and out of juvie. When she graduated high school and said she wanted to open a restaurant someday, we all thought it was a good idea to encourage her. Maybe the trouble was behind her. Two weeks after she turned eighteen she got her first DUI. The second came last month. California has harsh penalties for driving under the influence. If she gets a third, she's looking at jail time, and we can't protect her."

"She said she wanted to help Genevieve because Genevieve helped her."

"Even though her actions were illegal, I believe her

intentions were noble. When she got the second DUI, she spent the night in jail. I think she finally got scared. Her father asked if she could stay with us. He thought it would be good for her to be around my wife and me—good for her to have female role models around. That's why we asked Genevieve to help her out, too. Everything was planned to keep her busy and surrounded with strong women."

"That's why she said people were counting on her working there."

"Poly, I'm Kim's family. I know she's been in a lot of trouble, but I choose to believe her. If what she said is true, and if she takes responsibility, it shows a turning point for her. She needs people to give her the benefit of the doubt instead of suspecting the worst." He paused. "But I will make sure she tells the sheriff what she did. That's a promise."

I stood up. "Thank you for talking to me."

I let myself out the front door and walked down the sidewalk to my car. The neighborhood was so idyllic, it was hard to believe that inside this one house was a troubled teenager who was one drinking-and-driving infraction away from incarceration. What other secrets were hidden behind the doors of San Ladrón? And which door held the secrets that I needed to expose to save Genevieve?

I drove to Material Girl. It took five trips to carry the decoupage supplies and wood inside the store. I set the bags on the wrap stand and carried the musty voile panels up to the washing machine. It wasn't doing me any good to think about Genevieve. My brain was caught in a loop and nothing made sense. Maybe if I did something else to clear my mind, I'd be able to focus better.

I carried the bags of vinegar to the washing machine next. I fit as many panels into the machine as it would comfortably hold. It was about a third of what I'd cut earlier. I started the wash cycle and waited until the basin was filled with water, then added four bottles of white vinegar and a cup of Borax.

In thirty-three minutes, I'd know if the vinegar treatment worked.

I set the timer on my microwave and went back downstairs. Pins and Needles followed. I thought it cute how they still didn't venture far away from the other. I pulled the white school glue and Popsicle sticks out of the dollar-store bags and lined them up on the counter. At the bottom of the bag I found two felt mice: one royal blue, one yellow. Vaughn's surprise had been for the kitties.

"Look what Vaughn bought you," I said. I pulled the cardboard tag off each mouse and tossed them to the exposed concrete floor. Pins pounced. He caught the blue felt mouse in his gray striped paws and bit into the end with the string tail. Needles watched from a distance, as if he wasn't going to get involved until Pins proved it was worth it. Apparently the proof was established within a minute, because that's how long it took for Needles to join in the fun and attack the yellow mouse.

I pulled up a chair and stared at the supplies while the kitties batted the felt mice around the concrete floor. It was going on seven o'clock. How was I supposed to concentrate on crafting when my friend was in jail? It was for Genevieve, I told myself. I was working on this project for her as much as I was trying to find out who'd killed Phil.

I thought again about the shopping list on Genevieve's computer. Clark would certainly use it to secure his case against Genevieve if he found it. I needed to show that Genevieve's wasn't the only restaurant in San Ladrón who ordered croissants. It couldn't be that strange for her to order croissants, could it? If only I knew someone else in the restaurant business who I could ask.

But there was someone else I could ask: Topo di Sali.

I went through my messenger bag until I found his crumpled card. There was no address, only a website and a phone number. He answered on the third ring.

"Italian Scallion," he said.

"Is this Topo di Sali?" I asked. "This is Poly Monroe. We met at Tea Totalers on Tuesday and you gave me your card."

"I remember you. Cute girl in all black. Did your boss get my message?"

"My boss? I don't have a boss. Wait a minute. Are you behind the attack on my boss?"

"I'm not admitting to anything, but like I told you, it's a two-way street."

Twenty-three

"What does that mean?" I asked. "And what does any of this have to do with Giovanni?"

"Who's Giovanni?"

"My boss. Well, he's my ex-boss now, but—wait, don't you know?"

"I'm talking about Genevieve Girard. She wants to use my contacts, she's going to have to pay the piper. I'll give her a few more days while I'm in San Francisco, but you tell her I'm not going to wait forever. If she doesn't do business with me soon, she'll be out of second chances."

"But, Mr. di Sali—" I started, but the call disconnected.

I stood up. I felt like I was three steps behind a master plan that involved a handful of unrelated people. I kicked the blue felt mouse across the floor of the fabric store. Needles chased it and pounced. He chewed on the tail while I chewed on my thoughts.

Topo sounded like he was threatening Genevieve, but he

also sounded like she owed him something. Had they done business together that I didn't know about? And if so, why hadn't she mentioned it? Or worse—had Phil promised him something in private and now was taking that secret to his grave? That was something I might never know. What I did know was that I'd never gotten around to asking Topo about croissant suppliers. Even if he answered a second call, I didn't want to be in the uncomfortable position of owing him something myself.

I leaned back in my desk chair and ran my hands over the mail that had accumulated over the past few days. A flyer for the Waverly House caught my eye. Adelaide. She oversaw every aspect of running the restored mansion, and that included their award-winning restaurant. Maybe she could help me. It was a five-minute walk from the fabric store, and if I left now, I might still catch her at the mansion. I left the washer washing and the kitties playing, ducked under the long strap of my black messenger bag, and locked up behind me.

The Waverly House looked more impressive at seven in the evening than it did during the day, thanks to subtle lights that had been placed along the front exterior to illuminate the Wedgewood blue of the Victorian mansion. Vaughn had mentioned that Adelaide was in the process of prepping the grounds for the annual Midnight in the Garden party, and I could see the results of that work. I wondered how the battle between his parents was going. Secretly, I rooted for Adelaide. I found her passion for running the Waverly House inspiring. I hoped when I was her age I'd be as enthusiastic about running the fabric store.

I walked up three concrete steps and followed the sidewalk to the front door. The large Victorian house had at least two dozen windows facing the street, all framed in soft ivory casing. A turret rounded out the left corner, and the roofline sloped with gently curved gables. The front door matched the ivory of the windowsills. The front door opened toward me and a man and a woman walked out. Their laughter continued as they passed me and walked halfway down the sidewalk. Before entering the restaurant, I watched them veer off the concrete into the grass. The man put his arm around her and kissed her temple. She snuggled into him and they stopped under the large maple tree and hugged.

I gave the couple privacy and went inside. To my right was the pretty redheaded woman employed as hostess for the Waverly House restaurant. A few families stood outside the red velvet ropes, reading the captions on the black and white pictures that hung in the hallway. The pictures continued past the restaurant and into the historic building. Beyond the restaurant was a carpeted staircase that wound up one flight to the second floor, where bedrooms decorated in vintage Victorian design were available for viewing.

I threaded my way through the diners to the staircase, pausing only to take note of a film of dust on the dark wooden banister. I continued three doors down and stopped by the last door on the left. A light shone out of the door. I knocked lightly on the frame.

"Am I interrupting anything important?" I asked.

"Poly! What a nice surprise!" Adelaide said. She wore a mauve turtleneck sweater and a taupe pleated skirt that fell below her knees. A delicate gold-and-quartz chain hung around her neck, suspending a pair of reading glasses. She came around to the front of her desk, enclosing me in a hug. "You are exactly the breath of fresh air I need in here tonight." She looked at a clock on her desk. "Goodness. It's after seven? I haven't eaten since eleven. No wonder I'm having such a hard time concentrating on this document." She shook her head and the silvery-gray hairs that had already escaped her chignon waved around her face like filaments.

"I didn't know if I would find you here this late."

"It seems most nights I'm here this late."

"Vaughn told me about the trouble you're having with the city council."

"My son wouldn't have been that polite. He told you it was his father, didn't he?"

Adelaide went to a wooden cabinet that sat on top of an antique dresser. She turned the brass key on top of the cabinet and lifted the hinged lid. From inside, she pulled a bottle of a peachy-pink liquid and two small cordial glasses out and turned toward me.

"I make it a habit to only drink socially. Your surprise visit is a sign. Join me in a Sauterne?"

The last thing I'd expected from Adelaide was for her to offer me a drink. "I'd love to," I said.

She filled each glass with the rosy liquid. The label on the bottle read *Petrus Sauterne* in red letters across an aged cream label. She handed me one of the glasses and I waited to see what the proper Sauterne protocol was: Clink glasses? Let it breathe? Throw it down the hatch?

"Cheers," Adelaide said. She raised her glass to meet mine and, after a delicate clink, she sipped at the beverage. I followed suit. It was sweet but also strong.

Adelaide spun the bottle so the label faced her. "Your great-aunt gave me this bottle forty years ago. I've been saving it for a special occasion."

I was embarrassed. I wasn't at the Waverly House for a social call or even to see how Adelaide was doing in the fight against Vic McMichael, her ex-husband and the cosigner on the loan for my shop. I was there to ask her about croissants. Even though my mission was on behalf of Genevieve's well-being, it felt self-centered. Adelaide was one of the few people in San Ladrón who had been personal friends with my relatives. They had been great friends once. My family was important to me—generations who had created the fabric store long before I was born in it, along with my own parents who lived only an hour away—and I needed to make more of an effort to build a bridge to the past, to the people in my new hometown who knew my roots.

Temporarily, I shoved my own reasons for being there to the back of my mind.

"You're right. Vaughn did mention that his father is the person creating problems for you and the party. I admit, I don't really understand why he would do that, especially now. He must have known you've been planning the party for months."

"Oh, he's known, all right. He's aware of the entire planning calendar. And believe me, that's exactly why he waited this long. He added the change in the zoning bylaws to the city council agenda on the last possible day that he could. I've already spent months planning the party. It's an annual tradition! If we don't open our gardens for the midnight party, people will start to think that the Waverly House is having financial trouble."

"Are you?"

"Truthfully, things have been steady. We've booked six weddings for the summer, and five of those parties elected to use our restaurant and bar service for catering. That helps us project our profits and losses. But the annual garden party has been the centerpiece of our promotional calendar for years. The people of San Ladrón love having an event they can get dressed up for, but we also draw people from neighboring towns as well."

"Until I saw your flyer, I wasn't aware of it."

"It's our fund-raiser. We charge a flat fee, fifty dollars per couple. We have the most talented gardeners and landscapers working on the flowers around the Waverly House. It's simply amazing what they can do. For one night, the grounds are transformed. We add in outdoor bars, buffet stations, and a jazz quartet. Couples come expecting a romantic evening, and that's what we try to provide. What we clear after expenses determines our operating budget for the upcoming year."

"And Vaughn's father is making it so you can't promote

the event. And by not promoting it, you're not going to sell tickets. And by not selling tickets, you're going to have to lower your operating budget."

"You're very astute, Poly."

An idea formed in my head, slow and vague, like a cloud of steam from the dishwasher when the cycle was complete. I stared at the bottle of Sauterne, wondering if it had indeed given me remarkable insight and an idea that might help the people I cared about, or if it was a Toulouse-Lautrec-like thought, inspired not by absinthe, but a pinker beverage that had been aging for almost half a century?

"What if . . ." I started. My pulse ticked faster and I felt a buzz of energy. I looked up from the label on the bottle and made eye contact with Adelaide. "What if the garden party was held someplace else this once?"

"Dear, I don't think you understand."

"No, I think I do. I have an idea."

Adelaide looked at me with an expression of "why not?" and I realized she was exhausted, her energy probably spent from fighting the battle with her ex-husband.

"Like I said, what if the food-and-drink portion of the evening was held at a different location in San Ladrón, but the Waverly House was still the beneficiary? The catering and the beverages could be someplace else that has the proper permits. Like a restaurant. And maybe for one hour—midnight!— the gardens are opened up for people to view. No food, no booze, no city council to fight. The gardens are outside. If the gardens are open, then nobody can stop people from walking on the grounds. I mean, as long as the gates are open, the Waverly House gardens are public property, right?"

"In theory, it sounds wonderful, but I've planned the party for several years now. A business would have to close down indefinitely to prepare for something of this magnitude. I couldn't ask someone to give up business and expect the money to go to the Waverly House. I'm afraid it wouldn't work."

"I'm not finished," I said, cutting her off. She looked taken aback, but she gestured for me to continue. "I've been helping to renovate a local tea shop with fabrics from my store. Are you familiar with Tea Totalers? It's right around the corner. The store's been closed for about a week now and it's going to continue to be closed indefinitely. The hard part of the renovation is over: the measurements have all been taken and I'm using fabric from my shop, but what if the interior were transformed again? Instead of the French countryside look that I'm working on, we could do a temporary, one-night-only surprise setup? Your party is always called Midnight in the Garden. What if we called it Midnight in Paris, since the tea shop has a Parisian flavor? And ask other local businesses to get involved, maybe turn it into a festival down the length of Bonita Avenue?"

Adelaide sat back against the crewel fabric that covered her chair. Her fingers worried the delicate quartz-and-gold chain that held her glasses around her neck, running back and forth over the small pink stones while her eyes studied me. She dropped the chain and picked up her glass, took a sip, and then set it back on a cut-crystal coaster.

"I think it's a beautiful idea," she said softly.

"And it will work, right? I'll use different fabrics, velvet maybe, to take the new interior from day to evening. I can even use a heat-set technique to give the velvet a jacquard texture. The rest can be done with inexpensive glass votives and candles and flowers. I know Genevieve would want to help. We're already using toile and Provençal and voile. It's going to be beautiful," I finished.

"And it's going to cost you quite a bit."

"No, it's not. Like I said, I have the fabric in the store. I'll donate it. There are a lot of fabrics that aren't in perfect condition, and this is a great way for me to make good use of them. And it'll be good press for me, too. People will connect my store to San Ladrón. Honestly, it's a little self-serving, but if you don't mind, and Genevieve doesn't mind, then I'll take advantage of the opportunity." I didn't realize I was leaning forward until I stopped talking. I consciously relaxed into my seat and folded my hands in my lap, waiting for her to say something. I couldn't shake my nerves. I unfolded my hands and sipped the drink in front of me. Sweet apricot and honey flavors trickled down my throat, followed by a slight burn from the alcohol. I coughed once and set the glass back down.

"Adelaide, you probably know that Genevieve Girard's husband was murdered earlier this week. There is a lot of evidence against her, but I don't believe for a second that she killed him. I've been working on the store as a way to give her some distance, give her some time to deal with what happened. But the longer the tea shop stays closed, the more people are going to talk. Rumors of murder are going to be hard enough for her to shake. It would do her a world of good to know you agreed to this."

"I know of Genevieve's troubles and I feel for her. If this would help her, then it makes it an even better idea. But Poly, I won't begin to assume this is happening until I know I have her permission. As it is, I feel just awful for my part in the evidence against her."

"Your part? What do you have to do with Phil Girard's murder?"

"Nothing!" she said, sitting back. "It's just that a bit of my advice has worked against your friend."

"How?"

"When she was first getting started, she used to dine at the Waverly House. After several meals, I introduced myself to her and asked what it was that kept bringing her back. She told me she'd always wanted to run a French-themed tea shop and she was getting ideas of items she could add to her menu. She was embarrassed, as if I'd think her a thief. Such a sweet girl. I told her she could steal whatever ideas she wanted. That's the name of the game when it comes to business. I learned that from my ex-husband." She smiled ruefully and took another sip of her cordial. "She told me she always thought she'd serve tea and croissants, but she felt like a failure because her croissants weren't as good as ours. I told her our secret, and that's where the trouble comes in."

I leaned forward again, my lips loosened by the drink. "That's weird that you brought up the croissants. That's what brought me here tonight. I wanted to ask you about croissants."

"You came here to talk about croissants? That *is* weird."

I laughed at how odd it sounded to hear Adelaide use the word *weird*. "Please keep going. What's the secret with your croissants?"

"That we don't make then fresh!" She laughed. "We have them delivered from a distributor in Los Angeles. As far as I know, Genevieve uses the same supplier."

Twenty-four

"But that means anybody could have had access to Genevieve's croissants. Anybody," I said.

"Yes, I suppose that's true. Is that relevant?"

"Phil Girard was suffocated with croissants. There were crumbs in the back of the truck, and Sheriff Clark knows that Genevieve packed a basket of food for Phil before he left. One of the things in that basket was a sandwich on a croissant."

"Oh my, that's worse than I thought."

"What else do you know about Phil Girard's murder?" I asked Adelaide.

"What I read in the papers, I believe, and probably not even that much. I don't like reading about the murder of one of our local residents. He may not have deserved his wonderful wife, but he didn't deserve to die."

"So you knew he was cheating?"

"I suppose I did. He and Genevieve came here for dinner

one evening. Later that same night he came back with another woman."

"Babs Green?"

"Yes." She took a sip of her drink. "And worse, she dropped her shawl on the way out, which means she'll be visiting the Waverly House a second time when she comes to pick it up."

I thought back to the conversation Charlie had relayed about blackmailing Phil. It didn't fit. Why did Charlie have leverage with the knowledge of his affair, when Phil was parading his mistress around the Waverly House? It was another piece of information I couldn't justify.

"Do you know when Babs is going to pick up her shawl?"

"I suppose it will be sometime after I call her and tell her I found it. Funny, I never seem to get to that particular task on my to-do list." She giggled and took another sip of her drink. "But for Phil to bring her here on the same night that he dined with his lovely wife, well, it was an act of a true toad if you ask me. If Genevieve wanted to serve frog legs, she'd have had to look no further than him for supplies." She giggled again. "Did I say that?" she asked.

I looked at her, at the almost-empty cordial glass on the desk in front of her, and back at her. "I think the Sauterne might have helped."

"Poly, I do enjoy talking to you. You're a young woman, but you're an old soul. You don't make me feel like a seventy-year old woman. In fact, when I talk to you, sometimes I think I'm talking to my old friend Millie. She was a fixer just like you."

"What do you mean?"

"She saw problems and she tried to fix them. Vaughn notices it, too. I would never violate my son's confidence, but I suspect he's intimidated by your generosity and ability to do just about anything on your own. I daresay he doesn't know exactly how to treat you."

"He's doing okay so far," I said, immediately regretting it. "Did I say that?"

Adelaide looked between me and my barely touched glass. "I'm afraid I can't blame the Sauterne unless you drink at least half of what I poured you."

I sipped at my beverage and told Adelaide what else I knew of Phil's murder: about Rick Penwald and his fictitious delivery business, the empty tea jug in the back of the van, and Mack and the mix-up with the fabric. I told her about Topo di Sali's pressure to get Genevieve to sell out, and how Kim had faked the life insurance policy that had ultimately been the most incriminating piece of evidence. I kept hoping something would shake loose when I repeated everything to her. It didn't.

"I tell you what we're going to do," Adelaide said. "I'm going to talk to Sheriff Clark about the croissants first thing tomorrow morning. If you can get Genevieve's permission to let me use her shop, I'll get a press release out immediately and do everything in my power to halt the tide of public opinion from harming her while we put together this party."

"Then we have a plan?" I asked.

"We have a plan."

"Can I add one more thing to the plan?"

"What?"

"You give me Babs's address and I'll hand-deliver the shawl tomorrow."

"Is there no end to your generosity?" she asked.

"I might have an ulterior motive, but nobody else needs to know that."

She reached into a basket on the floor behind her desk and picked up a sheer black shawl with bright pink, blue, and green flowers on it. Long black piano fringe hung from the border. Adelaide handed the shawl to me. "Your secret is safe with me. Good luck."

Unlike when I arrived, Adelaide's eyes now sparkled brightly. She seemed to have forgotten about her battles with her ex-husband temporarily, or maybe it was because she viewed me as a new general in her army. That thought sent a shiver down my spine. It was one thing to help Adelaide find a way to host the annual benefit she had always hosted. It was quite another to feel like I was taking sides between two very important people in my new hometown, both of whom happened to be the parents of the man I'd kissed three times in the past week. Not that I was counting.

Adelaide and I walked to the front of the Waverly House. I was energized with ideas for the possible party at Tea Totalers. What we'd already done at the store would work perfectly for everyday, and with only a few modifications I could take it up a notch. It would be the kind of glamorous event I'd always wanted to attend. From what I'd been told about the annual parties at the Waverly House, this would be more than a night out for the town. It was something special. And because I was interested in becoming a part of San Ladrón, I was eager to be a part of the planning.

It had become dark while I visited with Adelaide. Instead of taking the shortcut down the alley that connected to the back parking lot of the fabric store, I walked to the gas station on the corner and turned right, keeping a brisk pace between streetlights. Most of the lights of businesses along Bonita were off, with the exception of Antonio's Ristorante and the Broadside Tavern. Both Tiki Tom and the Garden sisters had long since locked up their stores. A few cars passed me as I hurried along the sidewalk, past the local bank branch and an insurance storefront. I kept my eyes on my final destination, easy to spot thanks to the crack in the sidewalk where the heavy metal sign had landed earlier in the week.

I hadn't spent a lot of time thinking about that sign since Phil's murder, but I couldn't put it off indefinitely. I flipped through the recently dialed numbers on my phone and found the foreman. A machine clicked on after four rings, and I left a message.

"This is Polyester Monroe of the fabric store on Bonita Avenue. This sign removal and installation job needs to be finished tomorrow. I open for business on Sunday!" I stared up at the rusted bolts protruding from the façade. "Call me back." I left my number and hung up.

My business plan had included a loan to cover things like the sign removal and new sign installation, the acquisition of new inventory, and the expenses of running the store for six months while I built up momentum and generated a sales revenue. I had a little money in a Vanguard account, thanks to my ex-boyfriend constantly harping that it was never too early to start investing for the future, and that's what I relied on for daily expenses. The beauty of the fabric shop was that I could live in the apartment above it, which saved me money on rent, but there were obvious expenses I had to plan for: food, water, electricity, kitty litter.

I was a firm believer that if you created goodwill with the people around you, it would come back to you when you needed it. Karma, some people called it, but karma probably wasn't the immediate concept people thought it was. If it were, the people who cut you off in the grocery store line would be punished by their shopping bags splitting open on the way to their cars. Whatever it was called, I hoped it would come to me in spades when I needed it, as in, when the building inspectors took note of the crack in the sidewalk in front of the store and threatened to write me up for destruction of public property.

I heaved the gate open and unlocked the front door. A faint beeping sounded from the apartment. The microwave timer!

I'd forgotten all about the voile and the vinegar while talking to Adelaide. I ran upstairs to the washing machine and checked on the fabric. The scent was gone and the panels were all but dried—into the most wrinkled mess I could imagine. It would take hours to iron the creases out of them. Instead, I measured out a cup of detergent and ran the washing machine a second time. Hopefully, I'd get a do-over, as long as I decided to stay put. The clock said it was going on ten. No chance I was leaving again.

As much as I wanted a shower, I didn't want to compete with the washing machine for hot water. I waited out the cycle and moved the voile into the dryer and added a dryer sheet. I set it on cool tumble dry. Pins and Needles were nestled together on the bed, their heads sharing a watered silk pillow with marabou trim that Aunt Millie had made several decades ago. I ran my open hand over each of them. Pins raised his head off the pillow and croaked out a scratchy meow, and then went back to sleep. When the dryer beeped, I folded the voile and draped the panels over plastic hangers. When I was done, I took the long-awaited shower. Too tired to root around my closet and look at dresses, I slipped into a long black nightgown and pulled the sheets over me, my thoughts dissolving into dreams.

The next morning was cool. I pulled on a white cotton men's shirt, black cardigan, and black jeans. I found a pair of black-and-white argyle socks in the dresser, pushed my feet into well-worn black penny loafers, raked some styling gel through my hair, added a tinted sunscreen, mascara, and cherry red lip gloss. I stuffed Babs's floral shawl into my messenger bag and left. I was at Charlie's Automotive by nine thirty.

Charlie was drinking from a large red coffee mug when I walked into her auto shop. "What makes a better gift: a transmission flush or a lube job?" she asked.

"Those are car terms, right? Because they sound dirty."

"That's okay. It's for a man."

"What did this man do for you?"

"It's not what he did, it's what he's *going* to do."

"You don't strike me as the type to do preemptive gift-giving to a man."

"I just want to be prepared when the moment comes, that's all." She spun around and leaned back in her desk chair. She wore a cream Exxon gas station attendant shirt buttoned from the collar down to her ribs. The bottom four buttons were open, allowing the shirt to create an inverted V that showcased her pierced bellybutton. The waistband had been torn from her jeans, making them an even lower rise than they'd started out. The legs expanded into a boot cut that all but covered dingy square-toed motorcycle boots with silver rings and harnesses across the instep. Judging by the looks of them, they were almost as old as my VW Bug.

"Any news on Frenchy?" Charlie asked.

"Yes. The whole life insurance policy is another mess. Phil's brother Sam kept a policy drawn up in case they ever changed their minds. Kim forged the signatures and left a copy at Tea Totalers. That's what Clark found. Once Kim tells what she did, Clark has to acknowledge that maybe he doesn't have such a solid case against Genevieve."

"I wish I could be there to see the expression on his face when he finds out." She tipped back in her chair and rested the heels of her motorcycle boots on her desk. "Any word from the truck driver or the Italian Scallion?"

"I talked to Topo di Sali last night. He asked if my boss got his message, and I thought he was talking about Giovanni."

Charlie dropped her feet to the ground and leaned forward. "You think the Italian Scallion jumped your boss?"

"*Ex*-boss," I said automatically. "It's kind of a blur. He keeps saying to make sure Genevieve knows it's a two-way street. What's a two-way street? It's like he thinks he did her a favor and she owes him. I don't like the sound of that."

"You didn't ask him to clarify?"

"He hung up. But something else happened last night and I don't know how to tell you about it."

"Shoot."

"It has to do with your mother."

Charlie didn't want to talk about the fact that Adelaide had given her up for adoption when she was born. It was a secret that I'd only recently uncovered, and even though Charlie and I had established a friendship, we never spoke of it.

She scowled. "If you're talking about one of those two rich people who claim to run this town, she's not my mother."

I leaned against the built-in desk by the printer. "You really don't want to start a relationship with either one of them? Isn't that why you came back here when you found out you were adopted?"

"I wanted to know who the people were who gave me away. Now I know."

Secretly, I suspected there was more to Charlie's attitude. When she discovered who her birth parents were, she moved back to San Ladrón and established her auto shop. She didn't tell anyone who she was. I think she wanted to observe from afar, to try to understand what had happened all those many years before to make them make the decision they did. When she learned they were involved in more of a civil war than a relationship, I think she saw some of herself in both of them: the stubbornness and the desire to fight for what they wanted. She might have left town when she learned the true nature of their relationship, but I don't think she expected to find a brother in Vaughn.

"If I talk about her like she's a person in this town that you live in, can you handle that? Because it pertains to Genevieve."

"Shoot."

I shoved my fingertips into the front pockets of my jeans and kicked the heel of one penny loafer against the toe of the other. "Apparently Genevieve asked Adelaide's advice about running Tea Totalers and Adelaide let her in on a secret. She orders the Waverly House pastries from a supplier in Los Angeles. Including the croissants."

"So Frenchy doesn't make the croissants. That's good news, right?"

"Yes. Adelaide is meeting with Sheriff Clark today to let him know. That should explain at least one piece of evidence against Genevieve."

"You have something else up your sleeve, don't you?"

I pulled the colorful floral fringed scarf out of my messenger bag and swung it around in a circle. "It just so happens Phil took Babs to the Waverly House last week and Babs dropped this."

"So why do you have it?"

I opened my eyes wide. "I'm new in San Ladrón. When I found out that one of our local celebrities was missing her shawl, I thought the neighborly thing to do was to deliver it to her."

"Babs agreed to this?"

"I didn't make the arrangements with her. I made them with Adelaide."

I saw a flicker of emotion cross Charlie's face, a flash of vulnerability. I wondered if she really was okay with me building my own relationship with her estranged mother. I wanted to put them in a room together, lock the door, and not let either of them out until they'd figured out how to start over, but I knew this wasn't like a fabric project, where I could match up the edges and trim off any loose threads. It wasn't the kind of thing I could fix. The only thing I could do was respect Charlie's feelings and hope that in time, she'd come around. And if she didn't, I'd have to accept her decision.

"You want some company?"

"Considering the conversation I saw you two having, I'm not sure you'd be an asset." I grinned. "I'm hoping to find out what Phil was into. Clark is so sure Genevieve killed Phil that he's set on 'crime of passion.' But if Gen didn't do it because she was mad at her lying, cheating husband, then the question isn't just who killed him, but why?"

"Are you counting Kim out of the suspects?"

"Not yet. She's certainly had trouble with the law, so it's not out of character. Phil knew about her past. Maybe he was using her, trying to get her to do something illegal, and she flipped. Think about it. The one thing we've established by now is that Phil Girard wasn't exactly a good guy. That's the worst part for Genevieve."

"Why? He was a dirtbag. She's better off without him."

"But she loved him."

"She loved the idea of him."

"No, I think she really loved him."

"Frenchy and I spent some time talking while she was staying here. You know what I learned? They met at a tea convention. He played up his French background and she thought it was a sign. He said they could open the tea shop and he'd quit his job and they'd run it together. But he never quit his job. He started sleeping around. I got the feeling that Babs wasn't the dirtbag's first affair, either."

"And she clearly wasn't his last," I said, the undesired naked-with-a-Chrismas-bow image popping into my head. "If Genevieve knew all of this, why didn't she leave him?"

"Security. Bunch of bull. She gave him security, not the other way around. She runs that store herself." She picked up a pen from the desk and twirled it around in one hand while she spoke. "In one day I saw that she knows more about business than most people around here. She just downplays it because when people come in for a cup of tea, they don't want to talk about growth factors." She threw the pen like a dart against the side of the printer. It bounced off the hard gray plastic and landed on the desk, and then rolled to the edge and fell off.

I bent down and picked it up. "So when this whole mess is cleared up, she goes back to the tea shop and life goes on."

"As long as Old Man McMichael doesn't get his hands on her store."

"What does he have to do with anything?"

"That's the other thing she told me. He's been sniffing around her property. And if she can't pay her quarterly taxes in the next week, he's going to have a darn good chance of buying her out."

Twenty-five

I didn't think Genevieve's problems could get any worse. "If Mr. McMichael buys her store, she'll never be able to get it back from him. He'll sell it off without a second thought if a bigger investor wants that strip of land. We can't let that happen."

I set the pen on the desk gently, hovering my fingers over it until I was sure it wasn't going to roll down the slight slope of the desk again. This was bad—worse than bad. If Mr. McMichael found out that Adelaide was going to move the garden party to Tea Totalers this year, he'd have even more reason to gain possession of the shop. And Genevieve's troubles were bad enough. I wouldn't know how to break it to her that she might have to choose between bail and taxes. I thought about Topo di Sali's offer to buy out Genevieve's recipe. Just days ago I thought she'd never do such a thing. Now there was a chance the Italian Scallion held her only lifeline.

Unless he'd been the one to set this chain of events into motion?

A sick feeling twisted into a knot in the pit of my stomach, like I'd eaten too many slices of birthday cake. It's too bad Genevieve never learned to read those leaves she uses in the tea. If she had, she might have seen this mess coming. I couldn't let Genevieve's situation become another battle between Adelaide and Vic. I needed to contact someone who was good with money, someone who had no ties to the situation at hand. I knew who that person was a solid ten minutes before I gave in to the fact that I had to make the call.

The things you do for friends.

"I'm going to talk to Genevieve later today," I said. "Hopefully Clark will let her go after Adelaide talks to him, but I think it's still a good idea if she stays here. Whoever killed Phil is still out there, and she might be in danger."

"Why are you rushing off?"

"I have to make a phone call." I cut my eyes to the floor.

"You're not going to do something stupid, are you?" Charlie asked.

I avoided the question. "I'd rather not waste time defining stupid. There's a lot to do at the tea shop. I better get going."

I let myself out the front door of the auto shop and walked to the visitor center on the corner. I found a bench a few feet away from the road and sat down. This wasn't going to be easy.

I cued up my contacts and flipped to the Cs. Before I had a chance to regret it, I called my ex.

"Carson Cole's office," said a polite female voice.

"This is Poly Monroe. Could I speak to Carson?"

"Are you one of Mr. Cole's clients?"

"Yes," I answered without a moment's hesitation. Since when was he going by "Mr. Cole"?

She put me on hold for a few seconds, and then the call clicked back on. "Carson Cole," said a familiar voice.

"It's Poly."

"That's what my secretary said, but I didn't believe her." He paused. "She told me you said you were one of my clients."

"You've given me financial advice and I've taken it. I figure that constitutes *client*."

"Is that what you're calling about? You need financial advice? Wait a minute. Have you lost all of your money in that stupid store already?"

Sometimes it takes only a few minutes to remember why we made certain decisions.

"This has more to do with you than me. A friend of mine owns a café here. She's been dealing with some personal business and it's caused her to close temporarily. From what I understand, her quarterly taxes are due and if she doesn't make the payment she might lose the place. Is that how these things work?"

"Something like that. If it's a tax issue, there's nothing I can do."

"Well, technically, you could loan her the money, right? As an investment. With a really, really, really low interest rate as a favor to me?"

"Poly, you broke up with me and moved to another city. I can't think of a single reason why I would want to do you a favor."

"Okay, forget the favor. How about this? Right now, if she defaults on her taxes, Mr. McMichael is going to buy the property. If you loan her the money and she can't pay it back, the property goes to you, and you'd be in a position to negotiate with him. He's the big leagues, Carson."

"You're giving me a chance to go head-to-head with McVic?" He was silent for a moment. "Why didn't you go to his son? You're friends with him, right?"

Why hadn't I gone to Vaughn? He *was* the first person who came to mind. Only, I didn't want him to think I was using him for his money or that I was taking advantage of him in any way. And I didn't want to put him in an awkward position with his father. I didn't need Carson to know any of that.

"I have my reasons."

"What's the name of this café?" he asked.

I told him the name and address of Tea Totalers. It was probably just a matter of time until Carson figured out the nature of the personal business that was keeping Genevieve from running the shop, but he was going to have to do that legwork without me.

After exchanging a few more details, we hung up. I was confident he would look into the property purely for selfish reasons. I put my phone in my handbag and went back to the fabric store to pick up the panels of voile so I could finish the curtains. I carried several plastic hangers with fabric draped over them like a wedding shop employee would carry an expensive gown: hangers in my left hand held up over my head, fabric draped over my right forearm. If you took away the fabric, my stance was like the Statue of Liberty. I carried the panels to my car, took great care setting them in the backseat without letting them touch the gravel or the floor mats, and drove to the tea shop. I dropped them off inside, and then locked the shop up and headed back out to my car. Time to pay Babs Green a visit.

It was the tail end of rush hour and traffic was starting to thin out. I could hear "Bohemian Rhapsody" pouring out of one of the cars and the particular energetic musings of a morning talk-radio host from another. I made the mistake of exiting on San Ladrón Avenue, which meant I had to cut across two lanes of traffic and either make an illegal U-turn or turn left and circle around in one of the small residential lots on a side street.

I turned right instead of left, so I could get out of traffic. I drove past the Waverly House and the sheriff's mobile unit and turned right at the next road. I found myself on a two-lane street with a stop sign at every corner.

Even with the stop signs, I made better time than if I'd been stuck in the traffic on one of the main streets. I'd spent so much time driving up and down Bonita that I hadn't explored the rest of the neighborhood yet. I took note of the smaller cottages on either side of me. A few had signs out front advertising businesses that people ran from their residences, like Sam Girard. Tailor, seamstress, accountant, notary public.

Sooner than expected, I came to a cross street. I turned right, then left at the light, and cruised two miles until I reached Babs's apartment building. I pulled the scarf out of my messenger bag and smoothed my hands over the wrinkles a few times, my efforts wasted. The scarf was more wrinkled than the panels of voile I'd left in the washing machine last night.

The architecture of Babs's building was Spanish. A terracotta roof extended over a tawny stucco exterior. Thick vines of ivy hung from above the roof and swung lazily in the breeze. The door was framed by concrete-colored bricks that followed the entrance and met in the middle, kissing a keystone that sat at the top of the arch. To the left of the archway, a marigold tile set in mortar displayed the house number.

I passed into the courtyard and scaled a staircase of glossy Spanish tile to the second floor. Only one door had a number on it: four. I clapped the brass knocker twice. When the door went unanswered, I rapped knuckles against it. Was today like last Monday, when Babs was still sleeping off an alcohol binge from the night before?

I peered inside the window to my right. The front door opened and Babs leaned out of the doorway. She looked the opposite direction, toward the stairs, to see who had come knocking on her door.

She wore a sheer duster over a long satin nightgown that ended above delicate feet with a perfect fire-engine-red pedicure. Marabou trimmed the collar and sleeves of her duster. Aunt Millie had left a similar one hanging in the closet at the apartment. Babs's thick red hair was tousled, parted on the side, and falling over one eye. She held a Bloody Mary with a stalk of celery in it. Ice clinked in the glass as she turned away from the stairs and spotted me standing by her windows.

"What do you want?" she said.

It was a fair question.

I held out her scarf. "You left this at the Waverly House when you were there with Phil Girard," I said.

"And let me guess. You've been appointed the head of the lost-and-found department and you're an overachiever." She reached out and took the scarf from me.

"I'm Poly Monroe. I'm friends with Genevieve Girard, and I know you were having an affair with her husband before he was murdered."

She made a show of looking at the back of her wrist as though checking a watch that wasn't there. "It's a little early for blackmail, don't you think? Besides, Phil's dead. I hardly think our relations matter much anymore." She pulled the celery stalk out of her glass and took a long drink.

"Can we talk?" I asked, stepping forward.

"No." She stepped backward and shut the door in my face.

That hadn't gone well.

I hadn't traveled out here not to get information. I raised my hand and knocked on her front door again. "Ms. Green, it's important. Please." I waited about thirty seconds, and then turned away from the front door and returned to the windows. They were pushed up, with only a screen in place. Currents of air circled around the small second-floor landing, pushing her pink sheers inside for a moment. I pressed my face up against the screen and scanned the room. A secondhand sofa, a cart topped with full bottles of booze, and a coffee table covered in magazines filled the left-hand side of the room. On the right, a shiny baby grand piano sat unattended. I heard the refrigerator door open, a can pop open, and the sound of something being poured. Seconds later there was a thud, followed by the sound of glass breaking.

"Ms. Green? Are you okay?" I called through the window.

She cursed. "Can you come in here and help me? I'm surrounded by glass."

I entered her apartment and passed a row of open garbage bags before passing through her living room, and then into her kitchen. She sat on the floor surrounded by the tipped contents of a cobalt-blue recycle bin. She held one hand to her head and the other out front.

"What happened?"

"I tripped over the recycle bin and hit my head on the counter," she said.

I scanned the mess of tomato juice cans and glass water bottles that had spilled from her recycle bin. At least one of the bottles had broken, and the shiny green shards of a Perrier bottle covered the floor around her. Blood dripped from her hand. I helped her to her feet, turned on the cold water, and held her palm under the spigot.

"Do you think there's any glass in your hand?"

"No. I cut myself on one of the broken pieces on the floor."

I looked behind me and retrieved a pair of fur-trimmed slippers from under the piano. "Put these on," I said, and handed them to her. Once she was shod, she reached for a broom and dustpan from next to her refrigerator and swept the mess into a corner. As she emptied it into a plastic shopping bag and knotted the top, I scooped a handful of ice from her otherwise empty freezer, wrapped the ice in a white dish towel, and held it out to her. She traded me the ice for the bag of broken glass. She pressed the ice against the lump on her forehead and I carried the bag of broken glass to the other bags of trash in the hallway. When I turned back, I watched her pour a can of tomato juice into a tall glass.

"I'm sorry about the mess. I haven't had the energy to take

the trash out all week," she said. She bent over and scooped several cans and bottles back into the recycle bin and then rinsed her hands under the water again. Her eyes were blood-shot and her nose was red. "You really want to talk about Phil? Maybe I need to talk about him." She turned away and I followed after her flowing marabou duster. "Have a seat." She gestured toward the worn sofa.

I sat on the end, resting on the front half of the cushion. She waited until I stopped fidgeting to ask again what I was doing there.

"I'm Poly Monroe. I'm new to San Ladrón—"

"Polyester. You're the one who inherited the fabric store on Bonita," she said.

"Yes, that's me."

"Why are you here? To judge me? To vilify me for being the other woman? I'm sure that's what most of San Ladrón is saying. At least I'm sure the women are."

I considered how best to proceed. Truth was, I hated that she'd been helping Phil to cheat on Genevieve, but I knew it took two people to cheat. I also knew I was there to try to learn something. "Ms. Green, Phil was picking up fabric for me from Los Angeles the morning he was murdered. I'm trying to understand how this happened, so I guess that means I'm trying to understand what he might have been involved in."

"I thought he was getting supplies for his wife's tea shop?"

"He was. We both had things that had to be picked up from the city."

She tucked her chin for a moment and ran her fingers over her eyes. When she looked back up at me, a fresh tear trickled down her cheek. She let it ride the contours of her face until it dripped from her chin and landed on her sheer robe, leaving a dark wet spot on the silk.

"No one will ever believe this, but I loved Phil. I knew he was married and I knew he would never leave his wife. I didn't want him to. But he was a kind man who understood me. He accepted my act, my public persona, but he saw who I really was and he treated me like a lady . . . at least until Sunday."

My mind flashed to the garter belt Charlie had found in Phil's car. "What happened on Sunday?"

Her hand quivered as she took another sip of her drink. "He told me he reserved a room in Los Angeles. I reminded him that I had two shows booked Sunday night. I thought— hoped—that he'd wait until after my shows and we could drive to Los Angeles together, but he didn't come to the theater that night. When I called him, he told me he'd made other arrangements, that he'd met someone else. I couldn't believe it. The mistress—the exciting exotic-dancing mistress—gets cheated on with another woman." She downed what was left of her drink.

"Do you know why someone becomes the other woman, Poly?" I shook my head. "Because sometimes you take what you can get. And now I'm back to being alone. No companionship, no affection. The only things I wanted." Her hand shook as she held her glass to her lips for another sip.

"Is it true that you had someone from the theater drive you home Sunday night?"

"How do you know that?"

"I overheard some people at the Villamere talking."

She waved her glass. "To be honest, I don't remember much of Sunday. I'm afraid after I spoke to Phil, I found the companionship I sought in a bottle of champagne. I started drinking before my first show. My second show is a blur. I woke up here the next morning with my sleeping pills open on the nightstand. I must have taken some. There was a pot of coffee brewing and a blanket and pillows were on my sofa. My manager tells me one of the ushers drove me home, but he wasn't here when I woke up." Her voice shook as she talked, but instead of dropping her face into her hands, she raised her head like a queen and held herself proudly. I was surprised to feel her strength, that of a woman who has fought to make a reputation for herself, and now spends her time balanced between living up to that reputation and living it down. She set the empty glass on top of a straw coaster on the table and looked directly at me. "I should have crawled back into bed and slept it off."

"Why didn't you?"

"I don't like leaving my car in public parking lots. It's recognizable. People see it around town and they start rumors. I took a cab to the theater, but the manager wouldn't let me drive home until we'd had our weekly meeting."

"How did you find out about Phil?"

"The same way everybody else did. On the local news."

I thought about the morning I'd seen Babs at Charlie's Automotive. She'd been angry at Charlie for blackmailing Phil to keep quiet about their affair. Charlie hadn't known about Phil's murder. It made sense that Babs hadn't, either.

She dabbed at her eyes. "I know you're friends with his wife. I know you're prepared to hate me because I was the other woman. I'd like to thank you for giving me a chance to talk about him. It feels good to acknowledge my feelings out loud." She stood. "But now I really must ask you to leave. I have some business to attend to, and contrary to what people must say about me, I don't always conduct business in my negligee."

I stood, too. "Thank you for talking to me. I'll let myself out."

I walked to the front door, scanning the row of trash bags as I went. The only way one woman could amass that much trash was to let it accumulate. According to what I knew about her performance and subsequent meltdown, she must have been at the tail end of sobering up when she showed up at Charlie's Automotive.

I hadn't expected to hear Babs tell me she loved Phil. From what I'd witnessed at Charlie's, and what I'd heard about her from Adelaide and the usher at the Villamere, I'd expected to find a cold, calculating broad who had little regard for the marriage she was destroying. Instead, I'd found her to be just like every other woman I'd ever known with a broken heart. Had she become a recluse after hearing the news, returning to her home, shutting out the world, and grieving over her lover's death because she knew nobody else would acknowledge her feelings for him? Or was there something she was hiding that I still hadn't discovered?

Twenty-six

I drove back to Tea Totalers. The voile panels were where I'd left them, hanging from the curtain rod above the doorway between the kitchen and the front of the store. I checked around the interior and exterior for signs that Kim had come back after our argument yesterday. There were none.

While I was concerned over Genevieve's situation, I knew that taking care of her tea shop was as important as finding her husband's killer. If the shop folded while she was under suspicion, she'd have nothing to return to when this was over. I was down one helper and there was much work to be done. Not to mention the upcoming opening of Material Girl.

I didn't want to admit to anyone else that maybe there was a reason I was spending all of my time volunteering to help other people instead of focusing on my own needs. I was afraid that the store wouldn't succeed. I had watched the people around me make decisions that affected other people: Kim's impulse to fake an insurance policy because Genevieve was helping her get past her DUI conviction and Vaughn's father interfering with Adelaide's annual Waverly House event, putting their son squarely in the middle of their tug-of-war. I'd watched Genevieve get taken away to the police station because she was the likeliest candidate for her husband's murder, and I'd watched another woman mourn the loss of the same man. It wasn't fair and it wasn't right, but it was life. I would always want to help other people. That was in my nature. But I could help them more if my own life had purpose.

I tore the butcher paper down from one of the windows, careful to remove all of the masking tape that had secured the paper to the glass. I ran my hands over the voile, feeling the rough texture of the fleurs-de-lis woven into the texture between my fingertips. It was such an iconic French symbol, perfect for Genevieve's French interior. After removing the curtain rods from the windows, I tied ribbon bows around the wooden pole and rehung them. I replaced the curtains I'd made earlier in the week from the toile and tied them back with swags of Provençal.

The fabrics changed the interior of the tea shop. By the time I'd finished hanging all of the panels, I felt like I was in another country. The renovation spoke volumes about what could be accomplished by using fabric to change the appearance of a room, and in that moment, I knew if I could communicate that single message to the residents of San Ladrón, my store would be successful.

There was a knock on the front door of the shop. I pushed the curtains aside. Vaughn stood out front. I opened the door and he poked his head in. He was wearing a navy blue suit over a white shirt and paisley tie. His pants were narrow, ending in cuffs above cognac wingtips.

"You've been busy," he said, scanning the interior. "Genevieve's going to love it."

"That's what I'm hoping." I stepped back and held the door open wider. "Are you here to work?"

"Not today. I have to take care of some business. If all goes as planned, I might have good news tonight. I know this is last-minute, but are you available for a celebratory dinner?"

"I can't celebrate as long as I know Genevieve is in jail."

"My business has to do with her, too."

"You found something? You know something?"

He held up a hand. "I can't say anything yet." He leaned down and kissed me lightly on the cheek.

"What was that for?" I asked, surprised.

"I heard what you suggested to my mother. It's like you gave her a B-12 shot. She's full of energy and ideas and she's already contacted the media."

"She deserves to have her party and Genevieve deserves to show off Tea Totalers."

"And you deserve for people to know what your fabric store can do for them with the materials inside."

"It's not too self-serving, is it?"

"Are you kidding? It's a perfect solution and nobody would have thought of it if you hadn't suggested it first."

Embarrassed, I turned away from him and went inside. He followed and left the door open behind him. "Maybe I should have you come to my new apartment. I never even thought about using fabric in the interior. I've been absorbed in refinishing the molding and hardwiring the sconces."

"You can't ignore the fabric," I said. "All the molding and ambient lighting in the world can't provide the softness and texture of fabric."

He ran his hand over the toile curtain, holding the panel open so he could see the countryside scene depicted in the print. "Fabric always seemed so feminine."

"It doesn't have to be. Fabric is as personal as art. What one person responds to, another person doesn't even notice. It helps define people and can be used to create mystery."

"Like how?" he asked. He let the curtain fall from his fingers and turned to me.

"Here's an example. When people think about black leather, they think biker, right? But put black leather on a sofa, and it becomes modern. Change the color to cordovan, hunter green, or cognac, and you get a men's-club vibe. If you want to be unconventional, instead of a black leather sofa, maybe you go with black leather curtains—and there's the mystery. In a curtain, the toughness of the leather is countered by the volume of fabric needed to create the proper drape. It would naturally soften the appearance, but you'd have to compensate for the heaviness of the black leather in the rest of the room with lighting, maybe a tufted chenille sofa, lots of throw pillows, fresh flowers."

"Black leather curtains?" Vaughn said. There was an implied question in his tone. "Is that what you'd suggest for me?"

I tipped my head to the side and studied him. "I don't know what I'd suggest for you. I'd have to see this place you're fixing up and know what you were going for."

"As soon as I get the circular saw out of the living room, you'll have a standing invitation."

I turned away from Vaughn and looked at Jitterbug across the street. A black pickup truck pulled into a parking space facing me. Bingo! Rick Penwald got out of the cab and went inside.

"I need another cup of coffee," I said. "Can you watch the store for a couple of minutes?"

He looked at his watch. "If you lock up, I'll join you."

"No, I'd rather you stay here." I took a few steps away from him. "Look around. Tell me if you think I forgot anything." Before he had a chance to question my behavior, I was out the door and jogging through traffic.

I caught Rick inside the brightly colored shop. He was at the coffee and creamer station, pouring sugar into an otherwise dark-as-black beverage with one hand, stirring it with the other. He didn't see me coming, and judging from the look on his face when he recognized me next to him, he wasn't happy to see me.

"I need to ask you a couple more questions about Phil Girard," I said.

He pulled the stirrer out of the coffee, ran it through his lips, and tossed it into the trash. "I don't have to tell you anything." He turned and left. I followed behind and caught up with him by his truck.

"Your story has more holes than a bolt of netting. I know you didn't tell me everything the other day."

Rick opened the driver's-side door and set his coffee in one of the cup holders. He slammed the door and turned to me, pointing a finger in my face much like that hammer man from Western Extermination that Charlie had mentioned a few days ago.

"You need to mind your own business," he said.

I stood to my full height and looked him square in the eye. "I'm sure Sheriff Clark would like to know that your business doesn't even exist anymore. I called information and they said Special Delivery was a fly-by-night operation."

He stared up at the sun and squinted his eyes. I waited for his next move. We were in a public parking lot with plenty of people around us. He wasn't going to get away without telling me something. Rick took a deep breath and blew it out of his mouth. His breath was bitter from the coffee.

"Delivery jobs were few and far between before they all but dried up. I didn't need the expenses of maintaining the business, so I let everything lapse: phone, fax, office. I took jobs that paid cash, and when I did find work, I bought the magnetic sign and borrowed vehicles from friends. I used up the invoices I had left. When they ran out I bought generic ones from the office supply store and stickered my logo on them. I made ends meet."

"What happened on Sunday?"

"Like I told you, I was at a poker game. Drank too much, lost a lot of money. Crashed on a friend's sofa. Phil's call woke me up. He asked me to come to LA, get the van, and make the delivery here. He said he had something big cooking that he didn't want to blow."

"How'd you get your car back?"

"I got a ride into LA from a buddy of mine. He dropped me off, I got a cup of coffee, and I drove the van back."

"Does Sheriff Clark know all this? Has he questioned you? Because I can't see him taking your friend's word on all of this."

"He knows everything I just told you," Rick said with a smile not unlike the Cheshire cat's. "Sheriff Clark was the buddy."

Twenty-seven

Gone was the angry truck driver who seemed to be avoiding me, and in his place was either a regular guy who had been in the wrong place at the wrong time and just wanted to get on with his life, or a very wily man who had set things up so he was untouchable.

"Why didn't you tell me that from the beginning?"

"It's none of your business."

"But you or Sheriff Clark could have told me—"

"Like I said, Phil was a friend of mine. He helped me out. I don't want to believe his pretty little wife killed him any more than you do, but it seems as though that's what happened."

There wasn't much I could say to Rick to prove he was wrong. I had nothing other than my blind faith in Genevieve, and even though mountains of evidence pointed in her direction, I still knew she wasn't a murderer. I said good-bye to Rick and stood away from his truck as he backed out of the space and drove away.

Something wasn't adding up. I waited by the crosswalk for the light to change and strolled absentmindedly across the street when it did. When I got back to the shop, Vaughn was gone. Both the front door and back door were locked. I checked the Dracaena plant for the keys, but they weren't there. I wasn't surprised that Vaughn had left, and considering there was a killer out there framing Genevieve for the murder of her husband, I appreciated that he'd locked up before he had. Still, it put a damper on my work for the rest of the day.

I drove back to Material Girl. Boxes were stacked by the back door: more inventory. I dragged everything inside and pushed it up against the wrap stand to be dealt with later, then locked back up behind me and headed out to Charlie's. As I approached her shop, I saw Sheriff Clark talking to her in her office.

I pressed my back against the front exterior wall like a cat burglar in a comic strip and tipped my head to the side, straining to pick up pieces of their conversation.

"You're sure? Tonight?" he asked.

"I'm sure. This whole thing with Frenchy has been keeping her busy."

"Speaking of which, thanks for your help with that."

"Don't mention it."

I peeked into the window. Charlie crossed her arms over her chest.

"I mean it. I don't want word to get out about what I did. I have a hard enough time in this town."

I hadn't wanted to believe that Charlie was selling out our friend, but judging from what I heard, Charlie and Clark weren't at odds with each other. Her betrayal stung like an unexpected shock of electricity. I stormed into the auto shop and went directly to the office just as the sheriff reached up and swept Charlie's thick black hair off her shoulder.

"Just what the heck is going on here?" I demanded.

Charlie and Sheriff Clark looked horrified. I turned my

attention to Charlie. "I can't believe you. All along you've been feeding him information? When you said you were trying to expand your social circle and that I was a good influence on you, was that all crap?"

She turned to Sheriff Clark. "Later, Ryan. This is going to take some time."

Ryan? I looked around for a third person. Clark walked past me. "Ms. Monroe," he said, nodding his greeting. I followed him.

"Sheriff Clark, why didn't you tell me you were Rick Penwald's alibi?" I said to his back.

He stopped and turned around slowly. Behind me, I heard Charlie come out of her office.

"What did you say?" she asked.

"He's Rick Penwald's alibi. There was a poker game on Sunday night and Rick got drunk and lost a bunch of money. He crashed on Sheriff Clark's sofa. Phil called Rick the next morning and asked him to make the delivery. Guess who gave Rick a ride into Los Angeles so he could drive the van back?"

Charlie looked at Clark with fire in her eyes. Any anger she'd directed toward me shifted to him.

"You jerk," she said. "You should have told me."

"Charlie—"

"Get out. And find another mechanic to rotate your tires."

Clark didn't move right away. The tension between them was so palpable I felt as uncomfortable as if I were naked and wrapped in thick, itchy burlap. After several tense seconds, Clark stormed out of the middle bay. He turned left, the opposite direction of the sheriff's mobile unit, and disappeared from sight.

Charlie cursed. She turned around and punched her fist into a heavy boxer's bag that hung outside of her office. I'd always wondered exactly why it was installed there, and now I knew. She went into the small powder room in the corner and slammed the door.

I didn't care how long Charlie camped out inside her powder room; I wasn't going to leave until I had confirmation of what I suspected. Only, the longer I sat there, waiting for her to come out, my suspicions changed to something even less believable than her backstabbing Genevieve. But I needed to hear her say it. I needed to hear her tell me the truth.

After seventeen minutes, I approached the door to the powder room and rapped my knuckles on the outside. "Charlie, it's Poly. I'm not leaving until you come out here and talk to me."

"I knew there was a reason I installed that exit through the powder room," she said from behind me.

I whirled around. She set a flask of Chianti on the floor and pulled down the doors to each of the bays. The room darkened significantly. She locked the front door and flipped her sign from *Open* to *Closed*, picked up the Chianti, and went into her office. "If you're planning to join me, bring a couple of glasses from the cabinet next to Eddie."

Along the back of the auto shop was a large metal file cabinet. Hanging on the wall next to it was a poster of Eddie Van Halen. I opened the panels on the top of the cabinet, pulled out two glasses, and slid the panel shut. I carried them to the office and held them in one hand, resting against the door frame, staring at her.

"It's not what you think," she said.

"You and Clark are a couple? For real?"

"Okay, it *is* what you think. Give me one of those glasses."

I extended the glasses and she took them both and filled each about halfway. I sipped at one. She poured hers down her throat and refilled her glass.

"How long have you known?" she asked.

"About ten minutes."

"That long, huh?"

"It explains why Genevieve asked you to do something when Clark took her away. She must have figured it out. How long has this been going on?"

She shook her head. "About a month, I guess. He had a dead battery and I gave him a jump. One thing led to another. When Frenchy's thing happened, I thought I could run interference. Keep him distracted so you could find the real killer."

"That's why you kept saying to leave Clark to you."

She nodded. "I even asked him about Rick. No, you know what I did? I told him when you found out Rick's business wasn't real. I helped the bastard. He made a fool out of me, and I don't like looking like a fool." She slammed her glass down on the desk.

"Nobody likes looking like a fool, but Genevieve's situation is a little more dire than that."

"Are you any closer to finding out who murdered the cheater?"

"Right now I'd settle for finding out *why* someone murdered the cheater. Every single thing I find points to Genevieve."

"My money's on this Rick dude."

"I told you, the sheriff is his alibi."

"For what? Clark gave him a ride to the city and took off. Nobody knows what happened next."

"Charlie, you're involved with him. Do you really think he'd cover up for a potential murderer?"

She twisted in her chair and hung one leg over the arm. "No. He wouldn't. I'm looking for a reason to be even more mad at him than I already am, but that's not one."

"I think it's totally fine for you to be mad at him. In fact, I encourage it. He's after Genevieve, and she didn't do this."

"Okay, so what do we got?" she said, sounding like a female Kojak.

"Rick says Phil called him early Monday morning and asked him to come to LA to pick up the van. If that's true, then Phil was alive early Monday morning. Clark dropped Rick off and left. Rick found the keys in the ignition, money on the driver's seat. He bought a cup of coffee and drove back, and that's when I found Phil. Genevieve's produce was in the van, and the fabric was on top of Phil."

"What doesn't make sense is why he'd have the wrong fabric," she said.

"That could have been a mistake. Phil's body was under that velvet. And there were a couple of crates of produce in there, too. And the jug of tea. All of that suggests that something happened after he picked everything up but before Rick got behind the wheel of the truck to make the delivery. So, let's see. Phil packed the truck. Phil called Rick and asked him to make the delivery. And then what? Rick said Phil claimed he was on to something big in Los Angeles."

"You're sure it wasn't a woman?" Charlie asked.

"Both Babs and Genevieve said something that makes it sound like it was, but Phil was no Prince Charming. I'm not even sure how he got two women, let alone three." I chewed my lower lip and looked at the black-and-white cat clock on the wall of Charlie's office. The eyes of the cat moved from side to side, marking off the passing seconds.

"So whatever happened to Phil happened between him calling Rick and Rick showing up," Charlie said.

"It's like someone heard him call Rick. If somebody was watching Phil they would have heard him make those arrangements. It would be perfect timing for a murderer. Murder him and put him in the van. You already know someone's going to show up in forty-five minutes to courier the body to another town."

"I'd say it was genius, except it seems a little spontaneous. If Phil hadn't made that phone call, then the opportunity never would have presented itself."

"You're right," I said, dejected. "The other thing that bothers me is Rick. Why did he care so much about getting my signature on the paperwork? He acted totally normal. If you knew you were delivering a dead man with your cargo, would you act totally normal?"

"I like to think I don't know the answer to that question, not being a murderer and all," Charlie said.

I ignored her sarcasm. "We're still missing something. I just don't know what."

I said good-bye to Charlie and went out front. Across the street, a long truck with a wooden flatbed was parked in front of Material Girl. Two ladders were propped against the front of the store and men in hard hats stood on each ladder.

"Hey!" I called, jogging through the traffic like Frogger. A man stood by the truck, a hand keeping his yellow hard hat on his head, staring up at the men on ladders. He jumped when I put my hand on his arm, and his hard hat tipped to the side.

"You never called me back. What are you doing?" I asked.

"It's your lucky day. We finished our last job early. I had the permits for your job in the truck, so here we are. Should be done in about forty-five minutes."

"By 'done,' what do you mean?"

"All traces of the old sign down, new sign up and wired. Done."

"So I'll actually have a sign by the time I open on Sunday?"

"That's what you wanted, right? Don't you think you're cutting it a little close?" he said with a wink.

"Don't even go there."

I walked around the block and let myself in through the back door so as to avoid interrupting the hard-hatted men out front. I couldn't blame the interrupted schedule, or the rain, or the murder for not opening on time. This was it. Even if it was all coming down to the wire, it would be ready. I'd open on schedule, and I'd cross all of my fingers and toes that customers would show up.

The sound of the power saws cutting the remaining exposed bolts away from the façade of the store was uncomfortably loud. I put my earbuds in and cued up some Ike and Tina Turner. I grabbed one of the bolts of velvet still wrapped in plastic and dragged it across the floor to the wrap stand.

I cut the plastic open and lifted the velvet out of the wrapper. When I turned around, the foreman was standing by my back door. His lips moved but I couldn't hear him. I pulled the earbuds out and let them dangle around my neck.

"We're all done out front. You wanna come see?"

"Give me a minute to move the rest of this fabric." I went back to the stack and strained with the weight of another roll while moving it to the wrap stand.

"Jeez, lady, take it easy. You're going to throw out your back if you keep that up. You gotta lift with your knees, like this," he said. He crossed the store, wrapped his arms around the navy velvet, and hoisted it up. He stumbled forward a few steps, and then tripped over the bottom of it. The bolt fell out of his arms and landed on the floor. "Heavier than I expected."

He kept talking, but I didn't hear anything he said. I was too focused on the small, plastic-wrapped package that had fallen loose from inside the tube of velvet and rested on the exposed concrete floor.

Twenty-eight

I picked the small bundle off of the floor. It was in the form of a tube, as if it had molded to the interior of the cardboard where it had been stuffed. I set the package on the wrap stand and squatted down on the floor by the end of the fabric roll. There were more packages shoved inside.

"This must be what we're looking for," I said.

"What's that? Hash?" the foreman asked.

"I don't know. Is this what hash looks like?"

His expression morphed from curiosity to concern. "I don't know what you're involved in, lady, but I'm not sticking around to find out." He backed away from me a few steps, his eyes trained on the drugs. A few steps back he spun around and went out the front door. "Yo, pack it up. Job's over." He glanced over his shoulder at me. "Let's get out of here."

I grabbed my phone, ignored an incoming call from Carson, and hit Charlie's name.

"Remember how we thought Phil made a mistake when he picked up the wrong fabric?"

"Yes. Why?"

"I don't think it was a mistake. Get over here as soon as possible. Like, five minutes ago." I hung up.

I squatted by the end of the bolt of fabric and looked inside what should have been the hollow core. The cardboard tube had an opening of about three inches in diameter. I pushed my hand inside and reached as far as I could, made contact with an obstruction, and jimmied it until it was loose enough to remove. It was just like the first, a carefully wrapped and secured clear plastic package of something I was willing to bet wasn't legal.

I gave Charlie credit for how quickly she showed up. I was in the process of wrangling more bolts of fabric to the wrap stand when she came through the front door. "Drugs. In the velvet. Help me," I said between breaths.

She followed me to the back of the store. We struggled with the additional rolls, bringing them to the register one by one like a pair of lumberjacks carrying fallen tree trunks. Conversation ceased until we were done.

I scooted into the back room and grabbed two wooden yardsticks from a shelf. They were old, from the days when the fabric store had been thriving, and were printed with the original name: Land of a Thousand Fabrics. I didn't remember the last time I needed a yardstick while working for Giovanni, but I remember seeing them by each sewer's station, as if the ladies relied on their presence in case of a straight-edge emergency. I loved the nostalgic feeling of them and planned to use them as a promotional item when the store opened.

When I got back out front, Charlie was sniffing one of the small tube-shaped packages. I peeked inside the center core of the vibrant red velvet. Seeing nothing but darkness,

I reached my fingers in. I pulled out two more plastic packages from each end, and then used the yardsticks to poke at the center until I freed something and it fell out the other side. Charlie's hands were bigger than mine, so she left the task of emptying the tubes to me while she lined up our findings on the edge of the wrap stand. When we were finished, we had a large stack of bundles.

"What do you think they are?" she asked.

"I think they're somebody's motive."

"Do you think he knew they were in there? Do you think he double-crossed somebody?"

"Phil Girard wasn't smart enough to double-cross somebody. The man wasn't even smart enough to hide a garter belt from his wife," I said. I picked up a round package. It weighed about the same as the rubber-coated barbells I used when I worked out. "About five pounds each. And there were five packages in each roll of velvet—twelve rolls of velvet, so that's sixty packages. Times five pounds each, that's three hundred pounds of something. Add that to the weight of a roll of velvet and no wonder we're so out of breath."

"I think this kind of stuff is sold by the gram. Or the kilo. What should we do with it?"

"You know exactly what we have to do with it. We have to call Sheriff Clark."

Charlie followed me up the stairs to the apartment and flopped on the sofa while I made the call. I didn't waste time on details. I told the sheriff that I had discovered something that related to Phil Girard's murder and to come to the fabric store immediately.

After I hung up, I turned to Charlie. "We probably shouldn't mention Genevieve when Clark comes over. I'll give him the drugs and tell him how I found them. If he doesn't believe me, he can ask the foreman. He can't deny that Phil was involved in something that had nothing to do with Genevieve or the tea shop. At least this takes the heat off of her."

Sheriff Clark arrived quickly. I raced down the stairs in my argyle socks. Charlie followed slowly behind me.

"I better not find out this is a ploy to divert my investigation from Mrs. Girard," Sheriff Clark said.

"No ploy," I answered. "Come see for yourself." I led the sheriff to the wrap stand, where the sixty bricks were stacked. His eyes widened.

"Where did this come from?" he asked. He used the end of a pencil to poke at the plastic packages on the table. Charlie's arms were crossed over her chest.

"Inside the velvet." I pointed to the rolls propped along the side of the store. "This is the fabric Phil Girard was supposed to pick up, not the stuff at your station."

He picked up a plastic bundle and sniffed it like Charlie had done.

"From what I've figured, someone packed these drugs into my velvet and expected Phil to bring them to San Ladrón. He brought the wrong fabric—I don't know why—and he was killed because of it. Charlie thinks—"

Clark held up his hand to silence me. He pulled on a pair of white rubber gloves and stacked the plastic-wrapped packages into a brown paper shopping bag from the local market.

"Where'd this plastic come from?" he asked, pointing the eraser end of his pencil at the sliced-open plastic bag carcasses that littered the floor. They looked like oversized locust shells in a horror movie.

"The velvet was wrapped in plastic. I was about to throw it out."

"Don't."

Sheriff Clark went outside and said something in the radio that was attached to his dashboard. Minutes later, a dusty beige sedan and a white van pulled into the alley. The sedan parked next to my Volkswagen, and the van stopped in the middle of the lot.

I didn't recognize either of the men who arrived. Clark gave them instructions. They walked past Charlie and me and went inside the store. Charlie kept her arms crossed. I looked back and forth between the sheriff and her, expecting to see something that spoke of this secret relationship between them. Aside from the tension, there was nothing.

I watched as the plastic, the packages of drugs, and my new rolls of velvet were carried out of the store. After several trips, Clark and one of the men closed up the doors on the back of the van. The third man hopped inside, backed the van up, then pulled forward in a large arc and drove out of the lot to the alley.

"You can't possibly think Genevieve had something to do with this, can you?" I asked Clark. "She grows her own tea leaves and orders cases of Dijon mustard over the Internet. She probably wanted fresh vegetables and spices that are unique to French cooking. I'm pretty sure the one thing that wasn't on her shopping list was whatever that was. What was it?"

"Ms. Monroe, Ms. . . ." His voice trailed off as he looked at Charlie. I imagined that he hadn't put much thought into calling her by her surname during their time together.

"Charlie. The name is Charlie. Don't even *think* about using my last name." She stormed away from us. I heard her motorcycle boots clomp across the floor, and then I heard the front door open and shut.

"She'll come around," I said. "She needs time." Clark looked surprised. "Give me some credit, Sheriff. She's mad at you. You lied to her. She wants nothing more than for you to be wrong about Genevieve."

"My job is to follow the evidence."

"Okay, so how does this evidence factor into your case?"

"Maybe they were in it together. Husband-and-wife team. Maybe he couriers the drugs to San Ladrón and she moves them from her tea shop. She's got all kinds of leaves around there already. Nobody's going to question what's in her kitchen unless she gives them a reason to."

"But don't you see? You want to follow the evidence, but there's almost too much of it. Every single piece of evidence you found points to Genevieve and absolutely none of it indicates drug trafficking. Doesn't that set off any bells? That maybe someone did an almost-too-perfect job of pointing you in the wrong direction?"

"Ms. Monroe, thank you for your cooperation in this matter," he said as if he were reading from a manual. He turned around and left.

I picked up a spool of thread and threw it at the door behind him. I didn't know what Clark would do next, but I expected this new evidence would force him to reassess whatever it was he thought he knew about this case. Genevieve might have been his best suspect mere hours ago, but this new information, coupled with what he'd learned about the life insurance policy from Kim's confession and the croissant information that Adelaide had been planning to give him, would be enough to muddy those very clear evidentiary waters.

That meant Genevieve might very well be free by the end of the day. Free to reopen Tea Totalers. And I'd left it in a partial state of renovation. That was not what I'd wanted to do.

I decoupaged rectangles of fabric to each of the tray bases Vaughn had cut, using the white school glue from the dollar store. I poured an ample amount of glue on top of the fabric so the glue would seep through the weave, and then I used the side of a Popsicle stick to smooth out the bubbles. I left the wood panels to dry in the front window, where the sun beat down on them, and placed a sign on an easel that said, "Items from the fabric makeover at Tea Totalers. Come back on Sunday and find fabrics to inspire a project of your own!"

I found the cloth rooster images and wrapped the first around a damaged canvas that I'd gotten for a few dollars at Flowers in the Attic, stretched the fabric until it was taut, and staple-gunned the edges to the back. I repeated the process for the two additional rooster images in smaller sizes. When I was done, I loaded the canvases and the last of what I'd made for Tea Totalers into my car and drove to the tea shop. I was eager to see if it all came together.

Kim had finished the sanding and repainting of the outside tables and chairs, but I wasn't strong enough to carry iron tables to the front yard. As it was, it took several trips to bring the completed projects inside from my car. I dumped my handbag by the desk and carried everything else to the middle of the café, jumping right into it. I swept the front of the cafe and placed the interior tables and chairs that had been stacked in the kitchen to where Genevieve had kept them. After propping the rooster fabric art on the shelves behind the counter, I added baskets filled with silverware wrapped up in napkins made from scraps of the fabrics I'd used throughout the rest of the interior.

I found a bottle of lavender-scented laundry water among her cleaning products and misted the curtains. The light, fresh scent would fade to a mere hint within a short amount of time and would mingle nicely with the other scents Genevieve produced while baking and brewing her proprietary blend of tea. When I had finished all that I could do, I dug my phone out of my handbag and called Vaughn.

"It's Poly," I said. "I'm at Tea Totalers. Are you in the area? Do you think you can swing by? You had a part in this, and I think you should see it before the rest of the world does."

"I'm hoping to finalize something tonight. One more phone call should do it. You'll stick around?"

"Sure."

While I waited for Vaughn, I snapped pictures of the renovated interior, adjusting the placement of different items—a tweak here, a nudge there. Twenty minutes later I'd arranged baskets of fruit and flowers in a mismatched collection of glass jars and vases. There was a tap on the back door. Vaughn stood on the other side with a fist of wildflowers in one hand and a bottle of champagne in the other. I tossed my phone on the desk and opened the door.

"These are not for you. They're for the tea shop." He handed me the flowers. "This, however, is for you, assuming you're willing to share."

"This does call for a celebration, doesn't it? Or should we wait for Genevieve? Oh, heck, she'll get her good news later today and we can all celebrate again."

"How did you find out about the good news? I thought I was doing a good job keeping it a secret."

"I'm talking about some evidence I found hidden inside the velvet Giovanni delivered to my store. You couldn't possibly know about that."

"Sounds like you've been busy."

I walked to the east-facing window and pushed it up to let fresh air inside. "Earlier today I was working inside the fabric store. I knocked over the velvet that Giovanni delivered and found packages of drugs inside the cardboard tubes. I don't know how it all fits together yet, but like I told Clark, it doesn't fit at all with the rest of the evidence he has against Genevieve. That's enough to make him take a second look at the evidence he does have."

"Drugs? What kind?"

"I'm no expert, but they were small bags of dried-up leaves. The construction lead said it looked like hash. Funny thing is, we probably wouldn't have thought twice about it if they had shown up in a container marked *Tea Leaves*."

"You say it was inside the velvet your boss dropped off?"

"Yep. Phil must have known. He was planning on double-crossing whoever expected him to bring the drugs back to San Ladrón. There were loose zip ties in the truck by his head, and my fabric was bagged and secured with plastic zip ties. He could have hidden the drugs in my velvet, sealed them up, and left them to be picked up later. The fabric he brought here was labeled *100% Polyester*, so he could have played dumb and pretended someone else pulled a bait-and-switch."

"Either way, it seems that Phil was mixed up in some illegal business."

"And because of it, he ended up a dead man."

"We're going to have to stop talking about the murder before I pop this champagne."

"Deal."

Vaughn pulled two champagne flutes from the pockets of his blazer and set them on the table.

"You sure do come prepared," I said.

"Boy Scout motto." He popped the champagne and poured a little into each glass.

"You said you had good news that you were keeping a secret. Are you going to keep me in the dark?"

He handed a flute to me and tapped his against it. "As of tonight, Genevieve doesn't have to worry about her back taxes any longer."

I felt a shiver. "What did you do?"

"I made the payment on her behalf."

"But you can't do that. You can loan her the money and she can make the payment, but if it's a tax thing, you can't do anything about it."

"I didn't realize you knew so much about how it worked. Technically, you're right. Apparently a finance company in Los Angeles approved her for a loan. I paid them off. She's in the clear."

I remembered the missed call from Carson and the shiver turned to a full-on cold sweat.

"But I took care of that for her." I felt like I'd eaten a bad piece of fruit. "I didn't want her to have to owe anybody."

"She doesn't. What do you mean, you took care of this?" He set his flute down.

"I made arrangements with a finance firm in Los Angeles," I said.

"Why didn't you come to me?"

"I didn't want to be another person who came to you for money."

"This wasn't for you. I did it for Genevieve."

"I know."

"I know a lot of people in the banking business. Who's your friend? Maybe I know her."

"She's not a friend. She's not even a she." I braced myself. "It was my ex-boyfriend. I'm sorry I didn't tell you, but I thought I could trust him."

"You thought you could trust him?" Vaughn's face turned red. "Let me tell you about your ex-boyfriend's business methods. *He* called *me*. He said his firm had acquired a loan for a business in San Ladrón and they were willing to sell it to my father. When he said it was for Tea Totalers, I made the arrangements myself. Acquired the loan at the rate he named—which was above the going rate, by the way—and paid it off from my personal account. I can assure you, that's not the way my father would have handled it."

"I asked Carson for a favor. He was the only person I could think of asking—" I put my hands on Vaughn's arm and he shook me off and knocked his champagne flute from the counter to the floor. The glass broke on contact.

"The fact that you didn't think you could ask me says it all, Poly. Apparently, I was wrong about you." He turned around and walked toward the back door.

"That's not fair!" I called after him. "You told me what it was like to have money, how people expected you to foot their bills. You should have known I wouldn't be one of those people."

He stopped in the door frame and turned back around to face me. "You could never be one of those people. You're too darn generous to be one of those people. That's why I wanted to do this—not just for Genevieve, but for you, too. I wanted a chance to show you *my* generosity."

I searched for the right words to say, but none came to my mouth. Vaughn stalked to his car and took off.

Well, now, phooey. That wasn't how I wanted that to go. He said people used him for money. I hadn't. So why did that make me the bad guy?

But I knew the truth. The reason I hadn't asked Vaughn for the money didn't have anything to do with how people treated him. It had to do with me. In my world, money changed the playing field.

I kicked the toe of my penny loafer against the recycle bin and cursed. As much as I didn't want to admit it, I knew it was true. Vaughn's family and mine came from two different worlds. Why couldn't I get over this?

My problem was that I was too transparent. I didn't know how to feel about Vaughn having money. I didn't know how to act around him without seeming like I was taking advantage of him, which was the one thing I didn't want to appear to be doing. It wasn't like I wanted anything from him. He didn't have anything that I craved other than his company. When you took away the money, the family connections, and the trust fund, we got along perfectly. Resentfully, I confronted the real issue. I didn't want people to look at me and think I was with Vaughn because of his money. I didn't want people to see me as that kind of person.

I finished cleaning up inside the café. The bottle of champagne on the counter was mostly full. I sank down onto the floor by the kitchen cabinets and raised the champagne bottle to my lips. Bubbles overflowed the opening and champagne spilled down the front of my shirt and cardigan. I didn't care. I kicked my feet out in front of me and set the bottle down next to my left thigh. The blue plastic recycle bin sat empty inside the back door of the tea shop.

It was exactly where Kim had put it the day she threw away the produce and emptied out the refrigerator. I remember thinking she was trying to hide evidence. If she'd only just told me right from the get-go that Genevieve was doing her a favor by letting her work at Tea Totalers, I would never have suspected her. But she was too busy pretending to be someone she wasn't. The same could be said for Rick, pretending to own his own trucking company with fake papers and a temporary sign on the side of the van. What did these people hope to gain by pretending?

I took another swig of the champagne and then stood up. It was late and there wasn't anything else to do here. I poured what was left in the bottle down the drain, turned off the lights, and carried the bottle to the recycle bin. It was dwarfed by the empty expanse that should have been overflowing with signs of life from a bustling business.

And then I remembered another recycle bin that I'd seen recently. Overflowing with empty water bottles and cans of tomato juice and not much else.

That didn't fit with the story of Babs Green as boozer.

I straightened up and closed my eyes, trying to remember the rest of Babs's apartment. She had cut herself on glass in the kitchen and said she had made a fresh drink, but where was the vodka? Her cocktail cart had been full—I saw that when I looked through the window. Her freezer had been empty—I saw that when I got the ice for her head. She had enough trash lined up inside by the stairs to indicate she hadn't thrown anything out in a week, and she'd said as much. There hadn't been any booze bottles in her recycling bin.

I shook my head to clear my thoughts. Must be the champagne, I thought. So Babs didn't have empty liquor bottles lying around her apartment. So what? That was pretty far from saying she'd killed Phil.

But her alibi was that she'd been drunk, just like she wanted me to believe she was drunk today. She'd carried a Bloody Mary around with her while I was there. Was that for show? When I asked her about her performance the night of Phil's murder, she told me the second half of it was a blur. One of the ushers drove her home and stayed there until she was in bed. She claimed not to remember Sunday night, but the only reason anyone believed that was because she showed up still tipsy at the Villamere on Monday morning.

And the reason she showed up at the Villamere was to get her car.

Her recognizable car.

How many people had believed that Babs was at the Villamere all night because her car was there? And once people learned that she'd been given a ride home, how many assumed she was in for the night? Even the statement of the usher who crashed on her couch would have confirmed it.

I did some quick calculations. On a good day, it took about forty minutes to get from Los Angeles to San Ladrón, but Giovanni had made it even faster when he made the trip at night. Less than half an hour, he said. So thirty minutes to get to LA and however long it took to give Phil enough sleeping pills to make him go unconscious, suffocate him with croissants, and have a couple of strong arms load him into the back of the van and stack velvet on top of him.

It could have been done, but it wasn't the spontaneous act of a woman scorned. It was the act of a woman who had a plan—a plan to kill Phil Girard.

I heard a sound from the front of the tea shop. Like something tearing. I dropped to my hands and knees and crawled from the back to the front of the café. I hid behind the counter and watched a silver razor blade slice through the screen on the window I'd opened. Someone was breaking in.

I peered over the top of the counter where I'd set up the display of cloth napkins. Gloved hands pulled at the screen, tearing it away from the metal frame. I watched as the same gloved hands grabbed the window frame from the outside. Seconds later, a figure climbed in. Even though she wore a hat over her vibrant red hair, I recognized her. Babs Green.

I dropped down behind the counter and wrapped my arms around my legs. The old wood floor creaked. She was moving around the café. I felt my pockets for my phone. Not there. Where had I left it? I couldn't remember. If Babs saw it, she'd know she wasn't alone.

A flashlight beam bounced around the floor. Babs headed past me to the kitchen. I dropped forward to my hands and knees and crawled closer. She pulled a drawer open and then slammed it shut. She did the same for the next two drawers. On the third, she chuckled. She reached inside a black pouch that dangled from her belt and pulled out several pill vials. She stared at the labels for a few seconds and dropped the bottles into the drawer. She pushed the drawer shut and sat down at the computer.

What was she up to?

The computer was along the same wall I was hiding behind, and short of exposing myself, I couldn't see the monitor. Days ago I'd had the urge to delete the files that incriminated Genevieve. What could Babs possibly do on the computer that wouldn't expose her own presence?

But Sheriff Clark's case against Genevieve had fallen apart. It was just a matter of time until she was released and came to the store. It was just a matter of time until she came to the store. Whatever Babs was doing could be easily explained as Genevieve's actions. Nobody would know Babs had even been here, especially if her recognizable car was parked elsewhere.

Nobody but me.

Babs jiggled the mouse and typed on the keyboard using only her gloved index fingers. She looked to the left of the keyboard and stopped typing.

"Well, well. It seems someone forgot their phone." She rolled the chair backward and looked at the floor. "And a handbag, too. Maybe someone didn't forget their phone and they're hiding. Which is it, little Polyester?" she said.

I crawled toward the kitchen. When I rounded the corner, the chair was vacant. The computer screen was bright with the words *Online Pharmacy.* I stood up and peered at the screen. A pop-up window asked *Confirm Order?*

Babs's arms closed around me from behind. I struggled against her. I planted my feet on the desk and pushed backward. She let go. I fell. She lunged for the computer and clicked *Yes.*

"I knew you were going to be a problem," she said. "I knew it long before you came to my apartment. I had everything so well planned, it should have been an open-and-shut case against the wife."

"You claimed to love him," I said. I grabbed the door handle from one of the lower cabinets and pulled myself up to a standing position. Dry tea leaves scattered around the floor. I turned around and faced her. The desk chair had coasted backward and sat on the floor between us. She crept to her right and I moved, slowly, keeping her from getting too close.

"That was an act. You're so busy looking for integrity in the world, I gave you integrity. When you showed up, I knew it would be an uphill battle becoming sympathetic with you. The friend of the grieving widow. The one person in town who didn't believe she killed him. I had to play to that same need to see the good in people and it worked."

"Why did you do it?"

"I gave Phil twenty-five percent of what I made moving hash through San Ladrón. Twenty-five percent was more than generous. But he wasn't happy with our arrangement. He was pressuring me for a bigger piece of the action. There was no way I was going to go fifty-fifty with him. All he had to do was drive to Los Angeles, make the pickup, and drive back. Just like he'd been hired to do."

"But he didn't, did he?"

"No, he didn't. I've been moving hash through San Ladrón for years. My mistake was approaching him. His wife's tea shop would have made the perfect cover for us to move our product. All these leaves lying around in bins. Add in his van, and I wouldn't need anybody else to pick up the product. We could keep it between the two of us. But he knew the whole setup. And then he found out my contact and demanded an equal split. That's when I knew I had to get him out of the picture."

Babs deserved an acting award for how well she'd strung me along. She was still doing it. "What did you do?" I asked.

"I wanted out, but I needed a cover story. Something that told my contacts *I'd* been double-crossed—not them."

"You followed Phil to Los Angeles so you could kill him. You planned it all along."

"I gave him one last chance to back down, but he got greedy. He told me he knew his wife's tea shop was the cornerstone to my operation. He called me before he left on Sunday morning and said he'd expose me if I didn't agree to his new terms. I told him to book a room for us in Los Angeles and said I'd meet up with him at the hotel."

My eyes were trained on her, dressed in a black turtleneck, pants, and gloves. Her trademark red hair was pulled back in a thick braid that hung down her back. A black knit cap was over her head. I backed up against the cabinets and felt my breaths coming faster and faster, keeping pace with my racing thoughts.

"But you weren't there. Genevieve found him ready for— he thought you were coming, but you never showed up."

"I didn't know that. Wifey found him naked? That's an extra bonus. From the moment I hung up that phone after telling him I'd meet him, I set about establishing my alibi. Two shows at the Villamere. I pretended to be drunk and got a ride home from a starstruck usher. The kid slept on my sofa. Taxi ride to the Villamere the next day, then slept in my dressing room. I even had a fight with your little mechanic friend. Rock solid, I'd say. Nobody ever realized that I slipped out right under their noses. Left by five forty-five on Monday morning while the usher was asleep on my sofa. I even took the poor boy's car. I got to Los Angeles in time to see Phil load the fabric into the van."

"But the fabric in the van wasn't the right fabric. He called another deliveryman to drive that truck back to San Ladrón."

"I didn't know that at the time. I assumed the hash was already in the truck. I waited until he finished loading it and then I made him an offer he couldn't refuse." She smiled devilishly. "In the back of the van, can you believe it? I even convinced him to take a performance-enhancing drug so it would be spectacular."

My mind whirred. Did Sheriff Clark have the results of the tox screen yet? Was there evidence of this drug in Phil's system?

"The dummy didn't even question the pills I gave him. Prescription sedative stronger than a horse tranquilizer. The perfect performance. He was out cold in five minutes." She laughed.

"The police are running a tox screen on Phil Girard. If he took something, they'll know."

"Oh, I'm counting on that." She looked over my shoulder at the computer screen. I followed her stare and saw more clearly that she'd placed an order for a prescription sleeping pill on an account for Genevieve Girard. "Do you know how easy it was to set up the account in her name? And poor, poor Phil. When he gave me her personal information, he never knew it would come full circle back to him."

"So after he passed out, you suffocated him with a croissant?"

"And searched the van for the hash. When I didn't find it, I knew he'd already double-crossed me."

"But there were no croissants in the back of the truck, only crumbs. What did you do with the rest of them?"

"Tossed them in a public trash can. Everything went according to plan."

"What about the usher who slept on your sofa?" I asked.

"What's a little sedative between friends? He slept right through the whole thing. I woke the kid up myself when I got back. He took one look at my see-through negligee and went back to work with a heck of a story." She laughed again. "Establishing my alibi was a lot like a burlesque routine. A little sizzle, a little mystery. People think they see more than they do. There's a reason I sell out two shows a night. I'm good at what I do." She lunged across the chair for me. I leaned backward and her hands swiped at air.

"Don't you want to know where the hash is?" I said between breaths.

Confusion flashed across her face for a second. "Where? Where did he hide it?"

"In my fabric."

"No, he didn't. I looked."

"The fabric in the truck wasn't mine. Phil knew as long as he had the hash, he had power over you."

"And you have it now?"

"It's with the police."

Her eyes went wild and crazy. I lunged for the kitchen cabinets and pulled out the bin of catnip. The lid fell off. I threw the bin at her and tiny leaf fragments flew through the air. Babs swiped at them like a cat clawing a scratching post. I dashed past her to the sink. She spun around. I aimed the spigot at her. A shower of water drenched the leaves.

She grabbed me. I slipped on a patch of wet catnip. We both went down. She wrestled me on the slick, leaf-covered floor. We rolled until we were against the back door. She pinned me with her knees and pressed her wool-gloved hand against my mouth. I gagged.

The back door opened and a large blue-and-white piece of French pottery came down on the back of Babs's head. Her eyes fluttered for a second and then she collapsed against me.

Genevieve stood on the back steps. *"La nécessité nous délivre de l'embarras du choix."* She tossed the broken blue-and-white pottery against the concrete step. 'Necessity saves us the embarrassment of having to make a choice.'"

"What choice? Hitting the woman who killed your husband?"

"Sacrificing a perfectly good piece of French pottery."

She helped me stand. "How did you know we were here?" I asked.

"I didn't. I was released tonight and I wanted to peek at the store. I saw the two of you through the window and called Sheriff Clark."

In the distance I heard sirens. "For a couple of minutes there I wasn't sure I was going to make it."

"I wouldn't be so sure your troubles are over."

"Why?"

She pointed to my clothes, covered in wet clumps of catnip. "When you get home, Pins and Needles are going to tear you apart."

Twenty-nine

It was hard to believe how much happened after the showdown at Tea Totalers. Clark arrived and I gave him my statement. Babs returned to consciousness while we were talking.
When she saw Genevieve, she reacted like she'd seen a ghost.
Clark took Babs into custody, and a uniformed officer I'd never
met escorted her outside and into the back of a police car.

A medical examiner gave me a quick once-over despite
my constant repetition of the phrase, "I'm okay. I just want
to go to bed." He finally agreed and, just past midnight, I
was released.

When I got home, I cut the sleeves off my sweatshirt and
gave one to each of the cats. I put the rest of my outfit in a
plastic bag and threw it in the Dumpster out back. I showered for an hour and slept for fourteen.

When I woke, Pins and Needles were zonked out on the
bed. Their bellies were in the air, paws over their heads,
sleeping off the catnip buzz Cheech and Chong–style. I got

up, showered again, and made an afternoon breakfast of scrambled eggs, toast, and coffee. I called Charlie and told her what had happened, and then headed downstairs to work in the fabric store. It was Saturday afternoon. In less than a day, I'd be opening my doors to the public, and I had to use every second to make sure the place was ready.

I flipped on all of the interior lights and turned around. Since I'd been staying here, I'd gotten familiar with the interior of the store, but what would customers see? A large, open warehouse space. Walls lined in white shelves bulging with brightly colored bolts of quilting cottons, soft charmeuse, silk, wool, and jersey. Large tables in the middle of the store held stacks of fabrics rolled on cardboard tubes. One table held an assortment of faux fur; one held denim and camouflage. Others held suede, vinyl, and burlap.

I had lined the outside of the register stand with small two-shelf bookcases. The shelves facing the front of the store held how-to manuals and sewing supplies. Scissors, tape measures, pins, needles, bobbins, and thimbles filled the shelves on the side. Next to the register area were more fixtures, filled with zippers, thread, buttons, bias tape, and binding tape. The notions wall ran the length of the store and held more supplies for sewers at any skill level.

Most of the store was ready. Except for the front by the door, where I'd hoped to house my new bolts of proprietary velvet, the inventory was stocked. After what had gone down with Babs, I knew not to count on getting back my velvet—or not-my-velvet—any time soon. I looked at the rest of my inventory, trying to decide what to move to the empty space. Everything had been carefully placed. Everything except the fabric discards too damaged to sell. They sat by the back door, where I'd carried them. I hadn't been able to throw them away.

Maybe I didn't have to.

I moved the old inventory to the front of the store. I scanned in and printed up pictures from when Aunt Millie and Uncle Marius had owned the store, and wrote short blurbs explaining where the fabrics had come from. I created a history of the store from when they first opened their doors to the day I was reopening them as mine. When I finished, the front left corner of the store was a fabric museum, where patrons could come in and see what my family had built all those many years before. I ended the display with a large round trash can filled with bolts of the old, damaged fabric and signed it *Original Inventory. One Yard Free!* I doubted I'd get any takers, but it was better than throwing it out.

Sunday morning I dressed in a black turtleneck, black boot-cut pants, and my black riding boots. I pulled a pink apron printed with brightly colored spools of thread over the turtleneck and tied it in back, and then draped a matching pink tape measure around my neck like I'd seen my aunt do a thousand times when she was alive. There was a pounding on the back door. I unlocked it and found my parents in the parking lot.

"Surprise!" my mom said. "We couldn't let you open the store without us." She threw her arms around me. She stepped back and looked at my neglected haircut, then back at me, and hugged me again.

My dad handed me an arrangement of flowers. "Congratulations, Poly. Aunt Millie and Uncle Marius would be proud of you." He kissed me on the cheek and followed my mom inside.

She scanned the interior, her gaze falling on the display. "What's this?" she asked. She walked past the bins of fabric and studied the photos. Within seconds, she turned to my dad. "John, come here. You have to see what Poly made." There were tears in her eyes.

I couldn't wait any longer. I unlocked the front door and pulled the gate back. Out front I hung a sign: *Free Fabric! Inquire Inside*.

And then I flipped the *Closed* sign to *Open*.

Genevieve, Maria, and Big Joe walked toward me with Carlos and Antonio behind them. Big Joe pushed a two-tiered cart. The top held six carafes of coffee. The bottom was stacked with pink bakery boxes. The two young boys looked like they weren't happy about the prospect of spending their morning in a fabric store.

"Maria, Genevieve—"

"Poly, you need to learn to either say thank you or keep your mouth shut. You got that?" Maria said.

"Thank you."

"That's better."

Carlos's face was squinched up. "Where's our free fabric?" he asked.

"Carlos! We did not do this because we expected anything," his mother chastised.

"Maria, he's right. The sign out front says *free fabric*. Come with me," I said to him.

I led him to the section of the store where I'd set up the history display. I stooped down so I could look him straight in the face. "These pictures are from when my aunt and uncle owned the store a long time ago. They made a place that was really important to the city, just like your parents have made the donut shop. People came from all over the state to see the fabric in this store. Even moviemakers. They would buy special silk here because it came from Thailand, and cashmere that came from Scotland."

"Moviemakers came here to buy fabric?"

"Some of them did, yes. And some very glamorous women came here, too." I pointed to a picture of my great-aunt in a boucle suit with a pencil skirt. The picture was taken in the fifties, and I figured my aunt had been in her late twenties at the time. "See her?"

"Is she famous?" he asked.

"She's my aunt."

Carlos was mesmerized by the photos. His eyes scanned the rest of the display, until he spotted the bin of fabric at the end.

"That's the free fabric. You can pick any one and I'll cut you a yard of it to take home with you."

"For free?"

"For free."

He concentrated on something for a few seconds. "Can I look at the rest of the pictures before I decide which one I want?"

"Of course you can."

Genevieve was waiting for me at the register. "Thank you for everything, Poly. Babs was charged with Phil's murder, and Sheriff Clark contacted the Drug Enforcement Agency about the hash you found. Babs has been flying under the radar out here for years now. I can't believe she thought she was going to use my shop as her front."

I put my arm around her. "What about you? How are you doing?"

She looked up at me with a wan smile. "I still can't believe that I'm alone, that he's not coming back. There are so many things about Phil that made me mad, all of these secrets that I didn't know, but still, there's this hole in my life."

"Gen, it's going to take some time for that hole to go away."

"I know." There were tears in her eyes. "I know I'm better off without him, but it's hard to think that all of our plans were a lie. When we opened the tea shop, it was supposed to be our future."

"Tea Totalers is your future. Yours. From the moment I met you, I could see that you were born to run a French café. And now you can, and you can do whatever you want with it. In fact, I had this idea the other day . . ." I briefly outlined the Midnight in Paris concept for her and watched her expression change from sadness to enthusiasm. Genevieve's life was changed forever, but she had more to look forward to now than ever before.

"Poly, I owe you so much more than the next eight hours of my time."

"I'm sure we can work something out," I said with a smile. "But first, I have a question. What was the deal with the Italian food distributor?"

"Mr. di Sali? I told you he wants me to sell my recipes. Thanks to Vaughn, I don't have to consider that anymore."

"But why did he tell me to remind you that it was a two-way street?"

Her face colored. "He knew that I outsourced my croissants. He said if I would go into business with him, he could find me a different supplier and cut the cost in half. Poly, I was looking at everything I could to cut back on expenses, but that tea shop was my dream. I couldn't sacrifice the quality of the food to save a couple of dollars."

"Did you tell him that?

"I called him from Charlie's. He said if I ever reconsidered selling or buying, to give him a call."

I had to laugh. The world was filled with Italian Scallions and Giovannis: people trying to make money from other people's businesses. "It's a good thing you never took him up on his offer. The fact that you and Adelaide use the same croissant supplier really helped you."

"What really helped me was being friends with you."

"What about Kim? Is she going to continue to work for you?"

She shook her head. "Her parents felt that it was too much for her to handle, the job and school and her weekend community service. She's going to work full-time with her uncle Sam in the insurance agency. Who knows? Maybe she'll show a real flair for it."

"Stranger things have happened."

Genevieve draped a neon green measuring tape around her neck. "Enough about me. Tell me how I start to repay you."

I transferred the apron to Genevieve. "You can ring a register, right?" I asked while she turned around.

"Right."

I knotted the strings in the back. "Then that's your job."

There were four customers by eleven. By noon, at least a dozen. I lost track around a quarter after one and didn't look at the clock again until four thirty. My mom's hair stood up on one side and my dad was asleep in the corner thanks to donut overdose. We had given away several yards of fabric to people who wanted it because it represented a part of the city's history. Customer after customer told me how wonderful it was to see the inside of the store that had been boarded up for the past ten years, and a few members of the city's Senior Patrol shared their own stories: buying the fabric for their prom and wedding dresses here, making dresses for their children and now their children's children. I didn't want to jinx things, but if day one was any indication, it seemed as though Material Girl was going to succeed.

I sank into a chair to rest my feet for a few minutes. "Mom, thank you for cutting your vacation short to help me. I couldn't have done this without you."

She cupped her hand alongside my face. "Yes, you could have, but you didn't have to. This store is about family." She looked up at the front door. "Speaking of families, here comes one now."

I twisted my head and saw Adelaide and Vaughn enter. Adelaide smiled at me and said something to Vaughn. He looked at me, said something to her, and turned toward the historical display. Adelaide approached me.

"You've had a very busy forty-eight hours," she said. "I can't imagine what it took to open the store today."

"That's the one thing that I wasn't going to leave to

chance." I looked over my shoulder and saw Genevieve and Charlie reestablishing the foundation of their friendship. "Adelaide, have you given any thought to my suggestion for your annual party?"

"It's just about the only thing I have been thinking about."

"Genevieve Girard is by the register, and I bet she'd love it if you approached her about it."

"I will in a second." Adelaide looked around the interior of the shop, her eyes resting on the historical display I'd set up. She pointed to it. "You found a way to bring the past into the present," she said.

"Inspired by what you've done at the Waverly House."

"Do you mind if I go take a look?"

"Please do," I said.

I watched customers mill around the interior of the shop. Genevieve stood by the register talking to Charlie. They appeared to be on friendly terms again. I wondered how long it would take Charlie to be on friendly terms with Sheriff Clark again. If ever.

"Can you handle the cutting station?" I asked my mom. "I'll only be a second."

"I'll be fine. Go, take your time."

I met Vaughn halfway through the store by a bin of gabardine. He wore an ivory turtleneck, khaki pants, and his Stan Smiths. His hair was ruffled in the way that only the wind could do.

"I heard about what happened at Tea Totalers after I left," he said.

"Things got pretty crazy."

I expected him to apologize for storming out or for not coming back. He didn't. I liked him a little bit more because of that.

"Vaughn, would you like to go to dinner tonight? To help me celebrate the opening of the fabric store?"

He tipped his head to the side and studied me. I matched his eye contact and waited for his answer. I already knew

I'd offended him a few times recently. He could say no just as easily as he could say yes.

A lopsided smile played at the corners of his mouth and the light caught in his green-and-gold-flecked eyes. He gave in to the smile, revealing straight white teeth. "That depends," he said.

"On what? The restaurant? I hadn't given it much thought—"

"No. It depends on who's picking up the bill."

Before I had a chance to think up a witty retort, Genevieve popped her head into our conversation. "That's easy," she said. "Come to Tea Totalers and I'll provide a private picnic for two. My treat."

I looked at Vaughn and raised my eyebrows at him. "Does that work for you?"

"This time, but you owe me."

"Okay, then. I'll see you tonight." I turned to leave. He caught me by the arm and spun me back around.

"I'm not leaving yet," he said, "I've been thinking a lot about the value of a dollar and, well . . ." He paused.

"Well, what?"

"Well, before I leave, I want my free yard of fabric."

PROJECT: MAKE FABRIC PLACEMATS IN THE COLOR THEME OF YOUR CHOICE

Poly uses fabric to make over Tea Totalers, combining prints and textures with a French feeling. Here's how to make the same placemats that Poly makes. Select fabrics that match your own kitchen, but don't be afraid to mix and match! These instructions will result in a standard-sized 18 x 14–inch place mat.

1 yard of fabric #1*
1 yard of fabric #2*
1 package of 100 percent cotton crib-sized
    batting
1 package of double-fold seam binding in coordinating
    color
Pins
Thread
Yardstick
Sewing machine

Despite her love of blended fabrics, Poly suggests you use 100 percent cotton for this project. Fabrics with stretch will give you trouble when it comes to stitching them together and free motion quilting them into one item.

1. Lay contrasting fabrics on top of one another.

2. Measure a rectangle 18.5 inches × 14.5 inches.

3. Cut.

4. Measure a rectangle of batting 18.5 inches × 14.5 inches.

5. Cut.

6. Create a sandwich of fabric, batting, fabric, with both fabrics facing right side out.

7. Pin around all four edges.

8. Stitch layers together with ¼-inch seam allowance.

9. Drop the feed dogs on your sewing machine, then, starting at the back left corner of the assembled placemat, use a free motion to stitch over the entire mat by holding it taught and moving it with both hands while running the machine needle. This part can be lots of fun but sometimes feels a little crazy! Your object is to secure all three layers of the mat. You can move the fabric in a circular pattern, zigzag, or swirls, or all of the above. There are no mistakes here, just freeform stitch decoration. *(Poly says: if you are really scared of this step, you can take your placemat to a quilt shop and have them use a free-motion machine to "quilt" the layers together.)*

10. Unpack seam binding and measure 66 inches.

11. Press until flat.

12. With right sides together, sew the ends of the seam binding at a diagonal with a straight stitch, using a ½-inch seam allowance (this step will leave you with a circle of seam binding that is 65 inches in diameter).

13. Fit the circle of seam binding around the edge of the unfinished mat (with the fold of the binding against the raw edge of fabric and batting).

14. Pin into place.

15. Stitch the seam binding to the mat, keeping stitches close to the edge of the seam binding. Be sure the needle catches the binding on both top and bottom layers!

16. Voilà! Your placemat is complete. There is no top or bottom to the mat, so enjoy both sides, or better, make multiple mats out of several different fabrics. Coordinate them all with the same seam binding.

17. Invite some friends over and have an impromptu picnic!

Ideas for Fabric Selection

- Choose one print in several colors: a gingham or polka dot would do nicely!

- Choose several prints in the same color: combine stripes, dots, plaids, solids, and prints!

- Choose a theme: find several fabrics that relate to each other. Poly used a French theme for Tea Totalers, but other ideas could be: menswear fabrics, floral, or whimsical prints with pastries and cupcakes. Let your imagination run wild!

Turn the page for a preview of Diane Vallere's
next Material Witness Mystery . . .

SILK STALKINGS

Coming soon from Berkley Prime Crime!

The clock would strike midnight in two minutes. This was important for a few reasons, not the least of which was that the crowd of couples who filled the interior and exterior grounds of Tea Totalers, my friend Genevieve Girard's tea shop-turned-Parisian nightclub, would filter down the sidewalk of Bonita Avenue and make their way toward the Waverly House for their annual stroll through the historic mansion's gardens.

The other reason midnight was important was that the coordinators of tonight's event had synched every clock in our small town of San Ladrón down to the second. They were set to chime, ring, buzz, and otherwise announce the arrival of twelve a.m. It was one thing to imagine the impact of that type of alarm coordination, but it might be quite another to experience it. If the several hundred guests who sipped champagne and nibbled at petite fours and hors d'oeuvres at Tea Totalers had followed suit of the city and set their cell phones to ring, too, we could be looking at the kind of noise level that might launch missiles over Cuba.

Genevieve approached me with a flute of champagne. "Poly, things turned out better than I had hoped! We've gone through almost seventeen pounds of brie, and the crusty French bread disappears as fast as it comes out of the oven. I've served almost as much of my special blend of tea as I have champagne. And people are asking if I'll cater their parties. People who have lived in San Ladrón their whole lives are telling me they wish they'd come here earlier. This idea was genius. It's really putting me on the map." She handed me a glass of champagne and clinked it with hers. "It's putting you on the map, too," she added.

Genevieve had opened Tea Totalers a few years ago, with the help of her French husband. He was no longer in the picture, thanks to seedy business dealings with people who thought murder was an appropriate solution to a business dispute. Genevieve had been the number one suspect in her husband's murder, and I'd been instrumental in helping clear her name. In return, she'd been instrumental in helping me open Material Girl, the fabric shop I inherited from my great uncle several months ago. Tonight we were both reaping the benefits of hard work and creative marketing.

Genevieve spun around her café's interior with her arms out. The champagne in her flute spilled from the glass but she didn't seem to notice or care. "Can you believe it? It really does feel like we're in Paris at Midnight."

I followed her gaze around the newly made over café. I'd gotten the idea to use French fabrics from my shop to build upon the theme Genevieve had wanted for the interior. Long toile curtains framed out sheer panels of voile that had almost gone into the Dumpster behind my fabric shop thanks to a wicked case of mildew, but an intensive treatment with vinegar and fresh air had cleared the fabric of its musty scent and brought it back to life. The chairs had been recovered in gingham, provencale, linen, and even more toile, and napkins, placemats, and serving trays had been trimmed with the same fabrics. That was by day.

But tonight, for the Midnight in Paris party, I'd stepped things up a notch. Deep midnight blue velvet covered the existing butter yellow walls. I used a heat set technique to create a fleur de lis pattern on the velvet that mirrored the pattern woven into the voile sheers and I'd covered the chairs in luxurious velvet seat covers tied back with thick ivory grosgrain ribbon. Small tea light candles sat in clear glass votives on window sills, table tops, counters inside the café.

The organizers of the city's part of the event—decorating the street between Tea Totalers and the Waverly House—had hung strands of tiny white twinkling lights around the exterior of the buildings and in an arch over the street, creating a blanket of stars under which people danced to the jazz quartet on the corner. The local high school had crafted a scaled model of the Eiffel Tower that sat in the middle of the intersection of Bonita and San Ladrón Avenue. The roads had been closed for the night, so people could spill out into the street and enjoy the transformation of our small town.

"Are you heading over to the Waverly House when the bells chime? I bet Vaughn would love to see you in that dress," Genevieve asked.

I blushed. Since inheriting the fabric store and moving to San Ladrón, I'd spent enough time with Vaughn McMichael to get past the unfortunate first impression where I fell through a window and knocked him to the ground. We'd dined together, worked side by side, and even gone on a date. We'd also accused each other of having ulterior motives, resulting in alienation. And by we, I mean me, but I'd rather not get into that right now.

"I don't want to talk about Vaughn," I said.

"Didn't he have that dress made for you?" Genevieve asked pointedly.

"I don't want to talk about that either," I said to her. Much like the interior of Genevieve's shop, I'd stepped up my own appearance for the night. I usually wore black all the time, but I'd traded it for a shimmering gold gown with a sweetheart neckline, embellished on the shoulders with spirals of matte gold and silver sequins. The gown was fitted around my waist and hips and cascaded to the floor in a pool of fabric.

"Poly, you had just as much to do with the garden stroll at the Waverly House as you did here at Tea Totalers," Genevieve said. "You have to go."

I didn't know how to explain to Genevieve that I was nervous about showing up at the Waverly House for more reasons than I could count.

The Waverly House was the most significant historical building in the town of San Ladrón. A Victorian mansion turned museum, it had become a certified landmark years back and now boasted a restaurant, a monthly murder mystery party, and the most exquisite gardens in the town. Adelaide Brooks, the most energetic and elegant seventy-year-old I'd ever met, managed the building and the day-to-day business.

The annual party had been the landmark's major fundraiser for years, and the money brought in from this singular party determined their operating budget for the following year. People flocked to San Ladrón for the night to consider the Waverly House for weddings and parties. All would have been fine, except that this year, the most powerful man in San Ladrón had raised questions about zoning and put a scare into the suppliers who donated food and drink. That halted any planning that could take place. It didn't help matters that the most powerful man in San Ladrón was Adelaide's ex-husband.

Or that he was Vaughn McMichael's father.

Only a few people knew that I'd been the one to come up with the idea of changing the location of the annual garden party to Genevieve's newly reopened shop. Food and drink distributors had been happy to make their regular donations, and Genevieve had been thrilled at the opportunity. After applying for her liquor license (ironic in a shop called Tea Totalers), she had been pleasantly surprised by the outpouring of support from suppliers who donated food and drink for the evening, and local restaurants who loaned out employees to help.

Ticket sales for the Midnight in Paris cocktail party still benefited the Waverly House, as did separate ticket sales to gain entrance to the exquisite gardens behind the Victorian manse at midnight. Adelaide had sidestepped the zoning regulations by leaving the restaurant and bar open for paying customers. Landscapers had been hard at work on the grounds surrounding the landmark, and whatever it was that they were planning to debut had been kept a well-guarded secret. All Adelaide would say was, "it's more magnificent than I ever could have expected." The perceived success of the night would be determined to be true or false tomorrow when she would tally the money pulled in by selling tickets and subtract out any unforeseen expenses. I didn't want credit for the idea. I wanted everyone to get what they wanted—or needed, in the case of the Waverly House—from the event.

Bong-Bong-Bong-Ding-Bong Chime-Buzz-Clang-Ring-Bong!

Midnight arrived, announced by a cacophony of sounds that originated from a distance of several miles. The chimes, bongs, dings, and dongs were slightly off of each other, resulting in a white noise that mixed with the various cell phone alarms that went off from the pockets of people around us. A couple of people put hands over their ears, and a few kissed like it was New Year's Eve. Conversation became impossible.

The drummer struck up a rhythm on the high hat, and the man playing the upright bass plucked out a note for each strike of the clock. Cheers erupted from the crowd.

When the noise died down, I heard a voice behind me. "Let me guess. That's your cue to turn into a pumpkin?" asked Charlie. Charlie was a local mechanic, resident tough girl, and my closest friend in town. As a full-time mechanic with her own auto shop, Charlie favored work jeans, chambray shirts, and rock concert T-shirts, but tonight she wore a man's tuxedo over a white fitted T-shirt. The jacket was boxy, but the T-shirt hugged her fit body. The pants sat low on her hips and broke over red Chuck Taylors. "I heard you tell Frenchy you weren't going to the Waverly House. Good call. Wanna grab a beer at The Broadside?"

"The Broadside's closed. Duke and his bartenders are working for Genevieve tonight. Didn't you notice?"

"I just got here. This kind of thing isn't my scene."

"Which part don't you like? The free food or the free booze or the free ambiance?"

"The raising-money-for-rich-people part."

Rich people who gave her up for adoption, I thought to myself, but I didn't say out loud. Not many people knew Charlie was related to the wealthy McMichael family, and she wanted to keep it that way. I didn't judge her for her animosity toward Vic McMichael and Adelaide Brooks, but I wondered if there would be a day when she regretted not forging a relationship with her birth parents.

This wasn't the first time I'd thwarted a plan of Mr. McMichael's. When I first inherited my family's fabric store, he tried to buy it out from under me. We'd gone toe-to-toe a couple of times since then. My ex-boyfriend, Carson Cole, was a financial analyst in Los Angeles and maintained a fantasy about becoming Mr. McMichael's protégé, even after our breakup. When the businessman had threatened Genevieve's tea shop,

I'd called Carson to step in and save the day. Considering Vaughn was on his father's payroll, he'd been more than a little hurt that I hadn't asked him for help. Yet another reason I wanted to keep a low profile tonight.

"You're a liar," I said.

She raised her pierced eyebrow.

"Not a lot of people get away with calling me names."

"If you didn't care about this thing, you wouldn't have bothered to dress up."

"I'm meeting up with someone I haven't seen for a while. Thought I'd make an effort. Besides, you're one to talk," she said, scanning my ensemble from top to bottom.

Again with the dress.

"So I'm not wearing black for one night! It's not like it's a religion or anything."

She held her hands up and backed away. "It's a nice dress. You wouldn't be hoping to run into anybody while wearing it, would you?"

Before I could answer, Genevieve reappeared. "Hi, Charlie, are you coming to the Waverly House? I want to go and Poly won't come with me."

Charlie crossed the interior of Tea Totalers and looked out the front door. People filled the street, laughing and carrying on. A few policemen stood on the corners, trying to remain serious but failing miserably. One lady walked up to the town's sheriff, took his hand, and twirled like a ballerina. He let go of her hand and adjusted his hat. Charlie went inside and we followed her. A few minutes later, the front door opened and Sheriff Clark walked in.

"Is this a closed party or can anybody join?" he asked.

"Well, hello there, Sheriff Clark!" sang Genevieve, who might have possibly had too much champagne. She must have been thinking the same thing, because she handed her glass to him. "Help yourself to champagne. I can't stand it anymore. I want to go see the gardens!" She hiked her dress up so the hem wouldn't drag and ran out the front door. "Poly, lock up when you leave?"

"Sure," I said.

Clark took the proffered glass and drank half. He lowered the glass and scanned me. "Nice dress," he said. "You going to waste it by staying here in hiding?"

"You heard Genevieve, she asked me to lock up."

"It takes about four seconds to lock a door." He looked at Charlie.

"Yo, Frenchy, wait up," Charlie called. She ran past Sheriff Clark without an acknowledgment and went outside.

I looked at Clark and shrugged. He shook his head and walked out front. I found Genevieve's keys and grabbed my beaded handbag from behind the counter. Sheriff Clark waited while I locked up the doors and together we trailed after Charlie and Genevieve.

Sheriff Clark and Charlie had had a secret romance that fizzled over a miscommunication. It was probably just as well that they steered clear of each other. When I pictured them being a couple, I was reminded of what happened to the Gingham dog and the Calico cat.

Genevieve, Charlie, and I were among the last of the people to reach the Waverly House. Volunteers from the historical society stood in front of a ten foot tall version of the Arc de Triomphe, fabricated for the evening by the employees of Get Hammered, the local hardware store, out of chicken wire. Green Ivy and colorful flowers had been threaded through the wire. Couples walked under the arch to the luscious lawns behind the Waverly House, pointing at the gazebo, the white iron benches, and the brick pavers that had been carved with the names of each person who had made a donation when the building was in need of repair. They were trying on the location with their eyes, wondering how it would feel to celebrate a major event in the middle of all of this Victorian majesty.

"Excuse me," said a woman to my left. "Are you Polyester Monroe? Of the fabric shop on Bonita?"

"Yes, but I go by Poly."

"What's your shop called? 'Fabric Woman'?"

"Material Girl."

"That's right." She held out her hand and I shook it. "I'm Nolene Kelly. I've heard people say you were responsible for the transformation of the tea shop for tonight. Who knew you could transform a place with fabric!" she said.

"I hope people will be inspired to try it themselves," I said.

"It's a nice idea but it'll be a hard sell. People around here aren't used to making their own clothes or slip covers or curtains."

"I had a lot of help," I said modestly.

"But it was all her idea. Wasn't it amazing?" Genevieve chimed in.

"It was very impressive. And the fabric—that was from your store?" Nolene asked. She tipped her head as she posed her question and the earrings that looked like clusters of fruit set off a faint tinkling sound.

"Yes."

"Before you moved here, you worked in a dress shop in Los Angeles, didn't you?" It was odd to hear my recent history told to me by a stranger. "I'm afraid I've read up on your background. I'm the head judge of Miss Tangorli, San Ladrón's annual beauty pageant. Since you're new around here, you probably don't know much about it."

"You're right, I don't know much about the events of San Ladrón. This is my first time attending the Waverly House's annual party." I glanced around me. Genevieve and Charlie had migrated in separate directions: Genevieve toward the gardens, and Charlie toward a strange man who stood alone a few feet from the tea and juice station outside. He had a white ponytail and black leather blazer over a black turtleneck and black trousers.

"Rumor has it there wouldn't have been a party if it wasn't for you." Nolene winked. "But I'm not here to spread rumors. I'm here to find judges. I've locked in two so far."

Immediately I felt awkward. "I don't think I'd be qualified to judge a beauty pageant."

"Don't worry about that. I have something else in mind for you.

WELL-CRAFTED MYSTERIES
FROM BERKLEY PRIME CRIME

- **Earlene Fowler** Don't miss these Agatha Award–winning quilting mysteries featuring Benni Harper.

- **Monica Ferris** These *USA Today* bestselling Needlecraft Mysteries include free knitting patterns.

- **Laura Childs** Her Scrapbooking Mysteries offer tips to satisfy the most die-hard crafters.

- **Maggie Sefton** These popular Knitting Mysteries come with knitting patterns and recipes.

- **Lucy Lawrence** These brilliant Decoupage Mysteries involve cutouts, glue, and varnish.

- **Elizabeth Lynn Casey** The Southern Sewing Circle Mysteries are filled with friends, southern charm—and murder.

M2G0610